The stranger
LP-CF Mar

T49110

Help us Rate this book...
Put your initials on the
Left side and your rating
on the right side.
1 = Didn't care for
2 = It was O.K.
3 = It was great

DATE DUE

MAR 14 2019		
MAR 26 2019		
APR 13 2019		
MAY 24 2019		
JUL 10 2019		

me — 1 2 ③
LR — 1 2 ③
___ 1 2 3
___ 1 2 3
___ 1 2 3
___ 1 2 3
___ 1 2 3
___ 1 2 3
___ 1 2 3
___ 1 2 3
___ 1 2 3
___ 1 2 3
___ 1 2 3
___ 1 2 3
___ 1 2 3

PRINTED IN U.S.A.

THE STRANGER

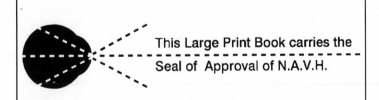

This Large Print Book carries the
Seal of Approval of N.A.V.H.

THE STRANGER

LINDA MARAN

THORNDIKE PRESS
A part of Gale, a Cengage Company

Farmington Hills, Mich • San Francisco • New York • Waterville, Maine
Meriden, Conn • Mason, Ohio • Chicago

GALE
A Cengage Company

Copyright © 2017 by Linda Maran.
Thorndike Press, a part of Gale, a Cengage Company.

**LIBRARY OF CONGRESS CIP DATA ON FILE.
CATALOGUING IN PUBLICATION FOR THIS BOOK
IS AVAILABLE FROM THE LIBRARY OF CONGRESS**

ISBN-13: 978-1-4328-6167-4 (hardcover)

Published in 2019 by arrangement with White Rose Publishing, a division of Peli

Printed in Mexico
1 2 3 4 5 6 7 23 22 21 20 19

To my Creator, the Source
of all creativity and to the
late Charles D. Farrell, for all
the times at your piece of
the Jersey Shore.

1

The car turned down a long dirt road that ran through a wide expanse of farmland. Silos, barns, and cows dotted the area as far as the eye could see. The road sign read, *Dillenback Road.* They made a left down a lane past a weathered black mailbox with the number, thirty-two, and the name *Wagler,* painted on it in white. Panic rushed through Kristen Esh and she turned to the driver, who'd introduced herself as Angela.

"No, no. I can't do this. Can you please drive me back? Now?"

"I'm sorry, honey. I can't. Your Aunt Elizabeth hired me to bring you here from your foster home. She said you're to be met by a family member." She stopped the car in front of a large weathered, white wooden house. "Ah, there's her son, John, on the porch. They're really nice people. You'll see."

They exited the car.

Kristen hesitated, heart pounding, and

stood back with her suitcase as Angela walked over to the blond man who waved. He wore a blue shirt, patched dark blue pants, suspenders, and a straw hat. His black shoes were covered with dried mud.

Angela motioned for Kristen to come over as John walked down the porch steps.

"You're all set, Kristen. I hope to see you again soon. Bye, John." She got into her car, waved, and drove off.

"*Hullo,* I'm John Wagler. You must be our cousin, Kristen. Your *mamm's* attorney said you'd be here today. Are you hungry?"

Kristen was tempted to bolt and run, but the kind expression of welcome on this man's tanned handsome face made her abandon the idea. For the time being.

"Uh, hi. No. I'm not very hungry, but I guess I need to eat something. Is this where I'm going to live?" Kristen took in the farmhouse, vegetable gardens, a big white-washed barn, and corn fields rustling in the breeze beyond it. She noted the mountains in the far background. They were the color of limes; a light new green on this bright, late June day. Storybook scenic, but not her beloved Jersey Shore. She didn't belong there.

"*Jah,* this is where you'll be living. Let me take that." John took Kristen's suitcase and led the way inside. He removed his hat and hung it on a peg in the foyer. A mass of mussed golden hair sprang free from under it.

"Sorry that my mamm isn't here to *velkum* you. She was called to help Irma Stoltzfus deliver her baby. She left me to wait for you." He placed the suitcase on the floor to the side of the door.

Kristen diverted her gaze from John's hair to his smiling blue eyes. "She delivers babies in homes?" Who delivered babies that way these days?

"Just helps the midwife every now and again."

She entered the kitchen, and John pointed to a chair at the large, rectangular wooden table. Kristen sat and watched as he washed his hands at a sink pump and then opened what looked like a large pantry closet that revealed a big ice chest.

"Mamm said to offer you lunch. She made sandwiches and potato salad to go with it." He placed both on the table, and then went back to the chest and brought out a sealed pitcher of what looked like lemonade.

Kristen did a quick three sixty scan of the kitchen. "Where's the refrigerator?"

"*Daed* never got around to getting us a propane powered one. Says this way has been fine ever since he can remember. I think he just likes to cut ice in winter for our ice *haus*. Mamm's working on him though."

"Propane?"

"Jah, natural gas. No electric. We're Old Older Amish. *Ach!* We need plates, glasses and forks, jah?"

Kristen nodded, hoping her disbelief wasn't too obvious. Seemed he had some kind of an accent.

"You can use the pump here to wash up or the one in the wash room at the back of the haus."

"Where is the water pumped from?" When she stood to head for the one at the sink, he looked at her as if she had four heads.

"Where else? From the ground. It's plenty cold, too."

He wasn't kidding. Kristen pumped the icy water onto one hand then onto the other. She used the lump of soap that resembled colorless play-dough next to the pump, lathered, rinsed, and dried her hands on a towel hanging nearby. "Thanks. Maybe later I can take a shower?"

"Sorry, cousin. We don't have any running water. It's just the two water pumps. That's the way it is in this district. We take a weekly bath and clean up at the wash room pump

10

in between."

"No running water? Um, so, there's no indoor bathroom?"

"*Nee.* We set up the basin in the kitchen and fill it with heated water, and . . ."

"No, I mean a bathroom . . . for when nature calls . . . you know . . ."

"Ah, the *briwwi*! Jah, we have an outhaus."

Out. House? As in outside? She'd used one when she was ten years old on a school weekend camping trip. Kristen winced. She sat again and tried to absorb what John had told her. Derick would have to rescue her from this place.

A sandwich with a dollop of potato salad on a white paper plate was set before her. She lifted the top slice of bread and frowned.

John cocked his head. A furrow tunneled in the center of his brows. "Something wrong?"

"Sorry, I don't eat ham. I'm a vegetarian."

He reached over and took her sandwich. "Here, I'll fix that."

He removed the ham and stuffed it into his own sandwich. Then he placed hers back on her plate. "Now you have a cheese sandwich instead of ham and cheese."

"But . . ."

"Can't be wasting food, you know." He lifted his fattened sandwich to his mouth and looked up briefly with a hint of a smirk on his face.

Kristen stared at her flimsy sandwich. "Hold on a minute. Give me your cheese then. That would be a fair trade for my ham."

John studied her with a glint in his blue eyes. "Jah, it would be." He lifted his bread, took out the cheese, and placed it on her plate. "Fair enough, then?"

"Yes, thank you." She put the cheese into her sandwich and took a bite.

John watched her. Then he chuckled.

"What's so funny?"

"You said you weren't hungry."

"I'm not. But what's fair is fair."

"You are a gutsy one, Kristen. The *dochter* of an Esh for sure and for certain."

"Why is that?"

"*Vell,* your mamm, my mamm, and two more of your *aenties* on the Esh side all have some headstrong traits." He lifted his sandwich and peered inside it. "And to think how much I was looking forward to ham and cheese all *morgen.*"

Kristen glared at him.

He burst out laughing.

"Just teasing, cousin. Enjoy your sandwich

12

as I will mine." Kristen couldn't help but warm up to him, but she didn't feel like laughing. Not at all. She picked up her sandwich again.

"So, were you born here?" Might as well make some small talk so as not to think about the water issue and the dreaded outhouse.

"Nee. I was born in Ohio and brought here to Stone Arabia as an infant after my mamm died bringing me into the world."

Her heart tugged. She couldn't believe her own mom was gone. "I'm sorry about your mother. You're adopted then?"

"Vell, my daed had farming to tend to and there was no time to care for a *boppli.* Daed had no dochters to do women's work and no female relatives in Ohio. I'm his first born. Your Aenti Elizabeth took me in. She was my mamm's closest friend and widowed only a year earlier. In the long run, the *gut* Lord saw to it that my daed and your aenti joined as man and wife. He sold his farm, moved here to upstate New York, and took on this place. She became my mamm for keeps. That was nearly twenty years ago. Nee, I don't consider myself adopted."

"Then that means that you and I are not really related." He seemed like someone nice to be related to. Sort of the big brother

13

she'd never had. Though his good looks and humor could make a girl want him for much more. She shook the thought from her mind. She didn't want to be here with him or with anyone else. Period.

John emptied his glass of lemonade. Then he cocked his head. His sky-blue eyes twinkled a hint of amusement as he jangled the ice cubes around in his empty glass.

"We aren't related by a single hair. But we'll be called cousins just the same, being that we are part of the same *familye.* That OK with you? Cousin?" His smile seemed a natural part of him as his gaze locked into hers.

"Yes. Cousin," she shot back.

John stood and began to clear the table. "Mamm will be here soon enough to show you up to your room. I have to get back to the fields now."

"OK. Thanks for the lunch." Kristen handed him her plate. John took it, nodded, and placed it in the trashcan. He grabbed his straw hat from the peg and twirled it in his hands as he walked backward until he reached the screened door, his large eyes upon her the whole time. Then he turned and darted out the door like a school boy at the ringing of the dismissal bell.

She didn't know whether to laugh or cry.

Her emotions were running high. Here she was in an unfamiliar place that would now be her home. And a complete stranger, nice as he was, yet still unknown to her, had just fed her lunch. At least her temporary guardians had been people she'd known all of her life . . . her best friend's parents. But these . . .

The sound of footsteps rushing up the porch steps stopped Kristen's thoughts. As she stood to see who it was, two women entered the kitchen.

They both stopped short and stared in her direction.

"You must be Kristen. I'm your Aenti Elizabeth and this here is your Aenti Miriam. Ach! You're the spittin' image of your mamm when she was your age. Ain't so, Miriam?"

Aunt Miriam gave a nod.

"I trust that John velkumed you and gave you some lunch? He seemed in an awful hurry. I thought he'd wait for us."

"He gave me the lunch you prepared. Thank you. He said he had to get back to work."

Aunt Miriam motioned for Aunt Elizabeth to step back out on the porch, her light blue eyes wide on Kristen.

Kristen stared back, amazed that these

15

women dressed in long dresses, aprons, and head coverings were her mother's sisters. Why had Mom never told her that she was Amish? All she'd ever said was that her dad had gone off not long after they'd been married and never returned. Was he Amish, too?

Aunt Miriam wore gray and Aunt Elizabeth, blue, both with brown aprons. For now the gray and blue helped Kristen keep their identities straight.

Her 'gray' aunt spoke hushed words to her 'blue' one, but her whispers rose loud enough through the screened door for Kristen to hear. Although she didn't understand the German-like language, the disapproval was evident in Aunt Miriam's tone.

Tears welled up in Kristen's eyes. Her mother and Ross were killed in a boating accident the day after school let out, three months before her eighteenth birthday, and now one of her aunts, Miriam in gray, obviously spoke about her as if she had the plague.

The feeling of being passed off to unknown relatives her mom didn't have anything to do with wasn't a good one. She'd been totally accepted while she stayed with Cindy's parents and was so happy that Social Services approved her temporary residence there. *Temporary,* being the key word.

Aunt Miriam and Aunt Elizabeth walked back into the house.

"Come, Kristen, let's get you settled while Aunt Miriam starts on dinner. She comes over a couple times a week and makes our childhood favorites. Ach, such a gut cook!"

Kristen followed Aunt Elizabeth up the stairs to a small, modest bedroom down the hall. It contained one bureau of drawers, a twin sized bed covered with a pretty green and yellow quilt, and a nightstand holding what looked like an oil lamp. An opened screened window adorned with a simple, sheer white curtain tied to one side faced the fields. Just about the same size room she'd had at Cindy's, except this room didn't have a TV.

"This is your room. We'll be getting a small desk in here for letter writing and such."

And for her laptop.

"Thanks. It's a nice room." But why would her mom want her in a place where she wasn't welcome?

"Now, you rest up, and I'll call you for supper. I'm making something special *tonacht.*" Aunt Elizabeth fluffed up the pillow on the bed, and then turned to her with

17

bright hazel eyes.

Such pretty eyes. The same shape as Mom's, only Mom's were brown, like hers.

"Will the others be here soon?" Kristen took a seat on the bed and discreetly wiped her sweaty palms on her jeans.

"Jonas, your *onkel,* is working with John out in the fields. Mary is working at the Farm Style Diner. And Daniel is helping out at Joseph Beiler's woodworking shop just outside of town 'til four o'clock. Then he helps his daed and *brudde*r with the farm work. They'll all be home for the evening meal. Our little Anna is over at her friend's haus the next farm over. Ach! She is so excited to meet her *Englisch* cousin."

Not like Aunt Miriam. How could Mom do this to her?

"Is there a fan? It's kind of hot." That was an understatement.

"We have a battery one. I'll bring it up. No electric in our haus. You know that, don'tcha?"

"Oh, right. John mentioned that at lunch. How come you guys can't use electricity?"

"It's our way. You'll learn more about it in time. There's a wonderful, gut breeze through the open window. Now, let me bring you that fan and a *nacht* gown for

18

tonacht. You'll be cooler once the sun goes down."

Aunt Elizabeth returned quickly with a small fan, a long, white cotton nightgown, and an armful of dresses.

"Being that you're part of the familye now, it's best if you wear some of these dresses around here. Mary sewed them up for you. Slacks are not fitting for Amish *maidles.*"

"But I'm not Amish! I brought my own clothes. There's nothing wrong with them where I come from. I have some dresses, too, if that'll be better." Kristen was downright insulted.

"Jah, sure, you can wear your own dresses, so long as you don't wear those tight jeans. Best to keep these dresses here just the same. You might need them if you come with us to Preaching, and it will make Mary happy to see them put to gut use."

She wouldn't be caught dead in those dresses. No girl her age would. At least, not a non-Amish one.

"Do I have to go to Preaching? Is that church or something?"

"Jah, it's our church service every other Sunday, held at the haus of a different familye each time. We'd like to have you join us as part of the familye. Even if you don't understand the High German, you'll be with the People on the Lord's Day. And you'll be meeting girls your age afterward, at the common meal."

Like she'd have anything to talk about with them! *Mom, what were you thinking?*

"Maybe one day," was all Kristen offered. Just enough to let Aunt Elizabeth know that she wasn't interested. Not now. Not ever! "If you don't use electricity that must mean that computers are off limits, too, right?" Kristen could barely control her mounting panic. Her laptop was in her suitcase.

"Vell, we can speak to Bishop Ebersol about that. Maybe he can arrange for you to go to an Englisch neighbor to use a computer, or you can use one at the public library in town. We cannot have one in our home. It's *verboden.*"

"Ver-what?"

"Verboden. Forbidden."

"But I have . . ." *one in my suitcase.* "Never mind." Unreal. How could she be happy living here? She probably had a hundred notifications on Facebook already. Maybe this was all a dream, and Mom would wake her from the sofa when she turned off the TV on her way to bed. In air conditioning. After Kristen's nightly swim in the ocean . . . with Derick.

A gentle nudge on the shoulder gave Kristen pause as to where she was. "Mom? OK, I'll go up to bed."

She received another nudge. This time she sat up and looked over at the source of the gentle push.

A small girl with honey-blonde braids stood there, wearing a sheer white head covering and a blue dress and apron. A miniature version of Aunt Elizabeth, except that her hair wasn't tucked into a bun, and her dress was a lighter shade of blue.

Oh, no! This wasn't a dream.

"Hi, I'm Anna. And you're Kristen, my Englisch cousin. Mamm said to wake you from your nap for supper."

The little girl's eyes shone with excitement and wonder.

"You have a pretty smile, Anna." Kristen felt a pull on her heart. No one ever made a big deal about her before. She wouldn't take her mood out on her sweet, young cousin.

The girl blushed, took Kristen's hand and tugged. "Let's go downstairs. We'll be eating soon, and I helped prepare the meal. Mamma said we can sit next to each other. Do you like fried chicken?"

"Um, I'm sure it'll be good." No need to explain her eating habits. She had no intention of staying long enough for them to question her choices. At least at Cindy's house, she was still able to see Derick. She'd text him later. He'd rescue her from all of this. He had to.

2

As Kristen and Anna entered the kitchen, two strapping men pulled out chairs and sat themselves at the table. Both wore blue shirts with the sleeves rolled up, darker blue overalls, and black work shoes.

Kristen looked toward the door and saw their straw hats hung on the pegs.

Aunt Elizabeth gave both the older and younger man wet cloths to wipe their faces and hands and then motioned for Kristen to sit across from them.

"Velkum, Kristen Esh, Emily's dochter. I am your Onkle Jonas, and this here is your cousin, Daniel."

Kristen nodded, not too comfortable having Uncle Jonas and her cousin looking her over as if she were some kind of oddity. Not to mention Aunt Miriam's ongoing glances of disapproval.

"Forgive the staring, niece, but we never had an Englisch relative that we know of.

Your Mamm left these parts many years ago, when she was just a couple years older than yourself. We never heard from her after that."

"So, why would she want me to live here if she didn't stay?"

"Better left unsaid," Aunt Miriam muttered.

Aunt Elizabeth paid no mind to the remark, not even looking Aunt Miriam's way to acknowledge it. She simply said, "Because we are your relatives, and your mamma knew we'd still be in Stone Arabia since our familye has been here for three generations now."

Kristen shrugged, her question still not answered.

"Did your *vadder* have any relatives?"

Aunt Miriam got up and walked toward the pantry, shaking her head back and forth as Aunt Elizabeth waited on Kristen's reply.

"I don't know anything about him. Mom told me he left before I was born, and they were married only for a short time. One day I might look into finding out who he is." She'd thought they'd know something. Guess her dad wasn't Amish. What a relief.

"Vell, no matter," Aunt Elizabeth was quick to say. "You've been through a rough patch, and it's time to get you on the mend.

A gut meal is a start, jah?"

Kristen nodded.

John walked in.

Butterflies swarmed Kristen's stomach at the sight of him. Odd.

"Sorry I'm late. I lost track of time finishing the mending of the fence behind the barn." His blue eyes momentarily locked on to Kristen's gaze.

"It's gut that the rain held off. Did you bring the tools back then?" Uncle Jonas gave John a lopsided frown as if he knew the answer.

"Nee. I have to get back out there right after supper to gather them up. I won't let them rust if it rains, Daed." Uncle Jonas nodded and unfolded his napkin, apparently a signal for them to bow their heads and say grace.

As Kristen bowed her head with the rest of them, she found herself wishing her father hadn't left them so she could have witnessed similar displays of family gatherings at her home. She remembered how she'd even hoped that Ross and her mom would fall in love, and how sad she'd been that it hadn't happened that way. What had she expected? He was the employer, and her mom was the live-in help. Nothing more to it, other than a friendship of sorts.

Someone cleared their throat and broke Kristen's reverie.

Then Aunt Elizabeth began passing the food.

Anna offered the platter of chicken to Kristen. She took it and held it for a long moment.

John looked over at her. No hint of teasing this time. "Kristen is a vegetarian."

Everyone looked over at him and then at Kristen.

"She told me at lunch today," he explained. "She traded her ham for my cheese. It worked out gut."

"Vell then, you'll enjoy the creamed potatoes and stewed zucchini." Aunt Elizabeth didn't seem affected by the news one way or another.

Kristen passed the platter back to Anna.

"Seems to me that the gut Lord gave us animals for our food. Why do you not eat them, Kristen?" Unlike her aunt, Onkle Jonas looked at her with both curiosity and what seemed like disapproval.

"I think if less people ate meat, we would have more land to grow other foods and be able to feed hungry people in the world that way. Cows and sheep take up a lot of land for grazing and to grow the food they're fed if they're factory farmed."

"Jah, in the Englisch world, but not these chickens," John told her. The teasing returned.

"And I coated all the pieces," Anna chimed in.

A twinge of guilt coursed through Kristen for disappointing Anna. She hadn't been a vegetarian 'til Derick urged her to join the Green Team at school.

"OK. Being that it's different with these chickens, maybe I'll taste one piece."

Anna was quick to hand the platter back to her.

"The Englisch do factory farming. The Amish here do not. Our animals graze and roam freely on our farmland. We only use what we need," Uncle Jonas informed her as she took a piece of the fried chicken.

Anna's face brightened.

Kristen had to admit that it tasted very good. Crisp and tender. Still, it unsettled her eating one of the chickens that obviously met its demise that day at this very place. So, this was what farm life was like.

"The strawberry pie is a special dessert I made for you," Aunt Elizabeth said. "I made two and already set aside a piece for Mary. This is her nacht for helping with the inventory at the diner where she works."

"Jah, otherwise she won't get a morsel.

Maybe we should see if we have other Englisch cousins needing a place to stay so you can make more of your special desserts." John's blue eyes sparkled with humor as he looked at Kristen.

Her pulse quickened and she looked away. John's good looks unnerved her, while his easy-going manner did just the opposite.

"Ach, go on now, John. We only got Kristen, far as I know." Aunt Elizabeth set the pie on the table.

Aunt Miriam went and brought back whipped cream. She sat at the opposite end from where Kristen was.

Why did this woman not like her? She didn't even know her.

"I better just have a small piece," Kristen said from habit.

"Ach! I made this dessert special for you. Go on. Take yourself a nice big slice. And if it's calories you're thinking about, like our Mary does sometimes, you'll be working them off around here in no time. Ain't so, Jonas?"

"Jah, that's for sure and for certain. Better eat yourself full. Your aenti will have you mighty hungry each day from all the chores she'll have you doing."

They all nodded. No one smiled.

He wasn't joking.

Finishing off her hearty slice of warm, sweet strawberry pie, with the creamiest cream she'd ever had piled high atop it, was no sacrifice for Kristen.

"Did your mamma make whipped cream to go with pie?" Anna peered up at Kristen with curious pale blue eyes.

But no answer came.

Instead, tears stung her eyes. The question brought the realization . . . all over again . . . that her mom and Ross were really gone. First, when she'd moved in with Cindy's family, and now, being with totally unknown relatives, honoring her mom's last wishes. The truth was too much to grasp. She couldn't bear to think what she'd do if Derick didn't pull through for her.

"Kristen, I'll put on some herb tea. It'll do you gut." Aunt Elizabeth stood and went to the cupboard. She returned with a cup and saucer. There was a momentary silence.

"Sorry. I just can't believe that my mom and Ross were killed in a boating accident like that. And how things are so different now."

"The Lord will heal you in His own time. You'll be making new friends here, and we'll keep you plenty busy. I grieve the loss of your mamm, too. Even though I haven't seen her in a long row of years, she was my baby sister. There's no need to be apologizing, ain't so, Jonas?"

"Jah, that's for sure, niece. You had to have a cry. Now that it's over, just take each day as it comes. We must remember the Lord saw fit to call your mamm from this earth, and we need to abide by His will."

Somehow Kristen didn't think being killed in a boating accident was the Lord's will. She attempted a weak smile while Anna patted her hand.

Aunt Elizabeth poured hot golden-colored water into her cup and stirred in a teaspoon of honey. It smelled like flowers.

"Go ahead. Take a sip. It's chamomile and tastes gut," little Anna encouraged.

John was quiet, but he looked at her with serious eyes.

Kristen blew on the hot tea and took a small sip.

Apparently satisfied, Anna flashed her a full-faced smile then happily resumed eating her pie, as did the rest of the family.

John looked up from his dessert once more as if to make certain Kristen was OK. She smiled more wholeheartedly to assure him. His expression relaxed. These people actually acted as if they cared about her. Of course, she knew they didn't. How could they? She was as much a stranger to them as they were to her.

Soon cups were filled with coffee and tea and conversation broke out again about chores and the latest news of various neighbors. The subject of her mom closed.

Kristen sighed and smiled at the same time. She thought of her dinners at fast food places or by herself with the TV on due to her mom's and Ross's work schedules. Tonight, it was kind of nice sitting at the table with other people. Not by herself. With . . . *family*? Almost a foreign word to her. An *Amish* family no less.

Once alone in her room, Kristen got her chance to text Derick while some battery life was left in her cell phone.

Hey, Derick. My phone might be dead by the time you get this. I'm in a totally backward place called Stone Arabia in Palatine, NY with the Wagler family on Dillen something Road. They're my mom's Amish relatives. Unreal, right? I need you to come take me back to stay at Cindy's. ASAP. Like, tomorrow by dawn. If you're not here then, I'll find a place to charge my phone so I can get your message and we can talk. I miss you like crazy.

A knock on the bedroom door pierced the almost too quiet room.

"Kristen? It's Aentie Elizabeth. Thought we'd chat for a short bit."

31

"OK. Come in."

"Voss iss diess?" Aunt Elizabeth's gaze immediately went to Kristen's pink phone lying on the bed. She didn't look too happy.

"Ah, my cell phone. I needed to contact a friend."

Aunt Elizabeth still held her frown.

"No electricity and no phone use either?"

"Jah, we have a phone shack over by the Byler farm. We mainly use it for emergencies or to contact far off relatives. Even those carrying phones are allowed by some now, especially for business. But not for idle talk."

"What exactly is idle talk to you guys?"

"Talk about this and that. A phone in the haus leads a person away from familye time."

"I wasn't even talking to anyone. I just left a text message for a friend to let him know where I am. Do I have to sneak around with this then?"

"Best you not use it in the haus for idle talk, is all I'm saying. Contacting your friend is fine, I s'pose."

Kristen rolled her eyes and crossed her arms. She was an inmate in a prison that happened to serve good food.

"We don't mean to upset you, Kristen, but this is the way of the *Plain* people. In

32

time, if you're not taking to things here, you'll soon be old enough to go your own way. But your mamm wanted you to be with familye, and I'm happy to have you for as long as you wish to stay. Gut nacht, child."

"Good night." Kristen sighed. Her response held more annoyance than she'd intended. Tomorrow was another day. But not here. Derick would take her away from this backward place.

3

A knocking sound awoke Kristen. Groggy, she turned over, but the knocking continued.

She grabbed her cell phone to look at the time, but it'd gone dead. She glanced toward the window. A glimmer of dawn overhung the darkness. Derick! Was he here?

"Time to get up, Kristen. We got breakfast to tend to."

Aunt Elizabeth sounded her usual cheery self and as wide awake as if it were noon. She made no mention of Derick. He hadn't come.

Kristen held back tears and forced herself out of bed. Not yet unpacked, she retrieved her suitcase from under the bed and took out her toothbrush, hairbrush, denim skirt, to abide by the no pants rule, and a striped polo. She slipped into the robe she'd laid out on the chair the night before and trotted off to the washroom downstairs next to the kitchen. The small area with a few hooks on the wall consisted of a water pump, a large rubber mat, a medium size basin, a chunk of the colorless soap, and some clean towels. No mirror. She'd never brushed her hair without looking at her reflection.

When she walked into the kitchen, washed and dressed, Aunt Elizabeth handed her an apron.

"You know how to scramble eggs, jah?"

"Yes, I've scrambled eggs for myself lots of times."

"Gut. Please use this bowl to crack the eggs into. Two dozen will be fine."

"Two dozen! That's a lot."

"Nee, not for seven people with the men taking seconds. While you do that, I'll fry up the bacon."

Kristen cracked the eggs and scrambled them with milk that Aunt Elizabeth had ready for her to add. She then went to the stove and poured the mixed eggs into two frying pans, careful to stir them around slowly, working side by side with her aunt. She hadn't cooked with another person since her pre-school days in Ross's kitchen with her mom.

A tall, pretty older girl walked in with a cheerful *Geode Mariye.* Her glance settled on Kristen. She gave her a warm smile

"Hullo, I'm Mary. Sorry I missed your velkum supper last nacht. It's nice to have another maidle in the kitchen to help get breakfast on the table. Can you please set out some jams and *budder* from the ice box?" Mary started to set the table.

Kristen glanced out the kitchen window. No Derick. She forced a smile back at Mary then went to the pantry where the chest was kept and retrieved three jars of different jams and a small tub of butter. She couldn't help but notice how full the ice box was, much like her mom had kept their fridge at home, before she began working a second job at the hotel. Then leftover pizza and Chinese food became the more common items found there. Scrambled eggs made for a quick home cooked dinner, when one of them remembered to buy eggs.

"Goede Mariye, Cousin Kristen," Anna said, bounding into the kitchen, all smiles and bright eyed as she headed toward the counter.

"Can I help make the *kaffee* again, Mamma?"

"Jah, you know where the pot is and how much kaffee to put into the basket. No need to be asking me each time. You can do it from now on."

Kristen marveled. One would think that

Anna just won a million dollars at being given this chore the way she hurried off toward the stove.

A wonderful scent filled Kristen's nostrils. "Is something baking?"

Aunt Elizabeth nodded. "Ach, just a couple of oatmeal pies. Later, we'll make cherry pies. I need to bring one to a quilting bee tomorrow. The leftover strawberry pie will go in everyone's lunch pails. Pies around here disappear faster than dust in the wind."

"I love pie." She was glad, at least, about the pie situation.

"Pizza pie, too?"

Kristen turned toward the voice and saw John walking toward the table. A slow smile claimed his handsome face. Her cousin. John. Who really wasn't her cousin at all. He was good looking enough all right. His blue large eyes, honey-blond hair and tanned skin were hard to ignore.

"Yes, I like pizza, too. I sometimes eat it cold right out of the fridge." Why did she tell him that? Well, he didn't have to know that it served as breakfast on those mornings that mom's hours were switched.

"How about warm pizza?"

"That's my first choice."

"The reason I'm asking is that I thought

you might like to go into town tomorrow after chores, it being Saturday and all. We could have some pizza there."

The room went quiet. The only sound Kristen heard was that of Mary opening the oven to take out the pies. Had John said something wrong?

As if on cue to her question, Uncle Jonas walked in.

"Did I hear you say you want to take Kristen to town for pizza?" He looked directly at John, with Daniel standing behind him, looking anxious to get past him.

"Jah. Figured she'd like to see the town and taste the pizza here. Said herself that she loves pies. Ain't so, Kristen?"

"Yes, I do love pie, especially pizza. At home we have our favorite place for pizza too." Mack and Mango's on the boardwalk. She'd be there soon enough.

Uncle Jonas took his seat at the head of the table while Daniel scooted around him to his seat. He pulled on his beard thoughtfully, keeping his gaze on John. "I s'pose it'll be all right. Give Kristen a chance to ride in the buggy, too."

"I've never been in a buggy before. Sounds like fun."

"Buggies are not for fun around here," Uncle Jonas said. "It's our transportation. If you stay on, you'll be driving one soon enough. Old Faithful is a reliable, calm horse. Rusty can be a bit excitable, but she is coming along better now. We use them both together with the family buggy and separately for the two smaller buggies."

"How will I get to the library to use the computer if the bishop says it's all right?" Kristen didn't know why she even asked. She'd be long gone before they knew it.

"Daniel and Mary can take you on their way to work. You'll squeeze in fine in the small buggy. Just need to be leaving a little earlier, is all."

"Jah, 'tis no trouble at all," Mary said, bringing one of the pies to the table. When she sliced it, a fragrant steam escaped that smelled exactly like oatmeal cookies.

"But you'll have to wait at the diner where I work for the library to open. Think it opens at ten."

"How did you get to the library and school where you used to live?" Anna looked into Kristen's face with her usual gaze of anticipation.

"At first I went with my friend, Cindy, and her mom in their car. Then Cindy got her driver's license. She's a year older than me. She drove us both to school and back home."

"What about your mamm?"

"She needed to sleep most mornings from working late at the hotel. And Ross left for work very early. He was also away a lot on business or with his lady friend, Mattie, on vacations."

"Your mamm went to work? Who's Ross?"

"Ach, I'm thinking that Kristen has to eat herself some breakfast, Anna," Aunt Elizabeth interrupted with a scolding frown. "How about you let her answer your questions later on? For now, let's eat, jah?"

After a short silent bow of heads, scrambled eggs, bacon, and pie were soon passed around with the conversation focused on a woman named Betsy who was holding the quilting bee the next day.

"Rachel Miller will be at the bee, too," Mary commented, her words directed at her younger brother, Daniel, causing him to blush.

"And I s'pose there'll be a whole crowd of men folk there just mulling about, jah?"

Mary rolled her eyes at his comment. "Nee, Daniel. But maybe you can drop me and Mamma off and then come pick us up. That-a-way you could say a quick hi to Rachel."

"No sense talking in circles, dochter. Let them get around to one another their own way and in the *gut* Lord's time." Uncle Jonas gave Aunt Elizabeth a small smile.

Kristen liked the quiet exchanges between them.

When breakfast was over, things took on a much brisker pace. Aunt Elizabeth gave Anna garden gloves and not more than a minute later, she was out the door. Daniel left the kitchen faster than Kristen could watch him go. Then Uncle Jonas and John each took a wrapped piece of leftover strawberry pie, shoved it into their pockets, and scooted past her. Mary cleared the table in record time, took two brown bags from the counter, and with a smile and a nod, dashed out.

Kristen heard a horse and buggy draw close to the house, some talking in the foreign language they used, and then John strode back inside.

"What is it, John?" Aunt Elizabeth looked at him with surprise.

His face took on a red tinge. He looked at Kristen for a moment, and then focused his gaze on his mother.

"We all headed out of here so quick, and being that it's Kristen's first morgen here, vell, I thought it would be fitting to wish her a gut day."

"Ach, you're right, John. Everyone rushed

41

out without a word to Kristen. Morgens are always a rushed time around here, no matter how early we rise. Didn't mean to make you feel unvelcome on your first morgen here."

"That's OK. I never gave it a thought. I was just surprised to see how quick everyone left the house."

"All the same, I wish you a gut first day here, Kristen Esh."

"Thanks, John."

Kristen appreciated his kindness but was too anxious about no sign of Derick to show it. A smile just wouldn't come.

"And you have a gut day too, Mamm," John added, and then scooted back out the door in the same school boy manner he'd exited the kitchen the day before.

As if on an automatic setting, Aunt Elizabeth had no trouble assigning work to Kristen. "We'll tend to the dishes first. I'll wash and you dry. After that, we'll sweep the floors, shake out the rugs, dust, and air the beds."

"I thought we were going to bake cherry pies."

"We'll be doing that, too, nearer to supper time. That-a-way we can have one for dessert. Chores come first. Anna will be eager to help with pie baking, that's for sure and for certain."

"What chores does Anna do?"

"Vell, this morgen she's out weeding our two vegetable gardens. She's our kaffe girl at breakfast time now, but before that she feeds the chickens. She gathers the eggs, cleans them, and keeps the pen tidy. Lately, she's taken to naming the hens. Not much sense in that."

"What about the chicken we ate last night? It was from here? It had a name?"

"Ach. Of course it was from here. We have laying ones and eating ones. Anna takes care of the hens we use for laying. Daniel the eating ones. She doesn't fuss with those."

"So, the eggs we ate came from your chickens, too?"

"Jah, they did. Most of the Amish around here keep them for eggs. You'll get to see all that we have over the weekend."

No, she wouldn't. She'd be long gone. "I'm supposed to go into town with John."

"Jah . . . with John." Worry laced Aunt Elizabeth's voice.

"Do you mind me going with him?"

"Nee, he's like a cousin, after all. But just so you know, I have an inkling that he is courting a young lady named Sadie Krantz. Best not to confuse folks, even though we keep these things quiet. Going out for pizza together, vell . . ."

"Don't worry, Aunt Elizabeth. I already have a boyfriend back in New Jersey." *And he'll be coming to take me back there . . . today. Please let it be today.* "Guys and girls go out for pizza together all the time. It doesn't mean they're a couple. At least not where I come from."

"Jah, that's the difference, Kristen."

4

The following morning, after another hearty breakfast and a lesson on making biscuits, Kristen headed outside with Anna to see the chickens. She tried her best not to show her disappointment about Derick not showing up. She needed to get her phone charged to find out what his plan was. She knew he had one.

"Do you know him?" Anna looked to the far left from where they stood, toward the road.

"Who?"

"That man sitting in the car over there. The one in the passenger seat. He's looking at you like he knows you."

Kristen's heart raced. Derick! She squinted her eyes against the new morning sun rising above the cornfields beyond the car. Once her eyes settled on the old car, she knew it wasn't Derick. He had a new Honda Fit. Her heart sank.

The car sped off, leaving a trail of dust behind. That was strange. Her stomach churned and her breakfast no longer sat very well.

"You feeling *grank,* Kristen?"

"Grank? What's that?" She stared at the lingering dust settling to the ground.

"Sick. Are you feeling sick? You look funny. Is it 'cause of that man who stopped to look at you?"

"No, no. I'm fine. And don't you worry about that man. Probably just a tourist who lost his way. That must happen here a lot, right?"

"Jah, sometimes. But that man was sure staring at you."

"Well, maybe that's because I look pretty today." Kristen batted her eyelashes, making light of the incident even though it set her on edge.

Anna giggled.

"OK, take me to see the chickens. Your mamma told me you gave them names."

"Just my favorites." Anna led the way to a fenced-in area of chicken wire.

"This is the hen haus, where they do the egg laying. That other pen and chicken coop behind these is for the chickens we eat. Daniel takes care of those."

Kristen was glad she didn't have to see

46

the ones they slaughtered if she was to eat them. She followed Anna into the henhouse. The ruckus from her presence as she walked in startled her. A few chickens were seated on perches, and the others were in their nest boxes like dedicated little mothers. Good thing she wore sneakers instead of sandals. Wood shavings covered the floor and coated her Nikes. It was way warmer than she thought comfortable. Then again, it was definitely too warm for her liking in the house, too.

"This here is Susie. She lays the most eggs and doesn't fuss when I take 'em from her. That one over there at the end is Missy because she thinks she's extra special, squawking and carrying on each time I tend to any of the other hens. And the one next to Susie is Sunny because she likes to go out only when it's sunny outside. I'm still thinking of names for the other five. Would you like to name one?"

"Well, sure. Let me take a better look at them."

"Jah, OK. While you're doing that, I'll name one of 'em after you. How about Kristie?"

"Oh, I like that. Which one?"

"That-a-one over at the end on the perch. She's a pretty one, like you, cousin."

"You're sweet, Anna. Now, tell me, which other one do you think is pretty?"

"The one at the other end."

"Well then, how about we name that one Annabelle, for you?"

Her young cousin beamed.

Kristen stepped out of the henhouse with Anna.

Uncle Jonas came toward them wearing a stern expression.

"Were you both in the henhaus all this time?" he asked, with a crinkled forehead and urgency in his voice.

"Yes," Kristen answered. "Anna showed me the chickens, and we . . ."

"Best you both head to the haus now."

"Is something wrong, Uncle Jonas?"

"Nee. Just don't go off alone 'til I say so. For the next few days, John will be going with you to feed the chickens, Anna. Kristen, you'll tend to the chores in the haus."

Kristen couldn't understand what exactly was happening or why. Then she thought of the men in the car.

"Is it something to do with the car that stopped by earlier?"

"What car are you talking about, Kristen?" Her uncle's eyes grew wide as discs.

"A car stopped by here when we were going to the henhouse."

"Did the driver get out? Did he walk on our property?"

"No. There were two of them . . . both men. I barely got a glimpse. When I tried, the car took off. Maybe they were lost."

"Would think they'd ask for directions then."

Kristen didn't answer, although her uncle's comment made good sense.

"The one staring at Kristen had a beard just like yours, Daed. He didn't look Amish though 'cause he wore a cap."

Uncle Jonas darted a quick gaze down the lane then nodded at Anna's comment.

"I'll be with John when I go into town while Aunt Elizabeth and Mary are at the quilting bee. Is that all right?"

He turned his deep brown eyes to her and said, "Just stay close to him and don't go rushing off anywhere on your own."

John noted Kristen's somber expression when she stepped into the buggy. He wasn't sure if she'd been told about the note left under their door. Should he mention it? He didn't want to worry her if she didn't know.

"Your dad was very upset this morning, as if something had happened to cause him to worry about my safety. When Anna and I told him about the men who stopped in a car by the road near the henhouse, that just made matters worse. Do you know why he's so worried?"

Relief washed over him when she solved his dilemma by speaking about it first.

"I wasn't going to talk about it if you didn't know. I don't want to cause you stress. But, jah, I do know the reason for my daed's concern."

"So, are you going to tell me? How bad can it be?"

"Kristen, someone left a note under our door saying that it would be better all around if you left Stone Arabia. It was unsigned."

"Oh. That's kind of creepy. Why would anyone want me to leave here? Is it because I'm not Amish?"

"Nee, it is not. We have never snubbed Englischers and many of them are our friends and neighbors. Besides, your mamm was Amish."

"OK, so I'm half Amish. Whatever . . . it only goes to show that I don't belong where my mother thought I did."

"Jah, you do. I know you'll learn to like this place and our ways once your hurt and grief settle down." John clicked his tongue and the horse began to trot.

"You think I'll live the Amish life? Not happening, John. I have Derick and good friends waiting for me. There are other places I want to see. Besides, I was supposed to go to college after I finished high school and earn a degree in accounting."

"You have a great interest in this?"

"Yes, I do. Ross was a CPA in his own firm and taught me a lot. I was always good with numbers. It pays a good salary. During tax time Ross prepared tax returns. Didn't have a minute to spare. Some clients were pretty famous, and he traveled to their homes. He did very well."

"Ach, Kristen, working isn't always about the money."

"I know that. But I like doing anything that involves numbers and seeing people happy and calm after their taxes are done. Many of Ross's clients were confused by the changes each year. He made it easy for them."

"Vell then, I think you'll make a fine accountant."

Kristen nodded with a weak smile then looked straight ahead onto the road.

John steered the buggy to the side to allow several cars to pass. One of the drivers took a photo, and the other two just drove on by. He wished they'd all do as the last two cars had done. He looked over at Kristen again. She seemed a thousand miles away in thought. He wondered if it had been wise to tell her about the note.

When they arrived in town, John hitched Rusty to the hitch rail by Sol's General Store and helped Kristen out of the buggy.

"I promised Anna I would get her a pretzel. They sell gut ones here." He held the door open for her as they walked inside.

"Would you like one?" John turned to her from the counter before giving his order.

"Not if we're having pizza. Too many carbs. Although they look so good."

"OK, next time we'll come just for pretzels." This meant he would take her to town again. A second time might not look proper. But when Kristen smiled and the gloom that had taken over her face lifted, John's worries about it lifted as well.

Then, as if she could read his mind she said, "You should have invited Sadie to come along. I'd like to meet her."

"Jah, that's a gut idea. How did you come to learn about Sadie?"

"Your mother said you're probably courting her. I think she's worried that I had some kind of romantic ideas about us. I told her that Derick is back home waiting for me."

52

John wasn't accustomed to such open talk regarding courting. It was generally kept secret in his world 'til published shortly before a wedding date. He found it refreshing and even a bit humorous.

"Is there anywhere I can charge my cell phone?"

"Sure, right here at the general store. The owner is not Amish, and there is electricity. Sol Yoder, who rents out the space, accommodates many Amish who require cell phones for business with battery charging. Let me have it, and I'll leave it with him. It should be charged by the time we get back from having our pizza."

Kristen handed the phone to John.

Minutes later John led the way into Gabrielle's Pizza shop, just a short walk from the general store. When they stepped inside, the wonderful aroma of freshly baked pizza tantalized his taste buds.

Kristen closed her eyes and inhaled deeply.

"Aw, the heck with the carbs. I think I'm going to have two slices. Is that OK?" She turned to him with a huge smile.

"I'd like nothing better. I usually have three." John motioned for Kristen to sit at one of the small tables and then went to place their order.

"When we're done, we can walk around town and after go back and get your cell phone." He set two sodas on the table.

"Thanks, John. I can hardly wait to hear my messages."

A waitress carried their pizza over on a tray. John liked the fact that Kristen paused for a silent prayer. Just as she was about to take a bite of her thick cheesy slice, he saw an Amish woman in a blue dress approach from the corner of his eye. He looked up and smiled.

"Hullo, Sadie. This is my mamm's niece, Kristen. She was just saying how nice it would be if you could join us, and here you are."

Sadie eyed Kristen with her light blue eyes then gave a friendly smile.

John pulled out the chair next to him, and she sat.

"So, you and John are cousins, then?"

"Not really. Because John's mom was Jonas's first wife. So no real blood relation," Kristen clarified.

John wasn't sure Sadie needed to know the details.

"Vell, I came to get my brudders some candy at the general store. Then I got a hankering for pizza. It's so nice to meet you, Kristen. I hope John is showing you a pleasant time. Many Amish sell from their homes, but on Saturdays an Englisch woman who runs a store called Country Commons lets Amish women set up bake stands in the parking lot. My sister brings her candles there to sell as vell. There are pretty Amish-made quilts in the store that you might like to see, too, although I'm not sure they hold interest for any of our men folk." She gave John a shy smile.

He read no discomfort in her eyes and felt a wave of relief wash over him. He returned her smile.

"Why don't you join us for pizza? I already have some here. Then we can show Kristen the home baked pies and quilts."

"Wouldn't you rather go to the hardware store?" Sadie grinned.

Jah, he would, but he had no intentions of disobeying his daed's wishes to stay by Kristen's side while in town.

"It's fine," he said, leaving Sadie with raised eyebrows.

She took a napkin and placed it on her lap.

John gave her one of his three slices.

He was glad Kristen and Sadie hit it off. Now Sadie would have no reason to be jealous if she heard that he and Kristen went somewhere together. Would she? Nee! For all intents and purposes, Kristen was his cousin, whether by blood or otherwise, and they would behave as such.

5

John tried not to roll his eyes over the fuss Sadie and Kristen made over the candles and later over those Edna Lucille soaps at the country store where the Englicsh owner sold many crafts the Amish made. Each weekend, weather permitting, the parking lot bustled with both Amish and Englisch women interacting as baked goods exchanged hands.

Kristen and Sadie spent more time than he'd anticipated sniffing all fifteen kinds of the soaps displayed inside The Amish Commons. He was ecstatic when they were ready to return to the general store.

Sadie went right in and headed for the hard candies for her brudders.

"This is a nice store. Why is there a FOR RENT sign on the glass?"

"Sol Yoder is moving to Pinecraft, Florida, next month. The landlord is looking for someone to take over the store," John explained. "I'll go get your cell phone. I'm sure it has a charge by now."

"OK. I'll listen to the messages in the buggy so that your mamm doesn't get upset with me doing it in the house."

"She's OK with it so long as it isn't idle silly talk. Your messages might be important."

"Kind of. I think my friends would want to hear how I'm doing. If I don't answer them, they'll worry, especially Cindy. She and I grew up together and her parents took me in after my mom and Ross died. Just the same, I'd like to listen to the messages while we ride home."

"Sure, that would be fine."

They headed inside the store, and Kristen went to check out the candy counter.

Sadie held a green candy stick and handed a purple one to Kristen. They giggled as they unwrapped them like excited school girls.

It was gut for Kristen to have another female friend, and there'd be no more concern about being seen with his pretty Englisch cousin. Now his only worry was why he couldn't keep Kristen out of his thoughts. She'd done nothing to lead him into any kind of romantic notions, and he'd had no interest in anyone else except Sadie for the past year. So, why was his mind full of how to make Kristen happy? Did he feel sorry for her? Could it be that he mistook compassion for some other emotion? Were his feelings for Sadie not deep enough for courting?

When John retrieved Kristen's cell phone, he bought a fresh pretzel for Anna and decided he'd eat the one he'd gotten earlier on the way home.

Outside, he untied the horse of each buggy from the hitching post.

"Are you all right riding home alone, Sadie? Or would you like Kristen to keep you company, and I can follow in my buggy?"

"Ach. I'll be fine. It's not the first time I've come here alone."

"Jah, that's true. I'll be seeing you tomorrow then."

Sadie nodded, got into her buggy, waved good-bye, and trotted off.

Kristen was already seated inside John's buggy when he handed her the cell phone.

"Thanks, John. I'll just be a few minutes getting my messages, OK?"

"Jah. Take as much time as you need. I'll munch on my pretzel."

"After pizza? It's a wonder that you're in such good shape the way you eat."

Her words flattered him, but he quickly dismissed his vanity. "It's the farm work that keeps most of us fit."

Kristen gave him a smile and then turned her attention solely to her phone. She had the nicest smile. And the blunt way she spoke to him continued to amuse him. He wondered what her beau back in New Jersey was like. Was she the least bit happy staying here in the Plain world? Judging by the way she anxiously punched the buttons on that phone of hers, he doubted it.

"What's the matter? Doesn't your phone work?"

"I don't know. Something must have happened to it. I have no messages. How can that be?"

"Maybe your friends want to give you a chance to settle in before they call." He didn't know what else to say. She looked as if she would cry any minute.

"No, I left Derick a message to call or text me. He'd have told Cindy and the others. And even if he never got the message, he would have called by now to see how I'm doing. And Cindy is my best friend. I don't get it."

"Why not try calling them now that the phone is charged to see if it's working properly? I can wait. There's plenty of time 'til supper."

"Really? OK. I'll be right back."

"Where are you going? I promised Daed I'd keep an eye on you. You can stay here. I'll step out of the buggy and wait next to it."

"No, that's all right. I like to walk when I talk on the phone, especially if I'm nervous. And right now I am. I'll be just over there by the store's porch where you can see me."

Kristen walked over to the bench outside the general store but never sat down. Instead, she paced back and forth as she spoke.

John finished off his pretzel while he waited and watched. After about ten minutes, Kristen was no longer speaking on the phone but stood as still as a tree trunk. He was about to go over and ask what the problem was when he noticed her wiping her eyes with a tissue.

What could have happened to make her cry? Had Derick or Cindy said something to upset her?

Waiting a few minutes before going to see if she was OK would be best. But no sooner had he decided that, Kristen walked over and got into the buggy without a word.

"Kristen, are you all right?"

"I don't know how I am. Let's just go back."

"Do you want to talk about it?" He surprised himself with the question. Since when did he or any other Amish person display such inquisitiveness?

"No. Talking won't do any good. Things are going from bad to worse. I just wish my mom and Ross were alive, and I had my old life back." She took out a new tissue from the pocket of her denim skirt and wiped at her eyes.

"Is it that bad being here?" He was almost afraid to hear her reply.

"It's just very different. I miss my mother so much. And my friends. At least I thought they were my friends."

"Why do you say that, Kristen? Of course they're your friends." He was doing it again.

"Ha! Yeah, right. Let's just go, please."

John couldn't understand what had caused such a change in Kristen. She looked absolutely crushed, and he was tempted to give her hand a squeeze as a caring gesture but thought better of it. Best be remembering that he needed to be keeping Sadie at the forefront of his mind. Why did he have to keep reminding himself to do that?

When Kristen and John arrived back home

it was four o'clock. The haus was empty. Kristen went straight to the washroom. When she entered the kitchen, John noticed that the tear stains were gone from her cheeks, but her eyes were still red. He decided to keep quiet about her crying episode. Instead, he went to the fridge and took out a pitcher of cold lemonade.

"Can you please get me a glass from the cupboard? Get one for yourself, too, if you'd like some."

"OK, thanks. I could use a cold drink. It's so hot here. I miss the ocean." She got herself and John a tall glass each.

"I've never been to the ocean, but we have plenty of streams, waterfalls, and lakes here." John hoped she'd be pleased to know that.

"I'm sure they're pretty, but there's nothing like the ocean."

So much for that.

"You can see way out to the horizon, and the air has a salty, fresh smell," she went on. "I can almost taste it just thinking about it. Oh, and the waves! Sometimes they'd soothe me to sleep when we'd keep the windows open in summer. I like the sounds of the gulls, too. I used to watch them swoop down onto the surface of the water for fish and then glide right back up to the sky again. And the awesome sunsets. Imagine, if you can, the whole beach turned to a golden orange. That's how it is, John. It amazes me no matter how many times I see it."

John stood quiet for a moment. Kristen's sentiments for the ocean moved something inside of him, the way she looked when she described it. Her eyes glowed with a sweet longing. He saw a glimmer of happiness come over her; something he hadn't seen on her face since she'd arrived.

"Kristen, maybe you can enjoy a few places here. I can show you a beautiful stream and the mountain fields with wildflowers if you like."

Kristen's face fell momentarily, but then she looked at him with her haunting dark eyes and smiled a half-hearted smile.

"Well, OK. I guess it's only fair for me to see what you love about this place if I want you to see what I love about the shore."

John thought it a gut idea to have a picnic in the meadow by the lake with Kristen and the familye next Saturday for a couple of hours. She needed to start liking the area if she was ever going to feel at ease here and think less about the ocean and her former home.

"Gut. We'll plan on a picnic with the familye for next Saturday. And maybe you can help make the sandwiches since you might still want to leave the meat out from yours," he teased. When he looked over to her with a chuckle, she was staring out the kitchen window.

"John? Who is that across the road outside?"

John followed her gaze out the window and saw a dusty car stopped by the entrance of their walkway by the mailbox.

"I never saw that car and I can't see the driver too gut. Maybe he's looking for directions. Let me go see."

"No! Don't go."

"Kristen, why would I not go?"

"It looks like the same car I saw when I was with Anna this morning. Why would they come back here?"

"Best I go and check it out then. You stay here."

As soon as John opened the screened door, the car took off. If this was the same car that Kristen told Daed about, he knew he needed to tell the familye at supper time. But right now, he didn't want her left alone while he tended to some chores in the barn. Kristen still stood with her gaze out the window when he turned toward her. He could see the worry lurking behind her deep brown eyes.

"How about you come with me to the barn to see how the cows are milked? We don't have many, but enough for our needs."

"What about that car?"

"It's gone. If it comes back again, we'll deal with it. For now, try to put it out of your thoughts."

"I'll try. I've never milked a cow before, so maybe that will take my mind off of things. Do you sell any of the milk?"

"Nee, we don't produce enough. We grow alfalfa to sell as feed for folks who have enough cows for milk selling. And soon we'll get a gut crop of corn that we'll sell at the farm market, too."

As they walked to the barn, Kristen turned and looked around her. Seemed things were mounting up on her nerves today. First, the mysterious car this morgen, then whatever happened with her friends on the phone, and now the return of the car.

"Kristen?"

"Yes?"

"You're safe here. I'll see to that."

When the family had finished their meal, Kristen saw Aunt Elizabeth catch Aunt Miriam's eye, as if it were time to do something.

"I have to go to Rebecca Bieler's tonacht

66

to help bind her cookbooks. Would you like to help me in the kitchen, Anna? This way I can get there sooner."

"Jah, sure, Aenti Miriam. Can I go with you to help with the books, too? They're candy recipe books. I'd like to see 'em."

"As long as it's all right with your mamm."

Aunt Elizabeth nodded her agreement.

"I'll help, too," Mary said as she stood.

"Nee, I think a familye talk is about to begin," Aunt Miriam explained.

"Can't we stay for the talk and then go to help with the cookbooks?" Anna looked to Aunt Elizabeth and Aunt Miriam with a pout.

"Rebecca has to have all the books done tonacht, so we need to get an early start. Besides, it'll be all grown-up talk here, and you'll get bored faster than a cat in a barn without mice."

"Jah, OK, Aenti Miriam. Maybe I can bring back one of those candy recipes for you to make, Mamma."

"That would be fine. Now go on with Aenti Miriam. Mary and I will take care of the dishes."

"*Denki,* Elizabeth. Come by tomorrow for tea, if you can."

"Jah, Miriam, I will. We'll talk more then." Aunt Elizabeth walked Aunt Miriam and

Anna to the door.

Aunt Elizabeth placed a pitcher of iced tea and a plate of lemon cookies on the table then she sat with a serious expression.

"I have something to tell you all. I wanted to wait 'til after supper so that our meal wouldn't be interrupted by anything upsetting."

"What is it, Liz?"

Aunt Elizabeth reached into her apron pocket and handed the yellow folded note to Uncle Jonas. Her uncle's eyebrows furrowed as he silently read the words. Then he put it down, scratched his beard and pushed the note toward Kristen.

"What's this?"

Aunt Elizabeth sighed then said, "When Rebecca dropped me off from her haus, I noticed part of the yellow paper sticking out of the closed mailbox as I walked toward it. You need to read it, Kristen. We don't want to hide anything from you. You're not a *kind* anymore. You can read it out loud if you want."

"Is this the note that was left here about me this morning?" Kristen looked from her uncle to her aunt.

"You know about that note?" Uncle Jonas looked at her with surprise.

"Yes. John told me on our way to town today."

"Vell, this is a second note that your aenti found in our mailbox."

"Another one? About me?"

John grabbed the note before Kristen read a word.

"John, what are you doing? Let Kristen read it. She needs to know what the notes say. I have the other one from this morgen right here in my pocket." He pushed it toward his son.

"She already knows what the first note says, Daed. I told her word for word."

"Can someone please clue Mary and me in to what this is all about?" Daniel asked from across the table.

"You'll both be knowing as soon as John reads the two notes to us." Uncle Jonas's voice held a hint of impatience.

"Jah, sorry, Daed. I just thought Kristen didn't need to be any more nervous than she might already be from the note this morgen, and, er, the car we saw stop here this afternoon."

Kristen looked up at John, and he held her gaze followed by a not-to-worry kind of smile. His quiet reassurance calmed her. The mention of the return of the car would cause more concern to them. It sure had her on edge.

"What car, John?" Aunt Elizabeth's brow creased.

"It was the same car that Anna and I saw this morning," Kristen was quick to say before John could reply.

"Jah, at the entrance to our walkway near the mailbox. So, whoever it was must've left the second note then," John said.

"Jonas, did you know about this car around here this morgen and not tell me?"

"I was going to tell you at bedtime, Liz. Didn't want to worry your whole day is all."

Aunt Elizabeth gave him a half-hearted nod then faced Kristen.

"We don't want you to be nervous and afraid, but none of us should keep any notes or news of seeing strange cars around here from you or one another. We need to be vigilant. Now, John, please read the notes to us like your daed asked."

John unfolded the first note and cleared his throat.

"It would be better all around if the girl is sent back to where she came from." Then he unfolded the second note, and without looking up, he read: "Take the girl back to where she came from. It is in her best interest. The notes will continue until she leaves Palatine." He put the note down and his

70

gaze rested on Kristen. She tried to keep her composure but her eyes began to water.

"Why would anyone not want our cousin here?" Mary asked.

"We don't know," Jonas answered. "But obviously someone does not."

"I think if we get more notes or see that same car around here, we should tell the sheriff," Daniel said.

Uncle Jonas stared at the notes in John's hands.

"You know we have to let the bishop in on this before we can do that, Daniel."

The bishop? This was turning into something bigger with each passing hour.

"Kristen, I don't mean to be unkind in asking you this, but when I showed your Aenti Miriam the note, she wondered if it could be your boyfriend trying to get you back to New Jersey?"

Aunt Elizabeth's voice held no accusation as she went on. "After thinking on it more, I came to realize that you are in a vulnerable position. You have nowhere to go until the estate is settled. You can easily fall prey to a young man's promise to take care of you. That's why your mamm asked for you to come here in her last wishes. If he doesn't have a job, Kristen, the responsibility would fall on his familye. You have familye."

Kristen's heart raced and hot tears spilled onto her face. All eyes were upon her awaiting her answer, but instead, she stood and ran from the room. If only Derick would have cared enough to be the one to do such a thing.

6

Kristen went up to her room. She couldn't hear any more talk of the notes and the mystery of the car. And for the life of her, she couldn't imagine why her mother would send her here if she'd be in any kind of danger. Too much sorrow was in her heart all at once. She thought she might burst.

"Kristen? Do you want to talk, dear?" Aunt Elizabeth was outside her door.

"No, thanks, Aunt Elizabeth. I just want to go to sleep. I'm OK now."

"All right. You have a gut rest and don't be worrying about things. We'll get to the bottom of it all. Gut nacht."

Kristen changed into one of the long nightgowns left by her aunt and pulled the sheet over her, leaving the quilt aside. It was too hot to sleep with even a lightweight one.

A low knock sounded on her door in what seemed like only minutes later. She looked at the time on her cell phone. It was 11:00

PM. She must have fallen right to sleep three hours ago.

"Who's there?"

"John. I want to talk with you for a few minutes. Can you meet me by the barn?"

"Now? It's so late."

"Jah, I know, but I'll be going to Lowville on Monday and want to talk to you before I go. Won't have a chance after tonacht."

"OK. Give me a few minutes to get dressed." She tossed the sheet off and got out of bed. What could he want? She didn't relish any more pity or concern over the notes, although John's calming effect was always welcome.

"Gut. See you outside."

Why was John going to Lowville? And why did she feel slightly panicked at the thought of him not being here?

Ten minutes later, after slipping on her denim skirt and a t-shirt, she gave a quick brush of her teeth, and went quietly out the door into pitch black. She wanted to go back and grab one of the flashlights she'd seen around the house. But the screened door squeaked, and she didn't want to risk waking anyone up at this hour and having to explain that she was meeting John.

She let her eyes adjust to the dark and walked slowly toward the barn. She could

74

now decipher the trees and the outline of the structure up ahead.

"Pssst. Kristen. Over here." John shined a flashlight her way.

She walked over to him and was glad he turned it off as she approached so he couldn't see her blush as she drew nearer to him. She wouldn't be able to explain it because she didn't understand it either. Blood relative or not, John was her cousin as far as the family was concerned. That little reminder gave her some respite.

"I'm sorry I woke you. Daniel and I are going to Lowville on Monday to buy some new tools and supplies at Jacob Mast's hardware store. Thought you might like to come, too. Mary and Sadie enjoy going to the Wal-Mart there."

"Mary and Sadie are going also?"

"Just Mary. Sadie has to work this Monday. I'll be spending most of the day with her tomorrow. So, this is my only time to talk with you about Lowville."

She tampered down the twinge of jealousy about John's plans for the following day.

"I already asked Mamm and Daed and they said it might be gut for you to have a day out."

"Even with the mysterious notes?"

"Jah. Seems whoever it is writing them

wants you out of Stone Arabia. Doesn't seem likely that a trip to Lowville would put you in harm's way. Mamm and Daed will talk more to you about it tomorrow. If you rather not go . . ."

"No. I'd like to go." She instantly regretted her quick enthusiastic tone. Calming her voice she then asked, "Is it a long trip?"

"Nee, it takes about two hours. We'll be back by nachtfall. The same driver, Angela, who drove you here, will be taking us. The three of you can shop, and then we'll all have dinner at Jacob's haus."

"What time are we leaving?"

"Angela will come by the haus at seven thirty. We'll be through with breakfast by then, and Daniel and I will have time to do the milking and a few chores before that."

"I bet Anna will be looking to help at the crack of dawn." Kristen smiled, thinking of Anna's enthusiasm for chores.

"You're starting to know this familye gut, cousin."

John was so close she could feel his warm breath on her face, but the dark night didn't allow her to look into his eyes clearly. She took a step back, not trusting the sudden surge of emotions that overtook her.

"I'm trying."

The realization then hit her that she was,

indeed, trying to fit into her Amish family. But why? She had no plans on becoming Amish and living there forever. As soon as she turned eighteen, she'd get her affairs settled with the attorney handling her mom's will and Ross's estate. She'd go back to the Jersey Shore. To her home town. To the ocean. To Der . . . no, not to Derick. And no, not to her lifelong friend, Cindy. How could she? They'd betrayed her. Her other friends from school probably didn't call because of that whole situation. Yes, she'd have a place and things to go back to, but not a soul in the world. Even when all was well with them, she knew deep inside that she'd always felt a sense of aloneness in her life.

"You OK, Kristen?" John's voice was gentle and full of concern.

"Sorry. I was thinking of Derick and Cindy."

"Did you ever get to talk with them?" The same concern held steady in his voice.

"I spoke to Cindy. She was crying and begging me to forgive her." Kristen stopped, afraid her voice would crack.

"Crying? Why? What happened?"

"She and Derick. They got together the minute I left Bradley Beach to come here. She told me that even though she loves me like a sister, she couldn't help falling for Derick."

"*Ach!* What a shocker that must be for you. I'm sorry, Kristen. No wonder you were so upset when you finished your phone call."

"Seems like this is my year for shockers. I'm afraid of what else might be in store for me."

"We'll pray that the Lord will have only gut things in store for you from now on."

How could she tell him she'd never prayed? At least not until she came here. And that was just at meal time.

"I think that you're one of the good things, John. You've been a wonderful friend."

"I'm glad to be a friend to you, Kristen." His voice was nearly a whisper. But the words rang louder than a tolling bell in Kristen's heart.

When John arrived at Sadie's, she was on the front porch setting out glasses on a little table between two white wooden rockers. He waved as he rode past her in his buggy to the hitch rail at the side of the house and then walked Rusty to their barn. It would be an all day visit.

"I have some sweet lemonade made here.

It's so hot out already." Sadie handed John a frosty glass of it as he took a seat in one of the rockers.

"Denki. You make a gut lemonade, Sadie."

Her pleased smile set the stage for him to tell her of his news. News that he and his familye had decided not to tell until they were sure they were able to rent the soon to be vacated general store on Main Street. John had all to do not to mention it to both Sadie and Kristen while they were there yesterday. When he got home his daed said it was all confirmed. The landlord left a message at the phone shanty. He hoped Sadie would be as excited as he was about this new business venture.

"Sadie, I have some news."

"News? I hope it's gut."

"I think it is gut. I hope you will think so, too."

Sadie nodded for him to continue. Her eyes set on his mouth for the words to spill forth.

"Our familye decided to take over the general store on Main Street. We will each contribute our Gott-given talents, and it will be a variety store for Amish folks. Course, the Englisch can shop there, too, but it will have items that we Amish need all in the one place. Besides Mamm's jams and pies, and Mary's hand sewn items, Daed will set up some hardware and seeds, too, and we'll have a section for staples such as flour, sugar, vanilla, and spices sold in bulk, unlike the Englisch stores. And a small candy section that Anna is excited to take charge of."

Sadie's face held an unreadable expression.

John waited for her response.

"What will your part be in this venture?"

"I'll tend to the stock and the books and keep the place maintained as needed. I still have the field work at home. If the store does vell, then we will have less worry about the weather and our crops in such a short growing season."

"Why did you not mention this to me sooner? We were just there yesterday."

"We weren't sure we'd get the store for the rent that my daed proposed to Jack Strean, the landlord. We agreed not to mention it 'til we were certain. I didn't mean to be keeping any secrets from you."

"I know that, John. I guess we should have talked sooner about our plans for after we are married. I know you want us to live in your *grossdawdi*'s haus for a time, so you can easily tend to the fields with your daed and Daniel, but something has come up."

"What is it, Sadie? Is everything all right?"

"Ach! Now I don't know, John. My onkle Samuel, in Lancaster, has asked if we could live with him in his haus after we marry so we can tend his farm. His *frau* is gone, and they never had any *kinner.* His two nephews, my cousins, Matthew and Zack, helped him keep the place up. The three of them made a nice living. But then each of the nephews married and moved away. He depends on help from neighboring farmers.

"Onkle Samuel is getting on in years and cannot manage the farm on his own. John, he is offering his haus and farm to us if you are willing to help him tend his crops and his cows. He would live in the *dawdi* haus. It hasn't been used in many years and he just painted it fresh and got some furniture and a new bed for it. My daed is going to tell you all of this at dinner. It was s'pose to be a surprise. I would not have said anything if you hadn't told me of your new venture. I don't want you to be in an uncomfortable position when the subject comes up."

"Seems I'm in an uncomfortable position any way you look at it. If I accept this generous offer from your onkle, it would mean we would have to move to Lancaster, and I could not be of any help to my daed with his crops and the store. I don't know if I am able to do that. If I don't accept the offer, then your onkle will be disappointed and in a tough spot. Is there no one else who can help him with his farm?"

Sadie lowered her head along with her voice.

"Jah, there is my cousin, Ruth, who will be married after us. Her beau, Micah, has three brudders working their daed's farm, so he would be able to easily leave to tend to Onkle Samuel's farm."

"So why the talk at dinner later and all the fuss about us moving to your onkle's farm? There is no problem if Micah is interested."

Sadie's face fell. "I think it is a fine opportunity to have a haus of our own and a farm to go with it. And I would have liked to be the one to help Onkle Samuel because he and my aenti Leah have been very kind to me and my familye when we were going through some rough times. He is like a second vadder to me. His offer is to us first, then to Ruth and Micah."

"You want us to do this, don't you?"

Without looking up, she whispered, "Jah, I do."

"Sadie, I would like very much to be able to do this for you and your onkle, but I can't see how my daed would manage. Plus, you know that I want to get away from farming to something more reliable. I want to farm just enough for the needs of our familye: some chickens, cows and vegetables. No more crops for selling and trying to make a living that way. It's getting harder and harder with the weather —"

"Jah, in Montgomery County it is," she interrupted. "It's warmer in Lancaster than it is here in Upstate New York."

"Not by much, Sadie. And lots of Amish folks there are selling and moving to New York and other states, like Wisconsin and Kentucky, where there is more land, less traffic and crowds, and not as much competition from other farmers trying to sell their produce. I don't think moving there is a gut idea in the long run. We will build our own haus one day, Sadie. And if the store does gut, you can help tend to the customers and bring your quilts to sell. It will be easier work, but not in the least way any less worthy."

Sadie lifted her head and looked at John. The warmth that shone in her blue eyes just minutes earlier was gone. She gave him a steely gray stare.

"I see that you have your mind set on this store venture and staying in Stone Arabia, John Wagler."

"Just as you have your mind set on moving to your onkle's haus and a life of farming in Lancaster, Sadie Krantz."

Kristen found the ride to Lowville to be pleasant while Angela kept up a lively conversation about her travels before she'd settled in Stone Arabia.

Mary sat up front and Kristen, John, and Daniel sat in the back. Whenever they drove over a bump in the road, John's leg touched hers. She scolded herself for wishing for more bumps and maybe even a pothole.

When they arrived at Jacob Mast's house, Mary went to the trunk of the car for the basket of zucchini bread and sweet rolls Aunt Elizabeth had sent along with a shoofly pie. Kristen took the pie from her and together they walked up the porch to the door, the others soon behind them.

They were welcomed and ushered inside by a jolly robust lady with rosy red cheeks. After greeting them, she turned her friendly green eyes to Kristen.

Mary stepped aside so Kristen could move forward and said, "Margaret, this is our cousin, Kristen."

"Hi, Margaret. Thanks for having me."

"Ach! It's a pleasure to have guests, especially any familye or friends of the Waglers. Here, let me take that pie from you. Mary, dear, can you please place the basket on the table? It all sure smells gut!"

"Is Jacob at the hardware store?" Daniel looked a bit antsy.

"Jah. He and my Eli. I'm sure they're waiting for you boys. Go on now. I'll be expecting you back here for the afternoon meal."

"Jah, we'll be here," John said, as he ambled toward the door.

"Would you like Kristen and me to stay and help prepare the meal while Angela drives my brudders to the hardware store?" Mary offered.

"Nee. I want you, Angela, and Kristen to have a nice time at Wal-Mart. I know they don't have one in your area." With a wide smile, Mary took Kristen's arm, and they headed back outside.

Angela drove them to the hardware store. She parked the car so Mary and Kristen could go inside with John and Daniel and say a quick hello to Jacob.

As they scrambled into the store, a bearded Amish man came forward and froze in place right before Kristen.

"Jacob, this is Kristen Esh, the cousin I told you about last time we were here. Kristen, this is Jacob Mast, Margaret's cousin and a gut friend of our familye."

"Uh, nice to meet you, Jacob. I heard a lot about your hardware store." She didn't know what else to say. His stare was so intense, she felt as if it might burn right through her.

"Ach! You are surely the image of your mamm You look exactly like she did when she was your age. I thought it was Emily herself walked into the store." Jacob kept his eyes fixed on her as he spoke the words. Then he stepped back and introduced her to Margaret's son, Eli.

"And this is Eli, my second cousin. He works with me here now."

"Nice to meet you, Eli." Eli was closer to her age and wore an easy smile. His eyes did not penetrate her as Jacob's had.

Jacob came toward her once again. " 'Tis a marvel how much you look like your mamm."

"Yes, everyone who knew her says the same thing. Had I worn Plain clothes, you might have thought I was a ghost." She laughed, but Jacob Mast did not.

7

Angela drove up to the Wagler house at 8:00 PM. Kristen was glad to find Aunt Elizabeth setting a large platter of cold meats and fresh baked wheat bread on the table. She was famished, hardly able to eat her meal earlier with Jacob Mast staring at her the whole time.

"Sorry we missed supper, Mamm. Margaret set out the afternoon meal a bit later than usual to give us more time at Wal-Mart, and then we encountered traffic at the midway point back," Mary said, as she opened the ice chest and retrieved relishes to go with the sandwiches.

"Jah, but after such a big meal, I don't think we would have been hungry two hours ago for supper," John commented as he took a seat beside Kristen at the table.

When Daniel joined them, they all bowed their heads in a silent prayer. Then John and Daniel forked out slices of meat onto their hunks of bread. Mary passed the platter of meats to Kristen. It felt great to be able to eat without anyone staring at her.

"What did Margaret serve?" Aunt Elizabeth sat with them even though she wasn't eating.

"Meatloaf with gravy, potatoes, peas, bread and budder, pickled beets, and the sweet rolls, zucchini bread, and pie you sent over." Daniel patted his stomach and laughed. "I'm hungry all over again."

"How did you enjoy your visit to Lowville, Kristen?" Aunt Elizabeth faced her with a curious smile.

"It was fine." Except for Jacob Mast and his dark staring eyes. Had anyone else noticed him staring at her?

"Jah? You seem preoccupied, dear." Aunt Elizabeth never missed a thing.

"What's the problem?" Uncle Jonas stood at the doorway that led from the living room to the kitchen. He must have overheard on his way in.

"There's no problem, Uncle Jonas, it's just that . . . well . . . nothing."

"Jacob Mast could not keep his eyes off of her. That's the problem." John made no effort to hide his disapproval.

"Ach! He probably hadn't seen an Englischer in a long time." Aunt Elizabeth waved her hand to dismiss John's annoyance.

"Can't be that. Englischers go into the hardware store, too. He needs to get himself a frau soon. Whatever his reason, I will not have such outright disrespect done to anyone in our familye like that again."

Aunt Elizabeth and Uncle Jonas exchanged quick glances. Kristen was flattered that John spoke up about Jacob in her defense, but she said nothing. All that mattered to her right now was that John had noticed. She almost broke a smile but decided to suppress it, given the serious expressions on everyone's faces.

"Not to worry, John. It's likely that Kristen won't be seeing Jacob for a long spell, if at all," Uncle Jonas assured.

"Maybe so, but if you were there, Daed, you might be expecting Jacob to offer an apology to Kristen. I had to stop myself from speaking to him about his behavior. I'm sure everyone at the table noticed it."

Kristen imitated Aunt Elizabeth's earlier wave-of-the-hand gesture. "It's fine, John. Just weird, that's all." Weirder than weird. It was as if Jacob drank in her every move and word.

"It was downright rude." John slapped a hunk of ham onto his bread as if to emphasize his point.

She'd better lighten things up, even though she agreed fully with John about the man.

"I had my eye on that piece of ham you took. Since I started eating meat again, I like a nice thick sandwich."

John looked up at her and then down at the fat slice of fresh ham on his bread.

Kristen fought to keep a straight face.

"So, you want this piece, then?"

Kristen nodded. Just as he was about to relinquish it to her, her lips began to quiver in an effort to hold back her laughter. John caught her eye and smirked. Then he began to chuckle, as did the rest of the family.

"I was ready to hand it over to you."

"I know you were. You're a true gentleman, John. Pout and all."

"I was not pouting!"

"Yes, you were. Wasn't John pouting when he was about to give up his ham?"

"Jah. That you were," Aunt Elizabeth said as the others nodded and laughed.

"Ach, vell, I'll still be a gentleman and give you my thick piece of ham on my extra thick slice of crusty bread." He placed it on Kristen's plate and then proceeded to make himself another sandwich, wearing an ear to ear grin.

"Thank you, John. And you're not even pouting this time."

He gave her another smirk and passed the relish and mustard to her.

All eyes were upon them.

All ears listened intently to their banter.

What were they thinking? Did it look as though she and John were . . . too friendly? No, it was a known fact that they both had feelings for someone else. He for Sadie, and she for Derick. No matter if Derick no longer felt the same. She still cried herself to sleep over him.

Kristen bit into her sandwich. Time to end the show. First Jacob Mast's prying eyes, and now her family's curious glances. She'd had enough introspection to last her a lifetime.

Something told her that this was just the beginning.

John tried not to be affected by Kristen's teasing and his family's raised eyebrows. Did the part of his heart that now held a special place for Kristen show through? He was still officially courting Sadie even though he saw no resolution to their different wishes for a future together. If he truly loved her, would he be so quick to dismiss her suggestion of going to Lancaster? Could they not go after the general store got on its feet? Would not a man in love give in to the kind of home that would bring his frau-to-be happiness and peace? On the other hand, would not Sadie want her husband to do the work he was best suited to do?

This had been a trying day. Best he wind it down on an ordinary note.

"I better finish up my sandwich and head up to bed. We have a busy week ahead, especially with it being our turn to host Preaching on Sunday."

"Jah. I have the meal already planned out. Aenti Miriam, Rachel Miller, Katie Mast, and Lucy Krantz will be here to help clean and prepare some of the food."

"And Sadie," Mary reminded Mamm. Sadie always came to help.

"Nee, not this time. Lucy said she'd be busy." Mamm's eyes turned upon John as she said it, waiting for him to elaborate on that piece of news. He just kept eating as quickly as his jaw would chew, so he could leave the table.

And this conversation.

"So, Kristen. You'll get to attend Preaching and meet some of our neighbors and friends on Sunday," Mary said.

Kristen merely nodded with a strained smile. She was not exactly excited about it.

That was obvious, especially since many eyes would be upon her. After the staring sessions she'd gotten from Jacob Mast, John wondered if she could take any more.

"Will you be wearing one of the dresses I made for you?" Mary almost looked as excited about it as Anna would be.

"Yes, I guess so. I don't really have any dresses long enough like the ones the women here wear."

"I have a kapp for you to wear, too. Your hair is just long enough for putting into a bun. I'll be glad to help you get ready."

Kristen gave Mary another of her strained polite smiles.

John knew she was dying to bolt from the room. He didn't have to wait very long.

"This was a nice meal. Thanks, Aunt Elizabeth. I need to get some sleep so I'll say good night." Kristen stood, took her plate and fork, washed them quickly, and headed toward the stairs. She looked weary for her almost eighteen years. He wished he could give her the happiness she'd lost so soon in life. Maybe *Gott* had led her to him for that very reason.

The next morning Kristen surprised herself by waking earlier than anyone in the house. Her denim skirt needed to be laundered.

She had no other skirt or dress that covered her knees. After she'd freshened up in the washroom, she went back upstairs and put on one of the dresses Mary had made for her. She chose a green one, pinned it where needed, slipped on her sandals, and headed downstairs to the kitchen.

The sun wasn't up yet, so she lit a kerosene lamp and began setting the table. The quiet was soothing, and she could hear the fabric of her dress swoosh as she walked. Imagine what Derick would say if he saw her now? But it wasn't Derick who walked into the kitchen and looked at her with such quiet admiration that she thought she might melt right through the seams of the wooden planks of the floor. It was John.

"Goede Mariye, Kristen. Mary will be pleased that you are making use of her dresses."

"It's a little stiff and the pins pinch. I must have done it up wrong. But it was either this or jeans."

"Mamm will be glad for your choice. You set the table?"

"Yes. This is the first time I got up before everyone else, so I figured I'd start breakfast."

John seemed to be appraising the table

and that familiar smirk began to curve his lips.

"What? Did I do something wrong?"

John simply shrugged, but the smirk remained.

Aunt Elizabeth walked in followed by Anna who ran out to the henhouse to collect some fresh eggs. The kitchen got busy in no time, and soon the scent of bacon and eggs filled the room. Mary walked in with a smile and morning greetings, and then did a double-take toward Kristen. "Ach, you're wearing one of the dresses I made for you, and it's not even Sunday. It fits perfect. I have a few with hooks and eyes, if that would be easier for you."

Oh! Thank goodness! "I think I'd like to try the hook and eye dresses next time."

Mary smiled, grabbed a biscuit, and explained that she was due at the diner extra early due to the other waitress being out sick for the morning shift.

As soon as she left, Daniel and Uncle Jonas took their places at the table. John was already seated, and Kristen, Anna, and Aunt Elizabeth joined them. They bowed their heads for a silent grace, and then an awkward pause ensued.

"Oh, no! The forks! I forgot to set them out." Kristen jolted up, rushed to the flatware drawer and grabbed a handful of forks. She gave one to each of them, nearly jabbing John as she handed him his. He avoided her eyes, but those lips of his were curved once again.

"Ach, I've forgotten such things many a time myself," Aunt Elizabeth told her as she passed the platter of eggs and bacon.

"Remember that nacht when you were in such a hurry that you forgot all the utensils, Lizzie? I thought we were having Frogmore stew." Everyone laughed along with Uncle Jonas, and Kristen's embarrassment eased. But her disappointment remained. She'd wanted to do it right. Being on her own for the first time in the kitchen was an opportunity to give back a little of the hospitality she'd been given. Turned out that she couldn't even properly set a table.

"Kristen, denki for setting the table." Aunt Elizabeth's warm smile seeped into her words. She amazed Kristen with her ability to read a person's heart.

"You're welcome." Kristen kept her eyes low to be sure she didn't look at John. She was still angry at him for not telling her she'd forgotten the forks. Normally, she'd think it was funny, too. But her emotions were so jumbled lately that anything could set her off and bring her down in seconds.

■ ■ ■ ■

As Kristen made her way to weed the vegetable gardens, John seemed to appear out of nowhere. He stood before her so that she couldn't walk any further.

"Do you want something? Maybe you've placed some plastic vegetables in the garden for me to harvest as a joke?"

"Kristen, I'm really sorry for not telling you about the forks. I was being a real *dummkopf.* I thought it would make for a gut laugh. Something we could all use to start the day. But it really wasn't funny at all, especially for you."

"No, it wasn't. I wanted to do it right, John. Do something nice for your mamm after all she's done for me." Her voice broke, and she looked away.

John reached over and turned her face toward him again. His blue eyes glistened.

She fell to her knees and sobbed.

It wasn't really about the forks. It was about everything. Her mom and Ross dying so tragically. Being uprooted out of her home by the ocean. Her friends not calling her . . . not a one. Derick, forgetting her like last week's meal. Aunt Miriam's dislike of her. The way she had to dress now.

Restrictions about her cell phone and the whole electricity thing. Her mom never telling her she was Amish. The mystery notes. Jacob Mast's deep stare. She just couldn't take one more thing. The fork mishap put her over the edge.

John knelt beside her. "I'm so sorry, Kristen. I'll never be so inconsiderate again." His voice was low and tender.

"Oh, John. It's isn't you. It's everything that's happened. My whole life is turned upside down. The fork thing just set me off. That's all. I just want . . ."

"What do you want, Kristen?" John whispered, his face only inches from her own.

"I want a normal life. But something new keeps popping up that takes me further away from that. I wake up afraid every day wondering what will happen next."

"When I dread the outcome of things, I remember the wise words your aenti Elizabeth often told me when I was growing up. To rejoice, pray without ceasing, and give thanks in all circumstances."

"I don't have the faith that you and Aunt Elizabeth have, John."

"Praying teaches us to have faith and to trust in Gott's plan for each day. Might not always go the way we want it to go, but if we do our best just the same, then we follow the will of Gott."

"Why would it be the will of God to have my mother and Ross die in a terrible accident?"

"It's not for us to question the ways of Gott. It's not always easy, I know. Pray more and trust."

"I never thought much about praying or trusting. It was hard to do that with things a tad unusual in my life."

John stood and Kristen followed suit. He stepped back as if to look at her more clearly. "What do you mean?"

"It was an unconventional household. I was alone most of the time because my mom went to work at a hotel when she finished her chores at the house for Ross. Once I began school, I rarely saw my mother except on the alternating Sundays when she was off. She'd say that she needed to save money for us to get our own place one day and that the two jobs combined would make it happen all the sooner. Not that she disliked living in Ross's home.

"He was a great guy. He let us use the pool and have free range of the whole house. Never said a word when I'd watch his large flat screen TV with my friends in the living room. But Mom said it wouldn't last forever. Ross was bound to get married or move as his business expanded to other areas. He was hardly ever home. So it was just me at the house most times."

"So, you spent a lot of time with your friends?"

"Well, I'd eat dinner over at Cindy's a couple of times a week and meet a friend or two at the pizza place on another night. The rest of the time, there'd be cooked dinners in the freezer that mom made for me and Ross. In summer, I'd walk over to the beach with my container of heated food and eat my dinner there most times."

"Are you saying you didn't ever eat meals with your mom? Or even with Ross?"

"They weren't there to eat with."

"Ach. I'm sorry you've been so lonesome."

"I got used to it after a while." She'd never admitted her loneliness until now. Maybe because the difference in family life was so different here, it was hard not to compare what she'd lacked to what she'd gained at the Waglers'.

She walked toward the garden.

"You won't be lonely in this haus. I can promise you that. You're with us now. And in Amish families, it's unheard of for a person to be alone so much."

"That's nice to know. But I'm not Amish.

The day I got here I knew I didn't belong here by Aunt Miriam's attitude toward me."

"She is not used to anyone different. That's all that was about."

"My mom left the Amish and that makes me an outsider, related or not. I don't fit in . . . anywhere. But soon, when I'm of legal age, I'll get myself a job and make my own way."

"Where will you go? This is where your familye is. Don't be minding Aenti Miriam. She's been riled ever since I've known her. Not a happy soul, that one."

Kristen's mind reeled, and she couldn't give John any logical answer about where she'd go. Lately, she wasn't sure she could go back to her beloved Jersey Shore with all the memories attached to the people who were no longer in her life. She wondered if she'd inherited Mom's savings or anything from Ross. If so, she could easily get her own place and have money to fall back on until she found a decent job. Maybe even take an accounting course at night. But the loneliness would follow her back there.

Right now, she needed to do the chores Aunt Elizabeth had given her for the day.

"Thanks for letting me cry on your shoulder."

He nodded with a warmth in his blue eyes

she'd never seen in anyone else's before.

"I better go do the weeding. See you later."

"Jah. Pick us some sweet peas for dinner if the deer left us any. You'll like those." He turned and walked toward the fields, his stride sure. He held his head erect and swung his arms just enough to give him a good pace.

She walked the few more feet to the vegetable garden and knelt down on a clump of hay Aunt Elizabeth had placed there. Then it dawned on her.

John really cared.

8

Kristen had never been inside a barn. She hadn't imagined barns to be so large, then again, maybe the Amish built them with extra room for holding church services during the warm weather, as her family would be doing this Sunday.

A mix of pungent odors enveloped her . . . the musty scent from the hay and a stronger one from the animals, but no one else seemed to notice. If they did, nothing was said about it. Must be a smell people with barns were used to. Like the fishy smell that the beach gave off on a low tide, foggy day. It didn't bother her in the least. In fact, she liked it. It was the familiar scent of home. She wondered if the smell of a barn would ever invoke the same feeling.

"It's gut that the farm equipment, harnesses, and tools were moved out of here at dawn. We have a nice early start now." Aunt Elizabeth handed Kristen a broom.

"Where are the other ladies?" Kristen asked as she began her dusty task.

"In the kitchen baking bread, and then they'll clean everything 'til it sparkles. We women tend to gather there after services, so it's nice to have it all scrubbed up."

"It always looks clean to me." Kristen had never seen a dish left unwashed or a smudge on the counter top. The sink nearly gleamed. Even the water pump had luster of its own.

"It's important for a frau to keep a tidy kitchen for her familye."

"What's a frau?"

"Ach, I forgot you don't know the Pennsylvania Dutch we use. It means, *a wife.*"

"What about an unmarried woman? Wouldn't her kitchen be tidy, too?"

"Jah, it would. Most Amish women marry, and those who are widowed or never marry, help other married women in their familye with chores and the kinner . . . children."

"Like Aunt Miriam?"

"Jah, like your Aenti Miriam. And Katie Mast. They are both a help to me."

"Then John was right about not ever feeling lonely here?"

"Did he tell you that?"

"Yes. When I told him I often ate meals alone because my mom worked so much.

He said I'd never feel lonesome in this house."

Aunt Elizabeth stopped sweeping, leaned on her broom and looked at Kristen with a deep crease in her brows.

"Your mamm was raised Amish. I am surprised to hear this news of you eating alone." She clicked her tongue and resumed sweeping.

"I am not." Aunt Miriam said, entering the barn.

"You are not, what?" Aunt Elizabeth asked, not looking up from her sweeping.

"I am not surprised that Emily did not raise Kristen with our ways. She left behind her Amish upbringing, or did you forget that?"

"I did not forget that she lived an Englisch life. But I thought she'd hold on to some of our ways. Many Englisch families eat together. It's a gut thing for Plain and fancy folk alike."

Kristen stopped sweeping and faced both her aunts.

"You might be interested to know that my mother held two jobs and worked long hours. She was never happy to leave me alone, but she wanted to save enough money to get us our own place. I'm sure if that had happened she would have been home to eat meals with me again."

"Ach, Kristen. I'm sure your mamm did the best she could in her situation. She was a gut *mudder.*" Aunt Elizabeth stopped sweeping and gave Kristen's shoulder a gentle squeeze.

Kristen forced a smile, and then moved to sweep the other side of the barn . . . away from Aunt Miriam and her comments.

Anna ran into the barn. "Come. The kaffee is ready and there's a loaf of bread set aside right out of the oven for us to budder and eat." She went over to Kristen and took hold of her hand. "I helped bake the bread this time." The flour all over Anna's blue dress testified to that.

Kristen admired the joy such a young girl expressed in learning to be a good Amish homemaker.

When she was Anna's age, she didn't even make toast very well. Always dry and burnt. Let alone make bread from scratch. Her mom baked her own bread once in a while but seemed sad each time she'd knead the dough, never asking help from Kristen on that task. Now, she was grateful that she wasn't asked to be part of the kitchen detail. Surely, she'd mess up on some important task, like forgetting to add the yeast to the water, or setting the oven to the wrong temperature. She knew how to scramble eggs only because she'd made them so often for herself before heading out to school. She hoped she'd get another chance to be up before everyone else again to redeem her fork mishap. She'd get it right the next time.

The kitchen smelled like a bakery, and Kristen's mouth watered.

Mary and an older woman cut thick slices of warm crusty wheat bread, and a tub of creamy, whipped butter and a variety of fruit jams graced the table.

Another woman Kristen had never met before stood at the stove stirring a pot of oatmeal. She turned when Kristen walked in.

"Hullo. I'm Lucy Krantz. You must be Kristen." Her light brown eyes sparkled when she smiled, and Kristen instantly liked her.

"Lucy is Sadie's mamm, Kristen," Aunt Elizabeth told her as they sat at the table.

Kristen had to make an all-out effort not to frown. The mere mention of Sadie had changed her mood. But why?

The older woman slicing the bread turned to her now. "And I'm Katie Mast."

"Any relation to Jacob Mast?" Kristen asked, almost quicker than her mind formed the question.

"Jah. He is my baby brudder. Raised him since he was born when our mamma passed. He's my only sibling. Never thought he'd move away from our familye home. I miss him so."

Kristen nodded. The older woman was attractive with gray eyes that contrasted well with the silvery gray hair that showed under her kapp. Why hadn't she ever married?

The sound of heavy footsteps caused Kristen to look up. John, Daniel, and Uncle Jonas stood there. They hung their hats on the wooden pegs and came to the table.

John's thick hair was mussed, and his face held the anticipation of a young boy at a candy counter as he eyed the steaming sliced bread.

Her stomach did a flip-flop. Maybe this was why the thought of Sadie caused her mood to sour. She didn't want to lose him. As a special friend, that is. They could never be anything more than that. Could they?

No, no, no. What was she thinking?

"Go ahead. Eat yourselves full." Mary passed the bread to her father, who then passed it along to the others. When all of their plates held bread and each bowl brimmed with steaming oatmeal, they bowed their heads for the silent grace.

Kristen wondered what they said to God in their silence. Were they thanking Him for the food? For a new day? For one another? And why didn't they say grace out loud?

After Kristen had buttered her bread, she raised her eyes and looked at Uncle Jonas.

"Uncle, why do you all say grace before and after meals in silence?"

"The silence gives us the reverence needed for prayer."

"What are you praying?"

Everyone looked up.

Did she ask such an unusual question?

"In the morgen, usually the Lord's Prayer. Other times, a simple prayer of thanks."

"Ah. OK."

"Do you know the Lord's Prayer, Kristen?" Anna asked with half a mouth of bread in her cheeks.

"Anna, swallow your food before speaking. You'll choke yourself gut," Aunt Elizabeth chided.

Anna chewed, and then swallowed, all the while her eyes upon Kristen awaiting her reply.

"Yes, I know the Lord's Prayer. I'd hear my mother say it sometimes. When I was ten, I asked her to teach it to me, and she did. She told me it's the only prayer I'd ever need. That it covers everything."

"Jah, that it does," Uncle Jonas said as he reached for another slice of bread.

"So, I'll say the Lord's Prayer, then," Kristen told them. When she looked up, John smiled at her. He looked pleased with her response.

"One day you might like to take lessons toward baptism into the faith. Then you'll better understand about our prayers and why we do things the way we do," Aunt Elizabeth said.

Before Kristen had a chance to answer, Aunt Miriam spoke up. "Very few Englisch can live the Plain life, Lizzie. Why, even some Amish can't, as we already know."

Kristen's hands formed into fists under the table. She was tired of Aunt Miriam's snide remarks and bitter attitude toward her and her mom. Time she spoke her mind.

"And maybe very few Amish, if any, could survive in the Englisch world. But my mother did. She must have ridden buggies here, but she learned to drive a car in the city. She probably walked these country roads all the time, but she also walked the confusing streets of the city and found her way around. She held two jobs and never missed a day. In my opinion, she was very brave to leave all she knew for a whole other way of life and make a real go of it."

For a moment it felt like prayer time again by the silence that ensued. No one uttered a word.

Kristen didn't care. She'd spoken her piece. Now, maybe Aunt Miriam would think twice before she opened her mouth to her.

John wanted to applaud Kristen for standing up to Aenti Miriam. Instead he remained quiet to allow the heat to settle some. Finally, he reached over and took the slice of bread from Kristen's plate.

"John, what are you doing?" Kristen reached to grab her bread back but missed.

"I'm giving you a thicker slice. That way you won't come after mine like you did the last time." He was determined to break the ice. When Daed chuckled, he knew he'd succeeded.

"That was ham, not bread," Kristen told him with a flushed face.

"Jah, and the bread the ham was sitting on was mighty thick, too. So, I'm thinking you might have your eye full on my piece here, since it seems I have the thickest slice."

Kristen's upset expression relaxed and a hint of a smile formed in her brown eyes.

"Suit yourself, John Wagler. Get me another slice then. With butter, please. And jam."

This time Mamm and Mary chuckled as they watched John fork a thicker slice of bread onto Kristen's plate, then pass the butter to her, followed by the jam.

"No, sorry, not the strawberry jam. The blueberry," she said with all the seriousness of a school teacher, her eyes focused on the jams.

"I'm thinking I should have left you with your original slice," John told her as he switched the jams, pushing the blueberry toward her. "Anything else?" He folded his arms across his chest and awaited her response, doing his best to repress the smirk pulling at his lips.

"Well . . . no. This is fine . . . for the time being." She smiled full force now as she buttered her bread.

Little Anna giggled, but Katie and Lucy, along with Aunt Miriam, wore stoic expressions.

She stood then chuckled as she made her way to the ice chest to get the container of orange juice.

Lucy cleared her throat and began to talk about the quilting bee that would be held at her house the following week while Daniel and Daed took a second helping of oatmeal.

Katie got involved in the quilting conversation and things seemed back to normal. Almost.

Aunt Miriam sat there. Silent. Still stoic, with a deep grimace across her face as she ate her oatmeal. She'd finally met her match in Kristen Esh.

After breakfast, Mary headed for work and John, Daniel, and Uncle Jonas went out to the fields.

Rebecca Miller showed up with a pair of rubber gloves.

Kristen, Elizabeth, Miriam, and Anna went back to the barn to make it as clean as it could be for Preaching on Sunday.

Lucy, Katie and Rebecca stayed in the kitchen to clean up and wash the floor.

"When will the benches come, Mamma?" Anna asked as she held the shovel for Aunt Elizabeth to sweep some pieces of cut hay and dust into it.

"The bench wagon always brings them the day before Preaching. We're almost done here. All we have to do is run a wet mop over the floor boards to get up the rest of the dust."

Aunt Miriam came over with a bucket of water and three mops. She handed one mop to Kristen and another to Aunt Elizabeth.

Then she took the third mop, dunked it in the pail of water, and started mopping at the other end of the barn. Without a word.

"Is that a car I hear outside?" Aunt Elizabeth looked toward the open barn doors.

"Maybe it's an Englisch neighbor, Mamma." Anna ran out of the barn to investigate. "Mamma, Mamma!" Anna screeched.

Aunt Elizabeth dropped her mop and ran. Kristen followed with Aunt Miriam.

"What is it, child?"

"Mamma, it's the same car that me and Kristen saw that morgen. The man threw something out of the car window and then drove away quick."

Kristen's heart raced in panic. She looked down the road, but there was no sign of a car. When she turned her gaze back to the house, Aunt Miriam held a white envelope in her hand.

Aunt Elizabeth and Anna were at her side. Kristen walked over to them.

"I found it on the ground here. It has a rock inside to weigh it down." She undid the scotch tape, removed the note, and handed it to Kristen.

"If you care for the girl, send her back to the Englisch world where she belongs." Her hands shook.

"Another one of those notes! Ach! Who is doing this?" Aunt Elizabeth threw her hands up for a moment, and then took the note from Kristen.

What did this mean? Was it a threat? Kristen wished she could go home to her mom. She had to face the hard reality that she no longer had a mother and no home other than this one. The very one that the writer of the mystery notes wanted her to leave.

She turned her eyes to Aunt Miriam. Aunt Miriam had told Aunt Elizabeth that Kristen didn't belong there.

9

Mary helped Kristen put her hair up into a proper bun and then placed a black prayer kapp over her head. She gave Kristen a burgundy dress with hooks and eyes, and then, with a reassuring smile, left to ready herself for Preaching.

Uncle Jonas and Aunt Elizabeth planned to show the notes to Bishop Ebersol after church service was over. She didn't know what the Bishop could do about the notes. But the family thought it best to alert the community so that there would be more watchful eyes out for Kristen's safety.

Still early, and once again, Aunt Elizabeth had made it to the kitchen before her. The table was set and pancakes sizzled on the stove. A dozen or so were already on a platter.

"Goede Mariye, Kristen. I see you are dressed for Preaching."

"Yes. Mary helped me. Do I pass for

Amish?"

"Ach, Kristen. You don't have to pass for anything. But I'm glad you decided to dress Plain for the service. It's best to blend in at such things."

"I figured as much. I had enough staring from Jacob Mast to last me a lifetime."

"I'm sure you won't have anyone staring at you today. Maybe a head turned your way now and again because you're a new face in the congregation. But once we introduce you at the common meal afterward, their curiosity will be satisfied."

"I hope so. Can I help you with anything?" Kristen walked over to the stove. The pancakes smelled wonderful.

"Jah, please get the container of juice from the ice chest and put it on the table. And the maple syrup, too. Have you tasted our pure maple syrup yet?"

"No. I love maple syrup. Do you make it here?"

"Nee, we buy it from a local Englisch farmer. He taps his own maple trees each year and runs a small business from his haus. Anna likes the maple candy."

"And I like the maple ice cream you make, Mamm."

Kristen turned to the familiar voice and smiled. John walked in and returned her smile threefold. His gaze lingered for a moment on her attire, and he smiled again. Not more than a minute later, Uncle Jonas and Daniel came in, followed by Anna, with a basket of eggs in her hand.

"Anna, please call up to Mary and tell her that breakfast is ready. I think she's fussin' too much for Preaching."

"Jah, OK. Levi Miller is back from Lancaster and Mary gets all red in the face when she sees him at Preaching." Anna giggled, placed the eggs on the counter, and scooted off toward the stairs.

"Levi Miller is a fine fellow," Uncle Jonas proclaimed as he took his seat at the table.

Aunt Elizabeth smiled without looking at him.

When everyone was seated, the silence for prayer ensued. Kristen recited the Lord's Prayer. As she finished, Uncle Jonas cleared his throat signaling that prayer time was over. The silence for prayer was exactly long enough to recite the words. A small step of progress in her newfound routine. She smiled to herself. She might get the hang of this yet.

John was readying the trough for the horses to have a drink when they arrived on this hot morgen. They would be hosting about ten families for the home church service, plus the bishop, deacon, and their families.

Their district wasn't very large, and John liked it that way. He remembered when they'd gone to a church service in Lancaster while visiting Daed's gut friend there. The district was much larger, and it took many hands to get the horses unhitched from the buggies to tend to them. The roads were congested going over to the haus with many Englisch drivers and all the buggies headed in the same direction. This was much better. No tourists. Hardly a car on the road, except the local Englisch who lived among them and respected the presence of buggies.

He couldn't imagine moving away from Montgomery County to Lancaster County. And he knew he had to make it definite to Sadie . . . today. They hadn't spoken since they'd had that conversation about Lancaster on her front porch last Sunday. The matter needed to be settled.

Once he readied the trough and checked the barn to make sure all the benches were arranged with enough leg room between each of them, he opened the barn doors wide. Whatever breeze there was outside would enter inside during the service and bring some relief from the rising heat.

Just as he finished, the bishop, his wife, and son arrived, followed by the deacon and his family. In the next half hour, buggies arrived within minutes of one another. Daniel came out to help lead the horses to the water trough and then guide them with their buggies off to the side, in the shade, to be tied securely to the hitch post. When they were about halfway done, Lucy Krantz walked over.

"Goede Mariye, John. I came to give you this note from our Sadie." Lucy wore her usual warm smile, but it did not reach into her eyes.

"Won't she be here today?"

"Nee. She's in Lancaster helping her onkle at his farm. Doing some cooking and haus chores for him."

John felt foolish for letting an entire week go by without contacting Sadie. He took the letter and tipped his hat to Lucy in thanks, saying nothing.

There was still at least fifteen minutes before the service would begin. He walked behind the barn to read Sadie's note in private.

Dear John,

    I decided to go help my onkle at his house with some cooking and cleaning.

He has always been so good to me. I would have told you I was leaving, but my heart felt sure that your decision about Lancaster is final.

Maybe a good frau-to-be would abide by her beau's wishes and forget all about her dreams and plans. I am sorry that I am not able to do that. I truly feel that God wants me here in Lancaster. That the remainder of my days should be here on this farm.

For this reason, I wish you well and thank you for the time we have spent together. You are a good man, John Wagler. You deserve a frau who will stand by you in your new venture, and I trust that God will find me a husband here who will stand by me in mine.

Sadie

John folded the note and stuffed it in his pocket. Sadie was gone. He assumed that her onkle already had a few potential prospects of marriage for her. If she was willing to leave so quickly, without even a good-bye in person, then she surely had made up her mind to go without him. He held no resentment toward her. He, too, had made up his mind. He would stay in Montgomery County. All Sadie had done was to make it official. Their courting was over now for sure and for certain.

When John walked back toward the entrance of the barn, most of the families were settled on the benches. The women and their children on one side, and the men and older boys on the other. His attention was drawn to his own familye. Kristen sat next to Anna, then came Mamm and Mary. Daed and Daniel walked to their bench off to the left where the men sat.

Kristen had her head down and looked as if she'd been Amish all of her life. Would she ever grow accustomed to their ways, to the mountains, the fields and streams, as she had her former home by the ocean? If she did, maybe she would consider being baptized into the faith. Maybe she would consider . . . Nee, he shouldn't be thinking of such things. Kristen was familye, even if they weren't related by blood, they were related by circumstances. Surely Mamm and Daed would not find his feelings acceptable. He must trample them down, like horses hooves on wet earth.

He took a seat at the back on the last bench so that he could go out every so often to check on the horses. Three hours was a long time for them to be untended in the warmth of this day.

About midway into the service, despite his resolve, John's gaze kept wandering toward Kristen. She shifted positions a few times, and he hoped she wasn't too uncomfortable with the backless bench. More than likely, she was bored, especially not understanding German.

Mamm looked over to her and smiled a few times. Mamm was elated to have her niece with them at Preaching, and he admired Kristen for her choice to come and to dress in the proper attire. She was being respectful of the Plain People and their ways by adapting herself to the situation the best she could. And even though her mamm had rarely been home to spend time with her these past several years, she'd obviously done a fine job in raising her.

His thoughts drifted back to the note Sadie had written to him. He was no longer her beau. He was an eligible bachelor. He could just hear Mamm and Mary making suggestions of whom he should ask to the next singing. Kristen had never been to a singing. Hmm . . . Would it be so terrible to take her to one? Just so she could experience it?

Probably. But right now, looking at her across the barn, sitting there in her Plain burgundy dress, he didn't care.

Kristen let her mind drift to her memories of the ocean so as not to focus on the uncomfortable heat and musty smell of the barn. It would do her no good to pay attention since she didn't know a word of German. The songs were sung from a book called the *Ausbund* and there weren't any instruments. Surprisingly, the people sang very well. Right on key and all in unison without the aid of any kind of beat to keep the tempo. She remembered how difficult it was to do that in music class, and she'd had the aid of the music and the teacher tapping his foot in time.

Right now if she were at the shore in Bradley Beach, she'd be on a sand chair sipping a cool latte by the water, waiting for Cindy to get out of church. Kristen's mom didn't go to church nor did she ever tell her to go, although sometimes she'd see her mother praying quietly in her room. A Bible had been in her nightstand drawer. Kristen came upon it while looking for an extra pair of sunglasses. A few of the passages in the New Testament were highlighted. Mom must have believed in God, and she had to have attended church services every other Sunday when she was her age. Probably had some services right in her home like they were doing this morning. She wished Mom had talked with her about her former life. Dad must have been quite the man to get her to leave her family and Amish ways behind . . . All that she ever knew and maybe . . . loved.

Kristen lifted her head and scanned the men's section across from her as discreetly as possible to see if she could spot John. A sea of male faces, most with beards, were looking into their books, singing, totally immersed in the words they were turning into praise. One of the men seated at the end of a bench in the back, bent over to pick up something his son had dropped, and there was John, behind him. Their eyes met. Her heart gave a huge thud and perspiration gathered at her brow and above her lips. She turned her gaze away and used the tissue Mary suggested she tuck into her sleeve to dab her face. She wondered if Mary would have to use her tissue when she spotted Levi Miller.

Finally, when Kristen felt she'd have to get up and get some fresh air, the people began to move about.

The service was over, and John, Daniel, Uncle Jonas, and several other men, began to carry the benches outside.

Kristen followed Aunt Elizabeth into the kitchen, her legs stiff from sitting so long. She wondered how the older women did it.

Her aunt turned and smiled at her for the hundredth time this morning. Then she said, "Glad the weather will let us eat our meal outdoors. The barn was getting stuffy after a while. Come. Let's start bringing the food out."

Soon, Lucy, Aunt Miriam, and Mary joined them in the kitchen, along with Rachel Miller, Katie Mast, and one other lady. They had covered plates of pickles, pretzels, sliced cheese, and jars of what they called church peanut butter, out of the ice chest and ready to go in no time. They worked so fast that Kristen just stood there baffled as to what she could do to help.

"Can you please start slicing the bread, Kristen?" Mary asked, as she headed out the door with a bowl of pickles.

Kristen nodded and walked to the counter where loaves of dark and wheat bread were neatly arranged in a row. She took the large sharp knife that was there and began to cut the bread into even thick slices, smiling, as she thought of John's teasing about her preference for the thickest slice. She filled one platter with what she'd sliced, which

Aunt Miriam quickly took and carried outside.

Then she started to fill another, when a sharp pain seared her fingers. Suddenly, there was blood all over the counter. Kristen grabbed a dish towel and wrapped her hand. The sight of her own blood made her woozy, and she didn't know if she should sit down or begin to clean the counter before any blood got onto the bread.

"Ach, Kristen! What happened?" Mary looked panic stricken. She ran back to the kitchen door. "Mamm! Mamm! Come, quick. Kristen cut herself."

But instead of Aunt Elizabeth, it was John who raced into the kitchen first, Aunt Elizabeth and Aunt Miriam on his heels.

John took her hand and unwrapped it.

The dishtowel was soaked with blood and Kristen became nauseated.

His brows furrowed and his hands trembled.

"We need to take you to the hospital, Kristen," he said, while Aunt Elizabeth opened a drawer to get out a clean towel. "Let me go see if Angela is home to drive us. Otherwise, there are two other Englisch neighbors we can ask."

"Jah, go, John. I'll get the first aid kit and dress the wounds. Maybe we can wrap her fingers tight with gauze to stop the bleeding some."

Aunt Elizabeth ran up the stairs.

Aunt Miriam came to her side. She reached over and held the towel tight with pressure. "Ach, niece. You cut four fingers." Her tone held not a trace of bitterness or scolding.

If Kristen hadn't had her eyes open, she'd thought it was another voice that spoke to her.

"You'll be fine. Not a one of us hasn't been bit by a bread knife, I'll tell you that."

Kristen tried to smile but her stomach roiled and her head swam. She closed her eyes to the soothing voice of Aunt Miriam.

The next thing Kristen knew, she was looking into a doctor's face. Had she fainted? She had no recollection of getting here.

"There, now. All patched up. You're lucky you let go of that knife when you did, or your fingers would be gone. Take it easy and keep the bandage clean and dry. I want to see you in three days."

Kristen nodded. Then Aunt Miriam spoke.

"Will she be prone to infection, Doctor?"

"No, I covered all the bases. Just make sure she keeps the wound covered and dry.

There's lots of stitches there."

Kristen sat up on the doctor's table and was helped to her feet by Aunt Miriam and the attending doctor. "Ooh, my arm!"

"That's from the Tetanus shot," the doctor told her. "Might ache for a few days."

"Can you walk OK, now, Kristen? Are you dizzy?" Aunt Miriam placed her hand under Kristen's elbow.

"I think I'll be OK. I was scared more than anything else. I never could stand the sight of blood, even my own."

"You lost a good amount," the doctor told her. "But not enough to be considered dangerous. Have something to eat when you get home and rest up," he instructed as they reached the door.

Aunt Miriam took a firmer hold on her.

"John is in the waiting room with Angela. We convinced your Aenti Elizabeth to stay behind and tend to the folks at the haus. She'll be anxious to see that you're all fixed up."

"Thanks for coming with me, Aunt Miriam." Kristen turned to meet her aunt's eyes. They were pretty when they weren't peering or squinting. A light blue under long light lashes.

Aunt Miriam nodded and her gaze softened even more. "It's what familye is for."

Knowing that Aunt Miriam had no family of her own in so far as a husband or children were concerned, Kristen assumed that this was one of the ways an unmarried Amish woman helped her married siblings, as Aunt Elizabeth had explained. She'd said that Aunt Miriam was a big help to her. Was she doing this out of obligation or because she genuinely cared about her?

"Denki, as you all say," Kristen said.

Was that a smile she saw gracing Aunt Miriam's face?

"You're my sister Emily's dochter, after all. My niece. You need someone to look after you, now that your mudder is gone. No matter how old we get, we need someone to look after us. It's a gut feeling knowing we're not alone, jah?"

"Jah," Kristen mimicked with a smile. Right then and there, she realized Aunt Miriam knew all about loneliness.

10

By the time Kristen was back at the house, all the buggies were gone and everything looked the way it had before.

Anna ran outside as soon as their buggy pulled into the drive. "How are you feeling, Kristen?" She gazed wide eyed at her bandaged hand.

"I'm fine, Anna. The doctor stitched me up and put special medicine on the cuts."

"Does it hurt?"

"Only a little when I move the fingers." It hurt much more than that, but she didn't want to upset little Anna, or John, for that matter. He was looking at her with the same worried expression as his youngest sister.

"Come. Let's get some hot tea and a nice piece of bread with church budder into you." Aunt Miriam guided her up the steps toward Aunt Elizabeth, who waited at the back kitchen door.

When they were inside Katie Mast was

seated at the table. She quickly stood and walked over to Kristen. Gently, she lifted her bandaged hand. "Seems they fixed you up gut."

Kristen met her gray eyes and nodded. Then the older woman took her shawl from the back of the chair and bid everyone good-bye.

"She waited to see how you fared with your injury," Aunt Elizabeth explained. "Now, let's see about you eating something."

"OK. I'm a little hungry, and I'm curious about this church peanut butter you all talk about."

"It's just peanut budder with *melassich*. That's, molasses, and some melted marshmallows. Some folks use corn syrup instead of the molasses, but we like the flavor the molasses gives," Aunt Miriam told her.

"I like a slice of cheese on top of mine," John's voice echoed in.

"Cheese? And peanut butter?" Kristen turned to look at him as he retrieved some leftover cheese from the ice box.

"Try it. You can always give the cheese to me if you don't like it." Smiling, he sat down across from her.

Aunt Elizabeth handed them both plates while Aunt Miriam got the peanut butter and bread.

"Here, let me make it for you. One hand won't do for a nice thick slathering." John took a slice of bread and smeared it with a hearty layer of the peanut butter. He then topped it with two slices of yellow cheese and placed it on her plate.

Aunt Miriam, Aunt Elizabeth, and Anna watched.

Kristen was surprised. "I've never had such thick sweet peanut butter, and the cheese gives it a slight saltiness that makes it just perfect. This must be the stuff that gave the expression of smacking one's lips."

"See, I told you!"

John looked as if he'd accomplished a great feat, and then took a hearty bite of his concoction. "The cheese makes it all come together," he added, placing another slice atop his bread.

"Aunt Miriam, aren't you having any? You haven't eaten all day either," Kristen said.

"Ach, Miriam. I'm sorry. I was so concerned for Kristen . . ."

Aunt Miriam put her hand up to her sister. "Don't worry, Lizzie. I'm not a child, you know. I can serve myself. But denki for thinking of me, niece."

John and Aunt Elizabeth looked at one another as if they hadn't heard right.

Kristen stood and went to the counter to retrieve a plate for Aunt Miriam with her good hand. She didn't want her aunt to feel forgotten. Although not intentional, she surely knew what that felt like most of her life.

"Ach, Kristen. No need to serve me, child. You have a bad hand."

"I still have a good hand to get a plate from the counter."

John's smile widened as he took another bite of the gooey bread with cheese.

Kristen wasn't trying to score points with him by her actions. She was only being what she'd wanted someone to be for her all these years.

Not until today did Kristen come to understand the bitterness that rose up like steam out of Aunt Miriam's heart.

A life of loneliness and rejection had caused it. Her role in the family was to be put to good use wherever there was a need, shuffled from household to household, it seemed. Not exactly the station in life a woman dreamed about. Maybe had she been less bitter, and offered a softer side of herself, her nieces, nephews, and close neighbors would act more loving toward her. That was the lack in Aunt Miriam. Feeling loved.

Kristen didn't want to end up the same way. She was young. There was still lots of time to be loved . . . someday.

She looked up from her half eaten bread to find John's blue eyes piercing through her. If she didn't know better, she'd think that John could read her mind . . . and heart.

After three days, Angela drove Kristen back to the doctor at St. Mary's Hospital. They both convinced Aunt Elizabeth and Aunt Miriam that they could go on their own and planned to have lunch out afterward.

"I'm so glad you got a good report, Kristen," Angela said as they pulled out of the hospital parking area.

"Me, too. I can't wait to get the stitches out in another week. Then I can get the hand wet and take a bath. Although I really haven't had a bath since I got here. I've been using the water pump in the back room since it's been so warm."

"I don't mean any disrespect to your relatives, but you're welcome to come take a hot shower at my house any time you wish."

"That's so nice of you to offer, Angela. But I want to abide by the ways of my family here. There's some part of me that feels at home being Amish. I wonder how I can do that in winter with a hand pump of icy water."

"In winter they heat the water in pots on the stove before using it. So you can sponge bathe that way during the week. I think Saturday night is bath night where they fill a huge basin with heated water."

"I remember John starting to tell me something about that when I first got here. Bath time must take forever!"

"It does. That's why . . . they . . . er . . . share the bath water, one at a time. Each person adds a pot or two of newly heated water when it's their turn to bathe."

"Isn't that unsanitary? Ugh! That's one part of being Amish that I'm not sure I'm up for."

"As far as I know, Kristen, no one has had any problem with it. They've been doing it that way for years. Maybe you can get a smaller basin just for yourself and ask if that'll be OK. It's well water, so they don't get a water bill."

"If I heat my own water and fill my own basin, I don't see the problem. Seems as if I've landed in another place and time."

"You have, in a sense. It's a matter of adapting — or leaving — when you're able."

Leaving? She'd almost forgotten that she had that option ever since her reliance on

Derick was no longer a reality. She'd wait 'til her mom's will was read to see where she stood financially. Then she'd start to make some decisions so she'd be ready the minute she was of legal age come October.

John. Why did he suddenly pop into her head? Had she become so attached to him already? She was barely over Derick. She wouldn't think about it now.

"So, where can we go for a bite to eat?" Kristen asked Angela, determined to burst free of her unsettled thoughts.

"There's a diner over in Fort Plain Village. One thing you'll certainly miss if you leave is the great food your Aunt Elizabeth cooks."

She'd miss more than the food.

That night after supper, Uncle Jonas told the family that the general store in town was now vacated and that they could begin to take it over.

This was the first she'd heard anything about the store being run by the Waglers.

"I almost forgot about the store. It's been a long time since you spoke of it," Aunt Elizabeth said as she poured a cup of tea.

"Jah, that's because I had to haggle with the landlord for a while about keeping the rent the same as it was. And even after he agreed, we had to wait 'til it was vacated. Sol kept changing his mind about moving south. He only left yesterday. Three days later than we'd agreed."

"It's officially ours now then?" John's eyes were wide with anticipation.

"Jah, it is. We can start cleaning it up as soon as there's time. I made a few keys so any one of us can go when we're able."

"I'm ready to go over there first thing after chores tomorrow morgen." John looked at Kristen. "Want to come? I know you can't use your hand yet, but you can give us some suggestions on where to set up things."

"Uh, sure. I had no idea about the store." How long had they known about this? And why didn't they think to tell her? She'd been left out. Proof again that she wasn't one of them. A sigh escaped her. "Sounds like you'll be changing it around."

"Jah, it will cater to the Amish community. We can't travel that far with horse and buggy, and some things require us to hire a driver. I'm hoping our store will make it more convenient to get some needed items locally. We're calling it Wagler's General Store."

Kristen nodded. Should she care?

"Kristen? Something wrong?" Aunt Elizabeth's question pierced through her apathy.

Was there ever a time she missed something?

Kristen shook her head.

But John's gaze steadied on her.

"We had a meeting as a familye to speak about the store before you came to be with us, Kristen. Had you come in April, you would have been at the meeting, too. So, do you have any ideas for the place?" John was so tuned into her feelings that it set her on edge at times. This was one of them.

She forced a small smile for him. "I'm not sure what Amish people need. Sorry."

Uncle Jonas turned his gaze to Kristen and pulled on his beard as he always did when contemplating something. "What about Englisch folks? They'll be coming to the store, too."

"Maybe some stationery items, like envelopes, writing paper, and computer paper. Some glue, scotch tape, pencils and pens, too," Kristen suggested.

"And crayons!" Anna said. Uncle Jonas looked at her and smiled. "Jah, Anna, crayons, too."

"We'll be selling a lot of things in bulk, such as flour, sugar, and nuts. And large jars of honey, molasses, and maple syrup," Uncle Jonas added. "Staples that are used at the haus for baking and making church budder and such."

"First thing we need to do is put in a hitch rail in the parking area. When any of us shop there, we have to tie our horse to the chain-link fence. It works OK, but the fence is all warped now," John said.

"You, Daniel, and Kristen go to the store tomorrow morgen after breakfast for a couple of hours and make notes on what needs to be done before we start ordering our goods."

"OK, Daed. We'll go right after I milk the cows." John stood, glanced briefly at Kristen, and then walked outside.

"It's still light out, so I'm going to sit on the porch. I like to see the fields turn orange just before the sun disappears behind the mountains. The day after tomorrow I get the stitches out of my hand, so I can help with the dishes again." Kristen directed her words to Aunt Elizabeth.

"No need to worry about that. It'll be gut to see your hand all healed up."

Kristen nodded and headed for the door. The sunset was a good excuse to catch John for a minute. He'd looked at her in a strange way before he left.

John went to gather a few mops, buckets, and wood cleaner from the shed next to the barn. He wanted everything ready to bring

140

to the store in the morgen. He intended to make Kristen feel useful there, even though she couldn't help with the cleaning. He'd bring a pad and pencil and have her take notes on where things would be placed when they were delivered in a couple weeks.

Despite his best efforts, he couldn't shake Kristen's forlorn look from his mind. Why hadn't he thought of mentioning the store to her? Why had he thought it didn't matter one way or another? It did. And the reason became as clear as day to him when he'd looked into her doleful dark eyes at the table earlier. For her it affirmed that she was not one of them. There'd been chances to tell her, and she knew it.

He could have . . . should have . . . told her the day she'd questioned him about the FOR RENT sign in the store window. Or the nacht he woke her about Lowville. Daed had gotten the thumbs-up go-ahead on renting it earlier that evening. But John didn't tell her then. Although the very next day he'd told Sadie. Sure, Sadie was his intended at the time. But Kristen was fami-lye, as Sadie would have been if things had worked out. They all knew about the store, even little Anna. He'd read the hurt on Kristen's face. And he felt it in his heart.

John set the cleaning items at the front of

the shed and closed it for the nacht. He heard the sound of a throat clearing, turned, and found Kristen standing there.

"I hoped I'd find you here."

He should apologize. Right now. "Listen . . ."

Kristen put her hand on his arm. "You seemed upset with me when you left the table before."

"Nee, I wasn't upset with you. I was upset with myself."

"But why?"

"For not telling you about the store. You're familye now, and it's a familye business. One of us should have at least mentioned it to you."

"But you said yourself that I wasn't here yet when the family decided to pursue the business. And you wanted to be sure it was definite before you said anything. Plus, with all the chaos I've caused here . . ."

"Chaos?" John interrupted. "What are you saying, Kristen?"

"Taking me in to honor my mother's wishes has caused this family nothing but trouble. The mysterious notes and that car coming around, scaring Anna, is not something any one of you need here. And my being Englisch as you call it, obviously makes me different, drawing unwanted attention.

Jacob Mast being one example."

"Kristen, my mamm is happier than you know about being able to have you here with us. You are her youngest sister's only dochter. Even if there wasn't a will that stated your mother's wishes for you, Mamm would have wanted you here. The car and those notes are not your fault."

"I can't even cut a loaf of bread right." Kristen held up her bandaged hand.

"Ach, the same thing happened to Mamm and to Aenti Miriam, and don't tell anyone I told you, but to Daed, too." John saw a glimmer of a smile flick into Kristen's eyes. But then it faded so quickly he thought he might have imagined it.

"John, I have to leave here eventually. I'll be fine with my inheritance, assuming I get one. Then come October when I turn eighteen, I can go."

John's stomach soured. "That should be soon, Jah?" Not too soon, he hoped.

"When I took in the mail the other day there was a letter from my mom's attorney, Riley Gallagher. He was a good friend to both her and Ross. He'll call when everything is in order, and then drive up with the details. He didn't say how long it would take."

"Vell, we best be going on that picnic we

143

planned. This Sunday is an off Sunday from Preaching. Wouldn't want you leaving here without some gut memories."

"John, I'm sorry if I made it sound as if everything is terrible here. It's not. I'm glad my mom wanted me to come."

He never thought he'd hear those words. His heart raced. "Me, too." More than she'd ever know.

"I hear a buggy coming down the road." Kristen looked past John.

"Maybe it's Aunt Miriam."

"No. Whoever it is isn't stopping."

Or greeting us. John thought that was odd. All the folks around here greeted one another as they passed by. The Amish tipped their hat or nodded, and the Englisch gave a quick wave of the hand. The driver of this buggy did none of those.

"Oh, look, the fields are turning orange. The last light of the day. My favorite time." Kristen waved her arm out as if revealing the sight before them.

John liked her love of Gott's splendor. "Want to walk some?"

"Sure. Then I think I'll have a piece of your mom's strawberry pie."

"Jah, me, too. On second thought. How about we skip the walk and go right for the pie? It'll be dark soon."

"Sounds good to me." Kristen laughed as they walked back to the house, but no sooner had her laughter begun, it suddenly ended.

She stopped in her tracks and pointed to a white bulged envelope in the grass next to the path leading up to the house.

11

John pulled out a chair for Kristen at the kitchen table, envelope in hand. He could hear Anna from the living room asking Daniel to play one more game of checkers. Everyone had gathered there to relax after dinner as they often did once nightfall came. By 9:00 PM, they'd all be in bed.

Should he call them into the kitchen about the note? He didn't like upsetting news before bedtime and figured as much for the rest of his familye. He'd wait until morgen.

He sat next to Kristen, opened the letter, removed a rock that was obviously used to weight it down, and together they silently read the words: *Please have the young lady leave Stone Arabia. It's only out of concern for her happiness and peace that I ask this.*

"It doesn't sound like a warning note this time, does it?" Kristen's eyes bored into his with her question. Their lovely soft brown and the long lashes that graced them were even more obvious when she wore her hair the Plain way, pushed back from her face under the kapp, as she'd been doing since Preaching. She was trying very hard to fit into this familye, and he wished he could end these regular assaults on her life here. The notes had to stop. He'd get to the bottom of it all.

"Nee. Sounds more like someone who is worried for you. But who? And why? Do you feel that staying here would ruin your happiness or take away your peace?" He was being quite bold in asking this of her outright, but he needed to know before he could pursue the matter any further. At least that's the reason he'd told himself.

"John, there wasn't a whole lot of happiness I came here with. And I don't know much about inner peace, unless you count sitting at the shore and feeling a sense of calm once in a while. Sure, I loved being near the ocean, but that's a different kind of happiness. I've had peaceful, happy moments here many times. I guess I just never said so. It's the notes that are ruining whatever happiness and peace I have here. Not this place or any of you."

John nodded, grateful that some goodness had entered her soul here.

"And I think some of your mom's strawberry pie might add to my happiness," Kristen said, getting up to open the ice box. She placed the half-full wrapped pie pan on the table and shrugged. "Might as well keep a sense of humor about it all. This particular note doesn't make me feel afraid."

Daed stepped into the kitchen. While he eyed the pie on the table, John quickly shoved the note and envelope into his pocket.

"Looks like we have the same liking to *aebeer,*" Daed said, getting three plates from the cupboard.

"Jah, strawberry is my favorite berry." John sliced three pieces. He tried his best to appear perfectly normal. The evening began to darken the kitchen, and Kristen seemed lost in thought as she ate. John got up to light a lantern.

When they'd all finished their pie, Kristen carried the dishes to the sink and began to pump water on them with her good hand.

"Mind if we step outside, John?" Daed must have seen him tuck the note into his pocket. Eyes like an eagle, for sure.

Once on the porch, Daed faced him and held out his hand. "Give me the note, John."

John pulled it out of his pocket and handed it over. "I planned to tell everyone tomorrow morgen. Figured it's no use upsetting anyone before bed."

Daed read it and handed it back to John. "Sounds like this is someone who knows Kristen. Maybe your Aenti Miriam was right about it being one of Kristen's friends in New Jersey."

"Nee. I don't think so, Daed. Her boyfriend there went off with her best friend, and none of her other friends ever called her. Seems strange to me that her best friend's mamm didn't call to see how Kristen is doing. Kristen spent a lot of time there for many years, not to mention living with them right after the accident before she came to us."

"How do you know all about her boyfriend and the friends not calling?"

"Kristen told me. We've had some talks."

Daed pulled on his beard thoughtfully. "The two of you are fond of one another. Sadie can get the wrong idea."

"Sadie is gone. She moved to Lancaster to help her onkle with his farm. If she marries a man willing to work the farm, it will be theirs. Our plans for a future are very different."

Daed looked at him quietly for a few moments. "I see." Then he glanced toward the haus. "Right now Kristen is all *verhaddelt*. Seems that she needs to find herself. That's probably why her mamm wanted her to come here."

"Mixed up? What are you saying?"

"I'm saying that Kristen comes from a different world. Now she is trying to be Plain and be part of a familye. It might not turn out that way in the long run. I think it best if you leave Kristen be for the time being. Give her a chance to work things out in her own self. Soon, she'll have to make some decisions."

"Me and Kristen are gut friends. Nothing more than that can come of it. She's Englisch, and I'm not jumping the fence. She'd have to be baptized and then . . . vell, no sense talking about it. Only Gott knows what will be."

"Jah, seems that way to me, too. And don't go forgetting that she's not yet eighteen. In the Plain world, a maidle is ready for marriage at that age, but in the Englisch world, eighteen is considered too young. Kristen might not be ready for such a commitment until way later."

John couldn't help give the dry earth a hard kick. Dust rose up as if to emphasize his frustration.

Daed stepped ahead of him and led the way back to the haus.

So much for taking Kristen to the singing.

■ ■ ■ ■

Morning came much too quick for Kristen. She hardly slept thinking of the latest mystery note. She wished she could turn over and go back to sleep, but she'd promised John she'd go with him and Daniel to the vacated store.

Kristen began to wear the Plain dresses every day now. It seemed easier than trying to choose something appropriate to wear from what she'd brought. Jeans were out. Short sleeves were out. Skirts or dresses above the knee were out. Besides her denim skirt, nothing else she had would do.

She was glad that Mary, true to her word, had given her several dresses that closed with hooks and eyes. It made dressing much easier to deal with than the pins, especially using one hand. She slipped on a dark purple dress and went to the wash room to freshen up at the water pump, careful not to wet her bandages.

When Kristen entered the kitchen, she smelled the familiar scent of bacon, eggs, and baked biscuits.

"Good morning, Aenti. Can I help with anything?" She walked over to the stove and waited.

"Ah, Geode Mariye, Kristen. Please take the biscuits from the pan and place them on a plate. How is your hand feeling?"

"Fine. I'm sure it's all healed, or the stitches wouldn't be coming out tomorrow."

"Still. I don't want you carrying or lifting anything heavy at the store later."

"OK. I promise."

Aunt Elizabeth nodded her approval then looked over at the table. "Everything is just about ready. Did I put the budder out?"

"Jah, the budder is there," John said, causing Kristen to swirl around. She met the familiar blue eyes, and he gave her an instant smile. But something about it was different. It wasn't his usual full smile. Maybe it was because he was about to reveal the latest note to the family this morning. More anxiety and trouble for everyone just because she was here.

When they were all seated and finished their silent prayer, John wasted no time in placing the white envelope on the table.

"Ach! Another note?" Mary gasped.

"Jah, last nacht as we were coming into the haus Kristen spotted it on the ground. We saw no car this time, just a buggy going by," John explained as Kristen sat there with her eyes cast down. She said an extra prayer that this topic would end soon.

"Should I read it aloud?" Mary asked, as she reached for the envelope.

"Jah, please do," Uncle Jonas said while Aunt Elizabeth nodded.

"Please have the young lady leave Stone Arabia. It's only out of concern for her happiness and peace that I ask this." Mary then folded the note and placed it back inside the envelope.

No one said anything for a while.

Hearing it again, Kristen felt more certain that the writer's words of concern rang true. But who was it? She knew no one in this area, except for her newfound family.

Daniel turned to his father. "Daed, I know how you feel about going on the outside for help, but this has to stop. The sheriff might assist us to make it happen sooner. Jah? Plus the bishop knows of the situation now."

"Jah, Daniel. First I will visit with the bishop and ask him about it. If he gives his approval, I will make a call to the sheriff." Uncle Jonas paused as if to allow anyone else their say, but no one said anything. "Vell, let's eat our breakfast. We have a busy day ahead." Uncle Jonas reached for the biscuits and everyone began to fill their plates. Business as usual.

Kristen liked their forge-ahead attitude. No getting stuck in the mud for this family.

She breathed a sigh of relief as she accepted the platter of scrambled eggs from Anna who wore a comforting smile on her rosy child's face. Kristen was glad the news of this latest note didn't seem to frighten her.

Maybe even Anna sensed that this particular note held a tone of care; concern from someone out there who was a complete stranger to her.

The general store looked very different vacated of all its merchandise. John knew they had a lot of work ahead of them before the deliveries started coming in.

Everything appeared old and dusty now. The mahogany woodwork that framed the counter by the cash register needed a good polishing. The Formica countertop where sodas and pretzels were served was worn and stained.

"Here's a job for you, Daniel." John knew his brudder could easily replace the Formica, being so gifted with woodworking and remodeling a room.

"Ach, that's not a problem. I'm thinking about the wooden sign I want to make out front. Should we have it on the building or posted in the ground?"

"So long as folks could see it, either way seems gut. What do you think, Kristen?"

John was not about to have her feeling left out of their decisions this time.

She turned from her inspection of the shelves to face them. A strand of dark hair came loose from her kapp, and she tossed her head to clear it from her eyes.

John found her lovelier with each passing day, and he wished he could tell her so. Daed's warning for him not to deepen their friendship shone like neon lights in his mind. For the time being. Now, he'd focus on finding the writer of the notes. Once all of the mystery was cleared up, his attempt to further their friendship would not seem like another thing she had to deal with. But instead, something that would bring her the happiness and peace that the writer of that note felt would be lacking if she stayed. Not if she stayed with him. He'd see to that for sure and for certain.

"What do I think about what?" Kristen asked, her eyes darting from John to Daniel.

"About the sign we need to put up that will read, Wagler's General Store. Should we put it on the building or on a post in the ground?"

"Maybe both. The sign on the post can just say, Wagler's. And the one across the top front of the building can say Wagler's

General Store, plus a short list of some of the items sold here. Dry Goods, Sundries, Seed. That kind of thing."

John turned to Daniel and saw his own smile duplicated on his brudder's face.

"That's a great idea, Kristen." Daniel's eyes danced with excitement. "I can picture it in my head. I'm going to burn the letters into the post sign, nice and big. And I will paint the sign for the building in green with black lettering."

"You do the lettering freehand?" Kristen widened her eyes.

"Sure," he said, his head tilted and his lips quirked.

John stifled a chuckle. Daniel didn't know the depth of his own talents. Woodworking and crafting came as natural to him as walking. His lack of pride was a tribute to his Amish upbringing and to the kind of person he was.

"I can't draw a straight line," Kristen told him, then shrugged.

"You don't have to draw to come up with gut ideas, like you did with the signs," John said.

"Thanks." She gave him a soft smile that sent a weakness running through him. Then she reached for a broom.

"Mamm told me to make sure you don't

do any cleaning or lifting. I brought this pad and pencil for you to write down where you think certain items should go."

Kristen turned to him and rolled her eyes.

"My hand is fine."

"Mamm said you promised her," John reminded, holding out the pad and pencil to her.

"Fine. I'll take notes, but if you don't mind, I'd like to take photos of the store with my cell phone, so I can study the different sections later. I'll never remember how many shelves there are and all of that." John was tempted to give her a playful smirk, but he needed to try to refrain from such flirtatious gestures.

"Here is a tape measure. Can you please measure the space between each set of shelves and jot it down? That will make it easier to decide what to put on them."

"I wouldn't have even thought of that." She slapped her forehead.

"I only thought of it because we've built things many times over and cut the wood to size for certain items. We decided to use the shelves as they are here to save on time and money."

"OK. I'll measure them all. No need to watch me. I know how to do it." She nearly glared at him when he failed to move along.

He didn't doubt her ability; he just liked being near her. He nodded and walked to the counter where he had some wood soap cleaner waiting. Best to keep busy and get his mind off of Kristen Esh. At least for the next couple of hours.

Kristen tried not to let her mind wander as she measured each shelf. She realized that Derick had taken a backseat to John in her mind these days . . . and in her heart. And all she could think of was what it would feel like measuring and cleaning up a home that would be hers and John's.

Of course, the thought was pure fantasy. He was Amish. She was not. He would not leave for the outside world, and she didn't know what she was going to do next.

Everything was on hold until she heard from Riley Gallagher on the status of her mom's will and Ross's estate. Even if she inherited a large sum of money, where would she go? As much as she loved the ocean, would she want to go back to a place where her friends had deserted her? The Jersey Shore would now remind her of being forsaken and taking her mom from her. Maybe she could live in a neighboring town. The ocean would always be a part of her heart, even if her friends and mother were no longer in her life.

"Kristen. Time to go." Daniel startled her. "John's out front in the buggy. We got chores to do back at the haus. Daed, Mamm and Aenti Miriam will be coming after we have lunch."

"Can I stay here and wait for them? I'm not finished with the measuring yet. I'll be fine on my own for a while." The fact was, she wanted some time alone to think and maybe to fantasize a bit more, uninterrupted.

"Don'tcha want to eat lunch?"

"I had a lot for breakfast. I'm not really hungry," she told him.

"Then I guess it's OK. I'll tell John you're staying. See you later." With that, Daniel was out the door.

Suddenly the place went quiet. So quiet, that she heard the wood floor boards creak in spots where she walked that she hadn't noticed before.

Kristen gazed at the work rags on the counter. Then at the clusters of dust in the corners of the floor. She went around the counter to a small sink to dampen a rag to dust with. No one had to know she'd dusted. Besides, it wasn't strenuous work.

An actual faucet! She turned it on. Running water. The owner wasn't an Amish man, so that explained it. Although, she'd heard that Amish were allowed running water at their places of business and even in the home if a good reason precipitated it. It was all up to the district's Bishop. Their bishop seemed nice enough when she'd met him at Preaching. She would see Bishop Ebersol every two weeks at future church services and wondered if he'd question her intentions about the faith. Well, his guess was as good as hers at this point.

After the hour had passed, Kristen was done with all the dusting. A damp rag did a good job on the shelves and worked well when tied around a broom to get the dust off the floors. She'd been careful to keep her bandage clean and dry by wearing one of the rubber gloves John had brought.

As she leaned back on the counter to appraise her work, the door opened. Aunt Elizabeth and Aunt Miriam entered, their expressions gloomy.

Kristen looked from one aunt to the other. "Did something happen to John?" She blurted out. "Or little Anna?"

They shook their heads.

"Come, Kristen. We need to go back to the haus. Aenti Miriam will stay here to clean. And you haven't even eaten any lunch yet." Aunt Elizabeth placed her hand on the small of Kristen's back and motioned her to the door. She had that look Kristen had seen the day her mom had died. A look of trying to cushion her from something bad that had happened.

When they arrived home, Riley Gallagher sat on the sofa with Uncle Jonas.

They looked up at her with strained smiles. She was beginning to feel a sense of dread.

"Kristen! You look . . . well, wonderfully Amish!" Riley rose to greet her.

"Looks are deceiving. I have a long way to go to become Amish. My aunt and uncle here can tell you that." She embraced him.

"That's not what I heard," he said as they parted. "Let's sit down. I need to talk with you about your mom's will and Ross's estate." Riley pointed to the oak rocker across from the sofa.

Aunt Elizabeth remained standing, fiddling with the strings of her prayer kapp. She did that whenever she was nervous.

Riley cleared his throat and then said the words that Kristen had to ask him to repeat.

"Are you telling me that Ross has a will, and I'm not in it at all?"

Riley nodded.

"What about my mom? Is she in his will?"

"No, she's not."

161

"And my mom's will?"

"Since she made me executor of her will, she told me about her wish for you to come here when we drew it up. I knew what her Last Will and Testament contained for several years now. She left you her savings. It's a nice sum. And she left some money to the Waglers for any expenses incurred during your stay here should she pass before you were of legal age to support yourself or marry."

So, they would be paid for taking her in?

As if Aunt Elizabeth could read her thoughts, she quickly put up a hand. "Ach, nee! Please add that money to Kristen's inheritance. We do not want money for having our niece here, ain't so, Jonas?"

"Jah. The Lord has blessed us with plenty to go around."

Riley smiled. "There is also a letter I'm to give to the bishop, and an item wrapped in brown paper for a Jacob Mast in the event of her death. I might need one of you to come with me to deliver these. Emily requested they be given in person, and I don't know my way around the Amish communities."

Jonas nodded.

Kristen's head reeled. "Jacob Mast? Why him?"

"Kristen, Jacob Mast was once your mamm's beau," Aunt Elizabeth clarified.

"What's in the package?" Kristen asked, thoroughly confused.

"We can't open it, Kristen. It's private and to be given directly to him, as is the letter to the bishop," Riley informed her as he stood to leave.

Where did the bishop come in?

"Riley, before you go. Who did Ross leave the house and his money to?"

"The bulk of his estate is willed to Mattie Cook, and a specified amount is to pay for the cost of an assisted living place for a widowed elderly aunt, Helen Maddok, in California."

"Ah, Mattie. Sure, he'd been seeing her for years and they were headed for marriage. Still, I don't understand why he would leave me out completely? I've known him since I was born, and we got along fine. He even named his boat after me." She hung her head in shame. Had she failed him somewhere along the line? The man who'd taken her under his wing yet did not deem her worthy enough to be part of his will?

"You can go to the house and collect whatever things you left behind if you like. Clothes, CDs, photos. Those are yours for the taking."

"I'd rather not go back there. Can you please mail me the few things that I'll list on paper? It isn't much." She suppressed the tears. Anger dominated her hurt, and she preferred to keep it that way. She refused to cave in to sentiments. After all, Ross Maddok wasn't her father or any relation at all. He was her mom's employer and friend, and they lived in his beach house because Mom was live-in help. True, he was her confidante many times, but never family. Or even like family. And now his will proved that.

12

The next morgen John hid his disappointment when Kristen's chair remained empty for the duration of breakfast. He'd come in several times from the fields with the excuse of needing some cold lemonade. Still no sign of her.

On his fourth time back to the kitchen, he spied his mamm going up the stairs with a tray in her hands. A subtle scent of chamomile lingered in the room. Mamm relied on chamomile tea to remedy nearly every ailment, especially those borne of sadness and nerves.

He could only imagine the pain Kristen was going through. The tragedy of losing her mom followed by one thing after the other. Now this. He wished he could make it all right for her. But how? Grief needed time to heal. She had much to grieve. He tried to imagine having to suddenly leave the farm and the home where he'd been raised, due to a tragedy. Then placed with familye members he'd never known. Without one item or memento left to him from his former life.

He'd told Kristen that it wasn't one's place to question Gott's ways. Now he wished he'd said more. Something personal and caring. Gott had always been his rock and he wanted Kristen to feel that same sense of surety in her time of struggle. But he suddenly realized that he'd never had such struggles as Kristen. Maybe it was too easy for him to trust in Gott's care given his circumstances — a happy, secure childhood with parents and siblings at his side. Jah, the loss of his birth mamma when he'd entered the world was, indeed, a sad thing, but he'd never known his mamma, and his step-mamm raised him with as much love and care as any kind could ever want.

From what Kristen had told him, most of her life had been a lonely one.

Until now.

He hoped her new familye here could fill up the empty places in her heart. More than that, he hoped he'd be part of what would replace the emptiness. A big part. Never mind his daed's thoughts on all of this. John would get around that, one way or another.

■ ■ ■ ■

The following morgen when John came in for breakfast, Kristen was at the stove with Mamm, dressed in a Plain, dark green dress. She stirred cornmeal mush while Mamm sliced the grain bread. The bread slicing reminded him that Kristen was due to have her stitches out yesterday but she still wore the bandage on her hand.

"Goede Mariye," he said as he walked to his chair.

Mamm turned and smiled, but Kristen barely acknowledged his greeting with a slight turn of her head and a nod.

"Kristen, if you need a ride to the doctor to get the stitches out, I'd be glad to take you. It's not too far for a buggy ride." He helped himself to orange juice.

She brought the cornmeal mush to the table in a large bowl. "Thanks, John, but I called Angela to drive me. She'll be here at nine thirty." She finally glanced at him just long enough to reveal red eyes underlined by dark circles.

His heart went out to her, but he said nothing of it.

"We have other errands to run afterward, so might as well kill two birds with one stone, as they say." She turned toward the ice box.

"Kristen wants to go with Attorney Riley Gallagher when he delivers the items her mamm left with him. He stayed an extra nacht at The Palatine Hotel 'til she was up to going. He'll be going with them," Mamm clarified.

"I can come with you if you like? You don't know your way around."

"Angela does. She drove us to Lowville, remember? Riley said he'd take care of paying for the driving and gas. He has his car but rather not chance getting lost. GPS doesn't get a reliable signal around here. Anyway, we worked it out." She placed a tub of budder and a jar of jam on the table.

Something had grown cold in Kristen. Her tone of voice was hard and empty. She didn't look at anyone when she spoke. She'd been broken. He wanted to fix her. Daed said only Gott could do that. Still, he wanted to help.

"If you change your mind, come fetch me from the store. I'll be there most of the day painting."

"Thanks, but we'll be fine." Kristen avoided his eyes and took a seat with the rest of the family.

Anna ran to the stove to get the kaffee

she'd made earlier. She set it on the table, and they bowed their heads in silent prayer. Too short for all John wanted to say.

When Kristen closed her eyes she saw the smiling face of Ross Maddok and the usual thumbs-up gesture he'd give her each time he'd leave for a trip . . . including the last and final one.

She opened her eyes with a start, and her glance fell on John. He looked right back at her. He should be praying, not watching her. She turned her gaze away. There was no point in nurturing her fondness for John. She couldn't become like him in her faith with all that had happened. She couldn't follow his suggestion to pray and trust in God's will. So far, the will of God had caused her nothing but grief. She knew that if they spoke about this latest setback, he'd bring up the topic of faith and encourage her to pray and trust.

Trust.

Now there was a word with a meaning she'd yet to experience from another. Well, maybe that wasn't altogether true. John Wagler certainly seemed to be the most trustworthy person she'd met so far in her entire life. But she'd thought the same about Cindy and Derick, her two closest friends. And look where it got her.

She'd trusted her mother and the choices she'd made for the two of them. But she'd been kept in the dark about her mom being Amish. She could have had cousins, aunts, and uncles while growing up.

Whatever made her think that Ross would will the house to her? Sure, he'd told her often that he'd wished he'd had a daughter like her. And she was always going on about how much she loved living by the beach. It didn't mean that she was entitled to his home. He had a life outside of their little beach house world where her mom worked and they happened to live. Ironically, they'd died only a few months before she'd soon turn eighteen and be of legal age to live there . . . if . . . Ha! If was just a fantasy. Mattie Cook owned the house now.

With ocean breezes, running water, and electricity.

And loneliness. At least here, she wasn't lonely. Family flanked her on a daily basis, especially John.

Should she begin her task to trust in God's will in this new life by placing her wounded heart into John's care? She wanted to. Maybe God wanted her to.

Kristen cleared her throat and then looked over to John as he reached for the corn mush. "Do you think you can put off a few hours of the painting to come along, then?"

John stopped spooning the mush into his bowl and looked up at her. His blue eyes widened with surprise. Did she see a spark of happiness ignite in his gaze?

"Jah, sure. I'll be at the store ready to go whenever you and Mr. Gallagher come by with Angela."

"Seems gut that someone in the familye will be with you, Kristen. Denki, John," Uncle Jonas said.

Aunt Elizabeth nodded her approval to her husband with a quiet smile.

Would Uncle Jonas thank John for his willingness to go along if he knew the feelings stirred up in Kristen's heart?

No matter. She'd committed this act of trust to God regarding John, and she intended to see it out.

When Kristen emerged from the doctor's office, she bent her fingers as if not believing they were still there.

"Think your hand is in working order?" John got up from his seat in the waiting room to have a look.

"Yes. It feels so good to move my fingers like this again. I better be extra careful the next time I slice bread. That is, if your mamm will ever let me do it again."

"Sure she will. Everyone has accidents now and then. They tend to make us extra careful, and I bet you won't ever cut yourself slicing bread again."

"Time will tell," Kristen answered, as she headed outside where Angela and Riley Gallagher waited in the car.

Time would tell. Those words spilled forth as naturally as a soft cascade of water. Kristen wondered if her subconscious had already decided to stay on in Stone Arabia. At least for a time.

The ride to Lowville was uneventful and the traffic on the interstate was sparse. As always, Angela talked about various topics to keep her passengers entertained.

Kristen was glad that she rattled on because she didn't want Riley to begin any sort of conversation about the whole estate issue. She wasn't up for it. All she wanted to do was be there when Riley gave Jacob Mast the package and Bishop Ebersol the letter. Not that she didn't trust Riley to do it without her presence. She simply wanted to be present while her mother's wishes were carried out.

As Angela pulled into the small parking area of Mast's Hardware, Kristen's insides tightened. She hoped Jacob Mast wouldn't glue his eyes on her as he had the last time. Surely, John wouldn't tolerate a repeat performance, and she didn't want any hard feelings to come between them for her sake.

To her surprise, Jacob didn't stare the way he'd done during her previous visit. Instead, he acted the complete opposite and barely looked at her, except for brief moments when she spoke. He was polite and pleasant, and she sensed an uneasiness come over him as he took the brown-papered package that Riley handed to him.

"Emily Esh requested that you be given this in the event of her death. This is her daughter, Kristen," Riley said.

"Jah. We already met. Hullo, Kristen. Again, I'm sorry for the loss of your mother."

"Thank you." She let herself take a good look at him. Jacob Mast was a handsome man, with medium brown eyes and hair to match. A hint of gray grazed the sides of the hair that showed from under his straw hat, but it didn't detract from his youthful look. *Mom's first love.* Kristen offered him a smile for that fact alone.

He looked surprised for the briefest moment then smiled back.

"I hope you can forgive me for the staring of you at my sister's haus. I didn't expect you to look so much like Emily . . . like your mamm. Denki for coming along to give me this." He looked down at the package in his hand.

Kristen thought she saw a tremor.

"You're welcome. I just wanted to see my mother's final wishes fulfilled."

John walked over. He and Jacob exchanged some small talk in Pennsylvania Dutch.

Riley cleared his throat, and Kristen was glad for the cue for them to be on their way.

When she looked back at Jacob, he smiled. It was a strained smile this time. Then he averted his eyes from hers and looked downward to the package he held.

Kristen turned and walked away. She wished she could see what her mom had given to him. Maybe old love letters. Or something of his she'd kept all these years.

Kristen wondered why his sister, Katie, didn't live here with him and his widowed cousin instead of alone in Stone Arabia. She'd ask Aunt Elizabeth about it.

Now it was time to deliver Mom's letter to Bishop Ebersol. If only she could read it. Was it an explanation for leaving to go work for Ross? Did Mom want her to become Amish as she'd been? What? Her mind raced with questions. Even after her death, her mother still managed to keep her in the dark.

Angela made good time on their way back to Palatine. She kept Riley occupied with the history of the area and how the Amish came to settle in New York State.

Kristen listened as intently as Riley.

How the influx was mostly Old Order Weaver and Andy Beiler groups from Wilmington, Ohio, with the recent incoming of some less conservative Amish from overcrowded Lancaster.

These were the things her mom should have told her. Now here she was listening about her lineage from the family's driver. An Englisch woman. The whole thing seemed a tad bizarre.

To prevent herself from bringing her thoughts to her lips, Kristen took out the sandwiches she'd made for everyone. A mouthful of food would be far better than a mouthful of resentment. Besides, it was nearly three thirty and none of them had eaten anything since breakfast.

When they pulled into the bishop's driveway, they'd just finished their sandwiches.

Kristen reached into her deep leather bag and handed everyone a small juice box. Her pocketbook seemed bottomless, which she liked. But it was time to buy a more reasonable bag to carry around. This one, her only one, was studded with stars in the black leather on the front side of it. She turned the studded part to face against her. Studded stars and her Plain dress didn't mix. Especially when visiting the bishop.

John held the car door open for Kristen and Riley to step out. A light shower had begun to fall. They hurried to the porch while Angela waited in the car.

When they reached the covering of the porch, Riley turned to John. "Thank you for coming. Having someone who is a member of the community with us might make for a more relaxed visit, don't you think?"

"Bishop Ebersol is very accommodating to all people. I 'spect that his greeting would be the same for each person who came to his door. Church member or not. After five or ten minutes, you'll feel as if you're at the haus of an onkle. We are blessed in this way. You'll see." With that, John knocked on the door.

Kristen drew in a shaky breath, and then the sound of footsteps drew near.

A young girl, who looked to be around nine or ten years old, opened the door.

"Hullo, Margaret. Is your daed at home?

We came for a short visit."

"Jah. He is." She opened the door wider and stepped aside for them to enter. Then she ran off to another room.

Minutes later, Bishop Ebersol appeared with a kind smile and a warm welcome. "Gut to see you, John. Hullo, Kristen."

Kristen nodded as John shook the bishop's hand.

"Bishop, this is Attorney Riley Gallagher." The bishop and Riley shook hands, and then Riley withdrew a white envelope and handed it to the bishop the moment they entered the large living room.

"I am the executor of the Last Will and Testament of Emily Esh. She wanted this letter to be hand delivered to you."

Bishop Ebersol took the letter and looked at it for a few moments in silence. Then his gaze shifted to Kristen. And he opened it.

Kristen hadn't expected the bishop to open the letter right then and there. She'd figured he'd wait 'til they left. Would he read it aloud? She, Riley, and John exchanged quick glances.

There were four typewritten sheets. The bishop scanned each one and then replaced them in the envelope. He looked toward Kristen . . . again. His smile had dimmed somewhat and his eyes held a serious pensive look. He said nothing for what seemed like a full minute. Finally, he spoke. "Would you be able to make time one nacht after supper to talk?"

Kristen really wasn't sure if she wanted to, but out of respect for her mom's wishes, she nodded.

The bishop then patted John on the shoulder and shook Riley's hand again. They never sat or had tea or coffee. She had heard the bishop was a busy man, and she was glad to leave.

On the way to the Palatine Hotel, John invited Riley to dinner, but he declined, saying he had to get on the road due to a court case the following morning.

Kristen thanked him for staying the extra day for her sake. She could see pity in his eyes.

Kristen hated pity.

She'd gotten that same look of pity from teachers and fellow students when her mom couldn't attend her plays or recitals due to working crazy hours at the hotel. She'd gotten the same look from Cindy's parents when she'd been greeted at their door for Christmas dinner, and later, when she was orphaned and moved in with them. Again, she was getting it now.

Aunt Elizabeth, Uncle Jonas, and even

Aunt Miriam, did not cast her pitiful glances. Nor did her cousins. They accepted things as they were and dealt with them. No judgments, no blame given to anyone. No pity. Good or bad, no matter, they thanked God and found a blessing in all of it. She wondered if she could ever be that way.

Kristen sighed. She didn't see as clearly with her soul as they did. Where was the blessing in this for her? She glanced over at John.

13

John convinced his daed that a familye picnic would be gut for all of them, even though his main intention was to have Kristen experience some time in their beautiful woods. He wanted her to like the area so that maybe she'd stay. But Daed didn't need to know that.

This off church Sunday was warm but not hot. The sun bright in a clear blue sky made for a perfect summer early July morgen.

He said a prayer of thanks for the cloudless non-humid day.

"The sandwiches are all made," Mamm told John as he stepped into the kitchen. "Can you get us the cooler from the shed?"

He held it up so she could see it. "I'm ahead of you, Mamm. I washed it out so it's clean and ready to fill."

"It'll be plenty full, that's a sure thing." She placed a pile of foil wrapped sandwiches into the cooler.

Kristen turned from the counter and aimed a smile at him.

He froze to the spot as if time halted along with the beat of his heart.

"We added cheese to the church peanut butter sandwiches." She had a playful glint in her eyes.

"Gut." He had to try his best to honor his daed's wishes and not cross the line of friendship. No teasing smirks, cute remarks, or discreet smiles.

"We have egg salad too," Mamm said, placing another batch of foil wrapped sandwiches into the cooler. "Mary made them last nacht."

Anna ran into the kitchen and went straight to the fridge. "Don't forget my fudge." She took out a pan of the white confection. "I have to cut it and wrap it first." She broke a small piece off and handed it to John.

"Umm, vanilla is my favorite. It's real gut, Anna."

She broke another piece off for herself.

Mamm looked over at her with a frown.

"I want to see how it came out too, Mamm." She bit into the fudge. "I might need another piece to be sure."

"Ach, Anna. Bring the pan here, please. I'll cut it up quick so we can get a move on." Mamm took the tray from her and began her task. Then when she thought no one was looking, she sampled a piece herself.

John cleared his throat and gazed at her with a smile and crossed arms.

Mamm waved her hand at him and chuckled.

"Too bad Daniel isn't coming. He loves Anna's fudge," John told her.

"Vell, I think that Rachel will have some gut things for him to eat while he's visiting with her and her familye," Mamm gave another chuckle.

John nodded.

Rachel must be as nervous as a cat chasing its tail since Daniel finally accepted an invitation to her home. He'd been avoiding the route of courting, even though he'd taken Rachel to several singings already.

John looked over at Kristen as she placed some of Anna's cut and wrapped fudge into the cooler. She'd fit right in at a singing, although she might not know the songs. But he had to get that idea out of his mind. For now.

Thirty minutes later, Angela came to drive them in her SUV as agreed. It was a tight squeeze with seven of them. Daed had said he'd stay home if Daniel was coming, being just as happy sitting on the porch reading the Bible and then the *Budget.*

John released a long breath of tension when he found himself seated against the car door with Daed on his other side, rather than Kristen. Being close to her would be pure torture. Sharing the same car and staring at the back of her kapp, bun, and neck was torture enough.

In forty minutes or so, they entered Glimmerglass State Park with its splendid woods, lake, beach, and picnic tables.

"We'll go to the picnic tables at the overlook like we always do," John said, as he and Daed each took an end of the cooler to carry. "It's an uphill walk on the trail, but it's not a long one." John looked at Kristen as he said that.

She nodded, and then looked at the scenery around her. If she didn't think this was special, then the Jersey Shore must be likened to Paradise itself.

"It's pretty, ain't so?" Anna asked Kristen as she took her hand.

"Very pretty. It has everything in one place. Mountains, water, a beach, and woods."

"Flowers, too, at the overlook," Anna added while Mary, Angela, and Mamm caught up to them.

John and Daed led the way onto the trail toward the overlook. It still hadn't gotten very hot, and the trail was shaded by trees.

John turned to see how Kristen was faring.

She listened to Anna tell of other things they would soon see while she looked out ahead of her.

And . . . she was smiling.

Kristen enjoyed the walk along the trail, and when they emerged onto the overlook, she understood the beauty John had tried to explain to her about the area. The expanse of the sparkling lake hugged by the green mountains made her feel as if she'd stepped into a painting. They stood in a large clearing of grass with several picnic tables scattered about and wildflowers flowing along the base of the surrounding trees.

"This is beautiful," she said, more to herself than to the others.

"Jah, the handiwork of God is before us," Aunt Elizabeth said.

They walked over to one of the empty picnic tables.

Two of the four were taken, and Kristen could smell a mingling of delicious scents the breeze carried her way.

A young couple sat on a blanket on the

grass, and an older man looked out over the lake with binoculars.

Mary unrolled one of the two worn quilts she'd carried and covered the picnic table with it while Anna and Aunt Elizabeth unrolled the other quilt onto the grass to sit on.

Kristen, Mary, and Angela joined them while John and Uncle Jonas took their seats at the table.

"Do you come here often?" Kristen asked.

"About twice during the summer, so we can visit the lake. We have some nice picnic spots closer to home, mainly fields with a few streams here and there. You'd like those spots, too," John answered. Kristen smiled at him, but he barely smiled back.

"I'm sure I would. Do people swim in the lake?" She directed her gaze to Mary this time.

"Jah, the Englisch do. But we just wet our feet, not taking much to swimming with our Amish dress code."

"You mean you're not allowed to wear bathing suits?"

"Nee. We usually wear an old dress if we go in the water. The men and boys can go shirtless. Women and men do not swim together."

Kristen was about to comment when her

cell phone rang. "Oops, sorry. I meant to turn it off. Riley said he'd call when he mails out some things to me so I'll know to expect them."

"Go ahead, Kristen. Answer it. It might be him," Aunt Elizabeth urged.

The caller ID on her phone was not Riley at all. It was Cindy's cell number. Kristen got up and walked off to the side to take the call. "Cindy? I didn't expect to hear from you again."

"Oh, Kristen, don't think that way. You're still my oldest and bestest friend, despite the whole Derick thing."

"Friends call and talk things out. They keep in touch. You never . . ."

Cindy interrupted her. "I'm here, Kristen. I'm sitting in a taxi in front of the house of your Amish family."

"What? But I'm not there now. We're all at a picnic about forty minutes away by Otsego Lake. Why are you here?"

"I need to talk to you about things. But I can't stay long because I need to be back by late tonight. My parents don't know I came."

"Then call them and say you'll be staying over with me. My aunt or uncle can speak to your mom, if you'd like."

"No, I can't do that, Kristen. I'll tell you

why later. Let me think . . . I know! I'll say that I'm at Merri's house for an overnight. Her parents are on vacation, and Merri will be home all night. I'll give her a call now and tell her to cover for me. When will you be back here?"

Kristen lowered her voice to nearly a whisper. "A few more hours, I think. We haven't had our picnic lunch yet, and we came here today mainly so I could see the area. I can't just tell them I need to leave."

"Where can I go in the meantime?"

"Hmm . . . sit on the front porch in one of the rockers. It's shady there. But first go see if the back door leading into the kitchen is unlocked. If it is, go inside and make yourself at home. Have something to eat and drink. OK?"

"OK. Thanks, Kristen. I'll send the taxi driver on his way then. See you later."

"Bye." Kristen returned her cell phone into the pocket of her dress then walked back to the blanket.

"Everything all right?" Aunt Elizabeth's ingrained perception seemed tweaked.

"I guess so. It was my friend, Cindy. She came to the house to visit me. I told her to sit on the porch or go inside if the door is unlocked and wait for us. Is that OK?"

"Ach, sure. Too bad she didn't tell you

187

she was coming sooner. We could have gone on our picnic another day."

"She'll be OK. I think she might have to spend the night being that it'll be a few hours before we get back."

"That would be fine. We'll have a simple but nice dinner together. Aunt Miriam will be joining us, too." Uh-Oh. Kristen hoped Aunt Miriam wouldn't take an immediate dislike to Cindy for being an outsider as she seemed to do with her.

"Speaking of dinner, I wouldn't mind having our picnic lunch now." Uncle Jonas peeked under the cooler lid.

Kristen's appetite wilted as she tossed around the possible reasons for why Cindy had turned up so unexpectedly. Was Derick OK? Why couldn't Cindy tell her parents she'd come to visit? After all, they'd known her since her early girlhood and acted as foster parents for several weeks prior to her coming here.

"Kristen? Have a sandwich." Mary waved her over to the table.

"And some fudge." Anna pointed to the foil wrapped confection.

She looked over at John, and his eyes locked on hers for a split second, but then he busied himself with the choices of food. He wasn't acting like himself. Seemed on purpose, too. Between John's changed behavior and Cindy showing up out of the blue, Kristen didn't know whether to cry or get up and run.

She opened the foil of her church peanut butter sandwich, and when she took a bite and tasted the cheese, she couldn't control her tears. Before anyone might notice, she took her sandwich and walked toward the view of the lake. Nothing unusual about that. The sight was pretty, and she couldn't take any more of John's distant behavior. Unless it was just her imagination. So much was happening at once that her emotions were all bungled up.

"Kristen?" She gasped a startle and nearly dropped her sandwich.

"John!"

"Sorry. I didn't mean to scare you. I just thought you might want a cup of lemonade." Kristen took the cup he held out to her. "And if you don't go and taste a piece of Anna's fudge, she might wear a frown the rest of the day."

Kristen laughed. "John? Are you upset with me or something?"

"Nee, of course not. Why should I be?"

"I don't know. You seem different, that's all." She kept studying his stoic expression and then it began to soften.

"Kristen . . ." he began.

"John! Kristen! Anna is waiting for you to have some fudge," Uncle Jonas called.

"Come. We best be going." But before John turned to walk back to the table, the warm full smile she missed so much graced his face just for her.

14

When they returned from the picnic, Kristen found Cindy and Aunt Miriam at the kitchen table having iced tea.

Cindy turned and looked at Kristen with an opened mouth and her jaw nearly hitting the floor. "Kristen! I almost didn't recognize you dressed like that." She sprang up from her chair to embrace her.

"Cindy. It feels like ages since I've seen you. So much has happened in these past couple of months." Kristen then turned to the others and made the introductions.

"Kristen tells us that you'll be staying over with us. We're glad to have you." Aunt Elizabeth smiled and put the picnic quilts down on a stool.

"Thank you. Had I known I was staying I'd have brought something."

"Never mind that," Aunt Elizabeth told her. "We're just happy that Kristen has one of her old friends visiting, ain't so, Jonas?"

"Jah, it's gut for friends to keep in touch."

Aunt Miriam cleared her throat to capture everyone's attention. "Cindy has come with some news, and I told her that it'd be gut if the whole familye learned of it along with our Kristen."

Uncle Jonas sat at the table and motioned for everyone to join him.

John cast a surprised look Kristen's way just as she looked to him for some kind of reassurance. He nodded with a faint smile, as if to say everything would be all right.

"Go ahead, Cindy. Tell us your news," Uncle Jonas urged as everyone settled into their chairs.

"I don't know where to start. I don't want to upset you, Kristen," Cindy began.

"Would you like me to tell them what you told me during our visit earlier?" Aunt Miriam asked.

Cindy nodded and brushed a tear from her cheek.

Kristen's heart began to race. She wasn't sure just how much more she could take.

Aunt Miriam turned to her with kind eyes. Something Kristen still wasn't used to. "Kristen. When you hear what I'm going to tell you, please keep in mind that you have a familye here and that your news is our news. Your happiness is our happiness. Your pain our pain. Jah?"

Kristen nodded. There was a wall of strength all around her like she'd never felt before. Still, she braced herself.

"The police are investigating whether or not the boating accident was really an accident at all. Seems that a woman named Mattie Cook came forward to the police with some news."

"Mattie? Ross's girlfriend?" Kristen said.

Aunt Miriam paused, and then went on. "Jah, she claims that she and Ross had a relationship for years and were planning to be married. But her son became angry that she and his father would now never reconcile. Mattie divorced him when her boy was just eight years old."

"Are we talking about Alex Cook? The boy who works at the boat dock for the Shark River Hills Country Club?" Kristen looked toward Cindy.

She nodded.

"Alex, jah," Aunt Miriam continued. "The newspaper article said that he'd told Mattie that he was still waiting for her to leave Ross, not marry him. Said he'd never step foot in Ross's haus. She relates that he became so angry at one point that he told her he'd be moving, and then stormed out the door. Mattie told the police that as he left, he yelled the words, 'I'll kill him. I'll kill him.'

"That's why after the boating accident, Mattie got to thinking that maybe her own son caused the boat to explode the way it did, being that he tended the boats at the country club where Ross docked his boat. She thinks he listened in on the other phone the night she and Ross spoke of going to lunch with Emily to discuss all of their plans. Ross said that he and Emily would meet her with the boat at the Seafood Harbor Dock, where they'd eat. So, Alex knew Ross and Emily would be on the boat that day, alone, to go meet his mom."

Cindy took Kristen's hand. "See, Kristen, all of this has been in the paper, and our parents didn't want us to call you or visit, because they were worried for our safety. At first, the tip was given anonymously, so no one knew who might be the suspect. And then a couple of weeks later, Mattie came forward and said she'd been the one who'd given the tip. She didn't want to be the center of a scandal, but her conscience got the best of her. And now Alex is a suspect."

"Cindy. How . . . how did he cause the explosion? I was told that it was an open container of gas that Ross had on the boat."

"According to the papers, it was gasoline

fumes that caused it. But not from an open container. There was a leak in the gas tank itself and it filled the hull with fumes. They said that any kind of friction could cause a spark and set it off, even static electricity. Thank goodness, you didn't go along with them that day." She handed Kristen a tissue.

"I can't believe all of this. I mean, Ross was seeing Mattie for so long. I'd seen her at the house many times, and he told me how much he liked her. But I had no idea that Alex was so against it. Did my mother know about this?"

"Jah, she did. And there's one more thing, niece. See, Alex accused Ross of being in *lieb* with your mamm and having an affair with her while also seeing his mother. He despised your mamm, too."

"That's not true at all. Ross and my mother never had an affair. No wonder Alex hardly spoke to me. All this time he'd thought . . . I wonder if anyone else thought the same thing?"

"People always find something to wag their tongues about, Kristen. I'm sure other homeowners there have live-in help. Jah?"

"Yes. But Ross was a single man, and no one probably knew that my mom was married, except for Ross's close friends and mine. What it looked like never occurred to me before now. I bet Alex had plenty to say to people at the country club about his take on it."

Cindy shrugged.

Everyone remained silent.

Then Kristen got up and ran upstairs.

John wished he could go after Kristen to comfort her. To console her. To hug her. Instead, he sat, trying to process all that he'd just heard. Day after day, week after week, more surprises unfolded for Kristen and the familye.

Mamm stood. Her eyes gleamed with tears, but she said nothing. She went to the cooler, took the leftover sandwiches out, and put them in the ice chest. Then she came back to the table with one of the sandwiches and a large pitcher of lemonade.

Aenti Miriam got some glasses from the cupboard.

"Have yourself a sandwich and some lemonade, Cindy. You've been waiting on us for a few hours." Mamm filled her glass.

"Thank you. But maybe I should go up to Kristen. I haven't been a very good friend to her these past couple of months. Things just happened so quickly."

"Are you talking about you and Derick?"

John regretted his boldness. A little.

Cindy turned toward him and nodded. "Yes, that, too. But mainly, I haven't been there for her during the most terrible time in her life. She and I go back a lot longer than she and Derick do. Besides, I was just a rebound person for him. We already broke it off. He really missed Kristen. Still does."

John's throat tightened. "Surprised he didn't come along then."

"I didn't tell anyone I was coming here. There've never been any secrets between Kristen and me. Not even about Derick. I had to come to let Kristen know what's going on. I need to talk with her one on one. Just the two of us, like old times."

"Vell, you eat something first, and then go on up and see how she's doing." Mamm unwrapped the sandwich and placed it on a plate.

"OK, but my appetite kind of closed up."

"Jah, I know. Just eat a little then. You've had a long day."

Cindy took a bite of the sandwich. "Thank you. It's good egg salad."

"Gut. Have yourself some of our Anna's fudge too." Mamm placed the foil wrapped goodies on the table. Anna ran over to unwrap them.

John didn't know what to make of Cindy.

She seemed sincere in her desire to make amends to Kristen, and the two girls had been friends nearly all of their lives. That had to count for something.

"Cindy, we have a cot stored in Mary's and Anna's room," Mamm said. "You are velkum to bring it into Kristen's room and spend the nacht there. That'll give you both more time to talk, too."

"That would work fine. Thank you. I'll go up now. Everything was delicious. You make great fudge, Anna."

Anna blushed beneath her wide smile.

"I can get the cot for you." John's offer was a gut excuse to see how Kristen was doing.

"OK. Thanks." John led the way up the stairs. His pulse raced and his stomach churned. He went into the bedroom where his sisters slept, got the folded cot stored against the back wall, and carried it to where Cindy stood by Kristen's closed door.

"I guess I should knock," Cindy said.

John nodded.

She did. No response. She knocked again. Harder. "Kristen, it's me, Cindy. John has a cot for me to sleep on later. Can we put it in the room?"

The door opened a crack.

Cindy paused then pushed it further and

found Kristen seated on the bed, her back turned to them, facing the window.

"Kris? John brought the cot for me to sleep on."

Kristen looked at John with reddened eyes, not at Cindy, as she turned toward them.

"Kristen, maybe you and Cindy would prefer to sit on the front porch instead of in here. There's a gut breeze there and you'll still have privacy to talk." John kept his voice as controlled and calm as he could manage, given the hammering of his heart as he witnessed her brokenness.

Kristen nodded and stood.

Cindy took her by the arm, and they both walked out of the room toward the stairs.

John turned and followed them down.

When they were settled on the front porch, John was about to head to the storage shed to gather more supplies to bring to the store.

Kristen placed her hand on his.

"Can you sit with us for a little while?"

Surely Daed wouldn't mind him being near Kristen during this difficult time. He couldn't very well turn his back on her in an attempt not to mean more to her than a friend. "Jah. I have some time before I go to the store."

Her sad eyes softened a bit and no one said anything for a few moments. A warm breeze brushed past them, and Cindy grabbed the tissues on her lap so they wouldn't blow away.

"When I was in my room before, I remembered the scripture from Preaching that I asked one of the ladies to translate into English for me after the church service here. All she said was, 'The truth shall set you free.' Do you think that in the end all of this bad stuff will do that for me?" Her soft gaze locked into his.

He swallowed hard and studied Kristen's pensive expression. She'd begun to think on her situation in a prayerful way. He thanked God silently right then and there. "Jah. I do, Kristen. Everything happens for a reason. It's gut that you are learning the truth about things, even though it's painful for you."

"I just don't understand why my mom never explained things. She was Amish and ended up living as live-in help to a non-Amish man. She had no romantic feelings toward him at all. I know. I lived there all my life. Maybe she still loved my dad, whoever he is. She had to have loved him a lot to go off and marry him and leave her Amish life behind. And then he goes and leaves her? None of it makes any sense to me."

"Maybe one day it will." Cindy patted Kristen's lap in a reassuring gesture.

"I want to know all about my mother's life here before she left. What she was like being Amish. How she came to meet Jacob Mast and why they broke it off. Maybe she met my father and fell instantly in love with him. I'm going to ask your mom and Aunt Miriam if they'll have a sit down with me about it all. They're her sisters. She must have told them things."

"Don't count on that. We Amish can live together under the same roof and keep certain things to ourselves. We don't tend to share all of our feelings as freely as the Englisch do. Maybe your mamm kept that trait even while she no longer lived among her own kind."

"You might be right about that. She had a reserved way about her, and she rarely spoke about herself. It's kind of sad that I really never got to know her. The way you and your mom know one another, Cindy."

"I guess it's just an Amish thing." Cindy looked to John for affirmation.

"Jah, some Amish women are very reserved with their emotions. Others not as much, like my mamm."

"I never saw my mom ever hug or kiss anyone at all. Just me," Kristen told him.

"You'll not see any hugging and kissing in public from any Amish, married or otherwise. It's just not done."

"Really?" Cindy stared at John as if he had three heads.

"That's for sure and for certain. Touching in public is verboten . . . forbidden." John emphasized *forbidden* to make his point.

Cindy shook her head in dismay.

Then they grew quiet again.

"Vell, I'd best be off to the shed for those supplies. I want to spend an hour at the store before dinner is ready." John stood and readied himself to go. Kristen grabbed his hand. The warmth of her unexpected touch startled him to pull away, but her hold was firm. Verboden or not, he was glad for it.

"Denki, John." She smiled up at him.

He wanted to bend down and kiss her smiling lips, but instead he returned her smile and gently took his hand out of her grasp. *"Bitte,"* he sputtered out, then quickly walked down the porch steps toward the storage shed, surprised that his legs could move at all.

Kristen watched John walk in the direction

of the shed behind the barn. She looked away to find Cindy's eyes on her.

"What?"

"You like him. A lot. But he's your cousin."

"No, he's not my cousin. His widowed father married my widowed aunt when he was just a baby. We aren't blood relatives at all. We're just part of the same family."

"Well, that puts a different spin on things. He's very handsome and seems taken by you. I can tell by how he looks at you." Cindy smiled one of her mischievous smiles.

"He's been there for me throughout everything since I've been here. In reality, he's been my only real friend. But it's not the only reason why I like John Wagler. He's a kind person with a good heart. He makes me feel cared for. Really cared for."

"Kristen, I've cared for you all of our lives. You're like a sister to me. The sister I never had."

"I was abandoned by everyone after I moved here. Everyone. Including you and your family, Cindy. I'm not mad now that I know the reason. Not even about the whole thing with you and Derick. It just proves that he never really cared for me like he claimed he did. But John wouldn't have turned away from me. In my heart, I know he never will. Whether as a friend or more than that one day."

"You mean you're actually considering staying here? Dressing in those clothes and following all the rules?" Cindy looked at her with widened eyes. If her jaw dropped any further it might hit the floor.

"My mother was Amish. I have Amish roots. And the rules don't really feel like rules once you start to live by them. At least that's how I feel about the clothes. It's just another part of living simple. Being Plain. And in my opinion, it's easier than having to decide what to wear. No more competition about clothes and hairstyles. It's really liberating in a sense."

"Kristen, it's a fantasy. This is not a practical life. It's hard work without any electricity and all the other modern conveniences. Your mother didn't leave for nothing."

"Well, I intend to find out why she left, sooner or later. At least here I have a real family, Cindy. You have no idea how it is to have no family around, especially for holidays. If it weren't for you and your family inviting me over, I'd have been alone."

"Kristen, you're like family to my parents and to my little brother, too. You know that. I bet they'd have tried to adopt you if you didn't have any relatives."

Kristen thought of the lack of contact from them. Of course, she hadn't known that it was because it no longer seemed an accident had claimed the life of her mom and Ross. Still, family would have rushed to her side. Not avoided her. Regardless of the reason.

"Thanks, Cindy. But after a while, I felt like a pity case. Not that you or your family ever made me feel that way. You'd have to be me to understand. I realize that I became a possible threat to the safety of you and your brother, and maybe that was why I was dropped like a hot potato. Still, I felt so alone. I don't feel that way here. These people are my blood relatives. It's as if I'm supposed to be here. I'm part of something."

Before dinner, Kristen clued Cindy in about the silent prayer said before and after the meal. She had Cindy tie her hair back in a ponytail, and secure the loose shorter strands with bobby pins. The clothes she wore were a far cry from Amish attire, but her jeans and light pink blouse were not flashy or indecent. Kristen had Cindy sit next to her and hoped that the family would soon unravel Cindy's obviously tense nerves.

After the silent prayer, the food was passed around and Cindy took a hamburger, a frankfurter, a bun for each, and some of the cold relishes and potato salad left over from their picnic.

"I wish I'd known you were coming. I'd have prepared a meal more fitting for a guest." Aunt Elizabeth turned to Cindy and passed some pickles.

"This is fine by me. I love burgers and franks. Thanks."

"Do you like cheese on your burgers?" John asked with dead seriousness.

"She does not." Kristen quipped.

John shrugged, got up, went to the ice chest, and returned with a package of sliced cheese.

"He puts cheese on nearly everything," Kristen told Cindy, "except maybe for pie and ice cream."

"Nee, apple pie tastes gut with sliced cheddar cheese. You ought to try it some time." He glanced her way as he helped himself to several slices of the orange stuff and placed them on top of his two burgers.

"I'm sure it does, but I'll pass."

"Ach, you don't know what you're missing. Just like it was with putting cheese on the church peanut butter. You thought I was *narrish,* but you really liked it once you tried it."

"You're still narrish, whatever that

means," Kristen told him.

Anna giggled while John smirked.

Cindy smiled, looking first to Kristen and then to John.

Did it show that Kristen cared for him the way she tried to be gruff with him? Was there something John was revealing that she couldn't see but that the others could?

Mary seemed to always smile, so it was hard to tell if she was just being herself or smiling at a specific comment.

Daniel placed all of his attention on his meal, practically oblivious to anything but the food.

Only little Anna paid them enough mind to squeak with laughter at their antics.

Although, Kristen had the distinct impression that none of it passed over the head of Uncle Jonas, and he seemed none too amused.

Aunt Elizabeth on the other hand, lowered her head now and then and smiled to herself.

"Lucky for you, Kristen, that it's more the season for peach and berry pies than apple," Aunt Elizabeth commented as she stood to clear some of the empty platters from the table.

"John will probably want cheese on those too," Kristen said, nudging Cindy with a chuckle.

John gave her another of his smirks, then looked over at his father and quickly went into a mode of seriousness. He ate the rest of his meal in silence.

15

Kristen placed a sheet on top of the cot for Cindy and gave her one to use as a cover. The summer heat still kept the nights too warm for a quilt.

"So, are you going to tell me what's going on with you and John? I mean, besides that he's been there for you?"

"Nothing is going on. Why?"

"Are you kidding me? The way the two of you tease each other at the table, it's hard to miss."

"Do you think my aunt and uncle believe something is going on?"

"I don't know. I'm asking you. Is there?"

"No, of course not. John wouldn't start anything up with me if he wanted to. I'm not officially Amish, even if I now dress and live like I am. Things are done a certain way here."

"So, if you officially become Amish, then would you and he become a couple?"

"It crossed my mind, but I'd rather not go there just now. I've had enough disappointments, and I'm not setting myself up for another one. Besides, he's nearly four years older than me."

"So what? My dad is nine years older than my mom. The guy is obviously nuts about you."

"Is it that obvious?"

"It's that obvious."

Kristen pulled down her sheet and crawled into bed. How much longer could this back and forth bantering, teasing, and even flirting, go on? Something had to give. Where were she and John headed? Maybe nowhere at all. She preferred not to focus on that possibility.

"Kris?"

"Yes?"

"Is there really no indoor bathroom here? When I asked to use one this afternoon, your aunt Miriam walked me to an outhouse in the back of the house."

"There really isn't any other one. But I've made my own version of a chamber pot under the bed, if you care to use it. And I keep a plastic jug of water up here for a quick freshen up."

"No, I will not use a chamber pot, thank you very much. I think I'd rather go to the outhouse. See you in a while."

"Cindy, take the flashlight on the bureau with you. There's no light in there."

"Wonderful. This has been one interesting day, I'll say." Cindy took the flashlight and stomped out of the room.

Kristen nearly laughed herself to sleep.

When John entered the kitchen, he patted his little sister on the head. Anna looked up from scooping coffee out of the canister. He stood there until she gave him the wide-eyed smile he looked forward to each morgen.

"Anna, how about you go up now and wake Cindy for breakfast. Then after we eat, you can make a few sandwiches for her to take along for the ride," Mamm told her as she began to fry up the bacon.

Anna scooted past John, off and running up the stairs and back a few minutes later to begin her kaffee-making task.

Not long after, Cindy came down, her hair pulled back the way she'd worn it the nacht before for dinner.

John admired her effort to be respectful of their ways.

"It smells wonderful in here," Cindy said as she took her seat at the table.

"You'll have a gut breakfast to hold you

for your drive back home," Elizabeth told her as she placed the cooked bacon on a platter of scrambled eggs.

"I usually just have coffee, so this will definitely hold me. Right, Kris?"

"That's true. Back home we never had big breakfasts. Now I rely on them to get me through the morning. Then again, I didn't keep as busy as I do here." She placed a plate of sliced grain bread on the table.

"What kinds of things do you do here?"

"Well, I weed the garden, clean, help with meals, and soon, I'll be helping out at the store when it opens." Kristen headed for the ice chest.

"I mean, what do you do for fun?"

Kristen put a pitcher of milk on the table and looked at her friend.

The room went silent.

"Let's see . . . on church Sundays we go to Preaching and afterward eat and visit with the other families in the district. And on off-Sundays, we go on outings and picnics, like the one we went on yesterday. Besides, I like doing all the things I do around here. I get to see the end results. I do things for someone else. And then I'm a part of something. At least it feels that way." With a reddened face, she turned and headed back to the ice chest. When she returned with the butter, she sat down and avoided looking at anyone.

John knew how she longed to belong. Somewhere. To someone.

"You're a part of this familye now, niece," Mamm affirmed.

"Jah, and it's nice to know you are happy, here, Kristen," Daed said, a wide smile brimming above his long beard.

As Mamm sat down, Daniel and Mary rushed in and took their seats. Then they all bowed their heads in prayer.

John's insides relaxed. Everything was going to work out just fine. Kristen was one of the Waglers, for sure and for certain. *Denki, Lord.*

"Why has Kristen not returned yet?" John inquired as he stepped back into kitchen after dinner had been over by at least two hours.

"I'm thinking it takes a long time to drive to New Jersey and back, what with traffic and all," Mamm offered.

"If she is not here in another hour or so, I will try to contact Angela on her cell phone at the phone shanty. With those notes we've been getting, we can't be too careful. The bishop advised to keep a close eye on her whereabouts. Why did we let her accompany

Cindy?" Daed shook his head as he got up and paced the kitchen.

"Vell, she's not here where the notes are coming. The note writer wants her back where she . . . came from." John's stomach lurched. What if the person writing the notes was someone she knew in New Jersey? Someone who wanted harm to come to her. Like that Alex fellow. She could be right in the lap of danger.

Mamm fussed with her kapp strings. "Kristen isn't alone, and Angela is very responsible. Let's give them a little more time. We'll have cherry pie while we wait, jah?" She stood and got down plates while Daed opened the ice chest for the pie.

"Denki, Mamm. We won't get to sleep 'til Kristen is home, so might as vell."

"Glad Anna is already asleep. Wouldn't want her upset." Mamm nodded in agreement with Daed. John had no desire for pie but took a piece to appease Mamm so as not to appear overly worried.

Daniel walked in and glanced at the table. "Isn't it a little late for pie? Something going on?"

"Kristen isn't home yet from accompanying Cindy with Angela to New Jersey," Mamm told him.

"That was over twelve hours ago."

"Denki for reminding us, Daniel." John frowned at his younger brudder as he forced another bite of pie down.

When Angela dropped Kristen back at the house, it was ten o'clock. The kerosene lamp shone through the kitchen window, and Kristen knew someone was waiting up for her.

Had she not taken a swim in the ocean they might have gotten back somewhat earlier, but still not in time for the evening meal. Just the same, she couldn't resist her beloved ocean and would now have to face the worried look that most likely hung heavy on Aunt Elizabeth's face.

First thing Kristen had to do before she entered the house was wash out the sand from her hair with the water pump at the back of the house. She had to look a sight the way she'd put her wet sandy hair back into a bun without brush or comb, hoping the kapp would hide the tangled mess. She was gritty and tired as opposed to the invigoration she'd enjoyed hours ago on the beach.

After rinsing off the sand, she brushed out her hair and put it back in a bun . . . wet . . . topped by her kapp.

"You could have come in the haus right

off. Enough time has gone by already. You had us worried half out of our wits. Mamm and Daed are beside themselves what with those anonymous notes about you these days."

Kristen spun around at John's reprimand.

"It's not like I could have called to say I was running late. I'll go in now to explain. I just wanted to appear presentable."

John looked her over. "You look fine." His face took on a light flush before he walked ahead of her toward the kitchen entrance.

"John."

He stopped and turned around.

"I'm sorry."

"Jah, I know. Just don't stay away so long again 'til we settle this note business, jah? We were close to calling the sheriff. And you know how rare that is around here."

Kristen walked behind John with her head lowered. She should have come straight back after they arrived at Bradley Beach. She entered the quiet kitchen to find Aunt Elizabeth, Uncle Jonas, and Daniel looking straight at her.

John held the door open for Kristen.

"Do you know that we're running past our bedtime waiting for you to come home and worrying something awful might have happened?" Daed was none too pleased with Kristen, although the look of relief upon seeing her safe was evident.

"I'm sorry, Uncle Jonas. It was still early when we got there, and Cindy offered to go home and return with a bathing suit so I could take a swim. I changed in Angela's van."

"Angela was paid to bring you and Cindy there and to return with you right after." The frown on Daed's face deepened.

"Yes, I know. She kept waving at me from the shore to come out of the water. I guess I got carried away. She wasn't happy with me at all and would have called the shanty, but her phone battery was low. Then when we got stuck in traffic due to an accident on The Garden State Parkway, she was really stressed. I promised her that I'd take the blame."

"Vell, we are glad that you are all right. But for the time being it'd be best if you don't take any more rides in Angela's car unless it's to a doctor or for some other important reason. Let's all head to bed now. Dawn will be here quick enough."

John went to get milk from the ice chest to go with the pie still sitting on his plate so he could linger after his parents and Daniel went off to bed. Mary and Anna were sleeping for hours already, and he was glad they were spared the tension.

"Maybe some warm milk will make you feel better?" John said after everyone else left the room.

"I doubt it. I have another black check against me."

"Kristen, no one is angry with you. We were worried something happened. I was nearly out of my mind when I realized you were in the same place as that Alex fellow." The words came quicker than he realized.

"Out of your mind?"

"Jah. Does it make you happy to know I was so worried?"

"No. But it makes me happy that you care."

John wanted to tell her exactly how much he cared, but it would do neither of them much gut if he went against Daed's wishes. He poured himself a glass of milk. "So, you had yourself a swim then?"

"Yes, it was wonderful." Kristen paused a moment, looking as if she were about to cry.

"Are you all right?"

A tear fell onto her cheek and John was tempted to wipe it away with his finger.

"Going back to the beach was not a good idea, John. It brought back a lot of memories."

"Were they bad memories?"

"No, they were good ones but remembering made me realize how much I miss those times. Being carefree with my friends. Having my mom. The walks she and I would sometimes take on the beach on Sundays, very early, just as the sun was coming up. I didn't get to see her much, so those were special times."

"It's nice to have gut memories, Kristen. They make the sad ones easier to bear. I'm hoping that you'll make some gut memories here, too."

A dull ache filled John's gut when Kristen revealed how much she missed her past. He poured some milk in a sauce pan to heat it. Maybe the warm milk would calm her. But it wouldn't change the fact that she might end up going back to her beach town when she turned of age and things got settled. Maybe find a job there and rent a room 'til she got on her feet. Get back with Derick.

Best not to think on it. He'd gotten used to having her around. Too much so. He couldn't imagine a meal without her now. Or a morgen not seeing her help Mamm and Mary in the kitchen. Nothing increased his pace in from the fields more than the anticipation of Kristen's soft brown eyes greeting him to breakfast. He wanted to see her every day. For the rest of his life.

"Maybe if you went swimming around here sometime, it would help with making some new gut memories." While John waited for Kristen to roll his idea around in her mind, he poured the warmed milk into a mug and placed it before her.

She wrapped her hands around it. "Thanks."

He hoped his gesture counted for something.

"Swimming would be nice. Is it far?" She took a sip of the milk. Her face had a rosy hue from the sun. She looked . . . beautiful.

"Nee, there are a couple small lakes not too far that you can swim in when the weather is warm. And there are stream beds to cool down in. Mary or Anna will show you."

"Would you come with me if I go?" John didn't expect her to want him to join her. He was elated and frustrated at the same time.

"I'd like very much to go with you, Kristen. But Old Order Amish men and women do not swim together."

"Oh yeah. I remember Mary saying something about that. So, you and I, or your mom and dad, or Daniel and either of your sisters can't swim together?"

"That's how it is, jah." Why did he ever mention the swimming? It wasn't something that would give him the opportunity to spend time with her as he'd hoped.

"Ach! I meant to ask if you'd want to help at the store in the morgen when we open." He needed to change the subject and this suggestion seemed a legitimate reason to be with Kristen. Perfectly acceptable.

"What would I do?"

"Tend to the customers. I'll show you how to work the register. It's not like the modern ones in the Englisch stores. You'll have to figure out the change."

Kristen smiled.

John's heart swelled.

"Since math is my strong point. I think I can figure out the change without a problem."

"You'll come help then?"

Kristen nodded.

"Anna will learn how to make change by the candy counter. We have a small money box there so the customers don't need to pay for the candy at the register if that's all they'll be buying."

"She'll love it, I'm sure. She told me that she and Daniel practiced." Kristen and John both chuckled simultaneously.

He looked into her smiling eyes. They

glowed when she looked happy.

"We have some plans then, jah? You'll be plenty busy around here for the making of some gut times to think back on."

"I didn't mean to sound as if I don't have any nice times here. It's just that some days I can hardly believe Mom is gone, and I have nothing of hers to hold." Kristen looked directly into his eyes and sighed. "You're a rock for me, John."

His heart sped up like a weather vane in the wind. Happy to hear her words while hesitant to encourage her any more than he'd already had, given his promise to Daed. "Gott is your rock, Kristen. Not me. Lean on Him with all your heart, soul, and mind. There's a reason for everything He allows. We have to trust in that, hard as it is at times."

A frown claimed her face and she seemed to contemplate what he had said.

"If God is my rock, then maybe you're supposed to be my road to the rock. Because something tells me that one day you'll be the bishop or a minister with the way you speak. You have a way of making sense out of things. At least for me." Her smile returned.

He swallowed, but there was no pie in his mouth.

16

The following day, Kristen did her breakfast chores as usual. No one mentioned the events of the previous day, and she made it her business to get to the sink first to wash the dishes. Not only did she want to prove her worthiness, but the task made her feel that this was really her home now. But was it? Is this where she wanted to live? As a Plain person? Why had her mom not been able to? She wanted to know the facts. Maybe later she could ask Aunt Elizabeth. She hoped she was receptive to her questions after the worry she'd caused her aunt the night before.

"I have to go to the shed and gather some more supplies to bring to the store tomorrow," John announced as he stood.

Everyone got up from the table then, and the morning rush out of the house began until it was just Kristen and Aunt Elizabeth left in the kitchen.

"I wonder if I can speak to you about my mother?"

"Jah, sure. We can talk while we wash the peaches for the pies."

"Peach pie? Oh, I love that. We used to go to a place called Delicious Orchards just for the peach pies."

"Vell, these peaches are from Sally Troyer who works with Mary. She gives us some from her orchard each summer. Mary placed a basket full at the door this Mariye. Can you please bring them in?"

Kristen got the peaches and placed them on the countertop. Then the two of them proceeded to wash and slice them.

"So, what is it you want to know about your mamm?"

"I want to know why she left the Plain life."

Aunt Elizabeth put her knife down. "I 'spect it was because she met your vadder. It must have been a big love that took a strong hold of her because she never looked back."

"What do you mean?"

"She never wrote to us. Not even to Jacob Mast, whom she'd been courting when she left. When Jacob came back from helping at his onkle's farm in Pennsylvania, she was gone. We didn't have much information to give him except she left for the Englisch world with an Englisch man."

"So, my dad wasn't Amish, then?"

"Nee. I think your Aenti Miriam thought Ross was your vadder. Now we all know that's not the case. She must have met him in New Jersey."

"If Mom didn't leave a note, how do you know she left with Ross?"

"She told your aenti Miriam when she saw your mamm and Ross talking friendly like at the farm stand. Your mamm gave her a note to give to our mamm and daed to break the news to them. I never saw the note, but Miriam knew what it said. Our mamma cried, and then they never spoke of your mamm again. Our sister, Emily, had been shunned."

"Does that mean she was like a black sheep to the family?"

"Nee, more like a stray sheep. Had she come back repentant for what she'd done, she'd have been velkumed into the church and at home again. It's a process, but she would have been forgiven and accepted. She never came back. And even though our mamma never spoke of it, we knew that her heart was broken. She missed her youngest dochter awful bad."

"Do you think Aunt Miriam can tell me more?"

"I don't know. She might not be wanting to tell you if your mamm asked her to keep a confidence. She never told me much more than I'm telling you now."

"Did my mother seem happy here before she left with Ross?" Maybe she had been so miserable she left with the first man who could take her away.

"Jah, she was always smiling and a happy sort. She loved to pick wildflowers and she could sew wonderful quilts. Took after her *grossmammi* with that gift."

"So, you don't think she left with Ross because she was unhappy here?"

Aunt Elizabeth picked up her knife again and shook her head before slicing another peach.

"It seems like a big mystery to me, especially since she never told me she was Amish. If she loved it here, why wouldn't she talk about her good experiences?"

"Maybe she was trying to forget her former life because she'd made a choice. It's a hard thing being caught between two worlds, I 'spect."

Didn't she know it.

Kristen nodded. Though this wasn't enough information to satisfy her hungry curiosity. She'd have to pay Aunt Miriam a visit with the hope that she would still be in a pleasant mode toward her.

She and Aunt Elizabeth brought the sliced peaches to the table where they were to add the sugar, molasses, flour, and butter her aunt had set out.

"I remember my mom baked great pies when I was little. Especially on holidays. But once she began work at the hotel, there wasn't time for her to do that anymore. I was too little to learn how to make them."

"You'll learn to make gut pies in no time, niece. It's in your blood."

"Did you all live here in this house?"

"Nee. This haus belonged to the familye of my first husband, Abe. Our mamm and daed went to live with our brudder, Amos, and his wife in Ohio. So it was only Miriam left at the haus we were grown in, which is where she still resides only a short ride from here. After our daed passed, your aenti asked our mamm if she could stay on and rent the haus. That was fine with Mamma, but she refused to take any rent from her dochter. Instead, she asked all of us if Aenti Miriam could stay on at the haus as if it were her own. All she had to do was pay for running the place. We all had our own homes, so none of us objected." Aunt Elizabeth looked up, as if calling back to past times.

"I've lived here since my marriage to Abe, even as a widow. We made some gut memories, even though the marriage was short-lived. Then after a spell, your Onkle Jonas brought John for me to mind after my dearest friend, Fannie, John's mamma, died birthin' him. Some months later, after much letter writing, your onkle came to join me here. We were both given a second chance and were happy for it."

"The two of you always look happy with each other without even saying a word. That's something I wished I could have seen between my mom and dad, whoever he is."

"You mustn't be bitter, Kristen. We don't know who or where he is and what happened between him and your mamm." Aunt Elizabeth gave Kristen a wad of dough to roll out. "Dust it with some flour first so it won't stick to the rolling pin."

She did as her aunt advised. "I never questioned my mom about him much. She'd just say the same answer each time anyway. By the time I reached my teens, I stopped asking. But now I feel as if I need to know exactly why he abandoned us."

"Maybe we'll find out something later at the bishop's haus."

"The bishop's house?" Kristen stopped kneading the dough.

"Jah. Seems he wants to read your mamm's letter to us as she'd instructed in her will."

That might be an easier way to get answers to the questions she couldn't release. Either that or she'd find out things she might not want to know.

Dinner was quiet. John kept thinking about his self-righteous response to Kristen, that he was not her rock. At least she hadn't seemed offended. He was only trying to stop himself from hugging her hurt away. Honoring his daed's wishes by keeping her at arms' length. Literally. Although, he truly believed that God was, indeed, her rock; his rock, everyone's rock. He wanted Kristen to know the peace of the Lord in her time of trouble. But he also wanted to be by her side and be a support to her. Yes, like a rock. He should have told her exactly that. She reached out to him, and he'd shrunk back.

"Kristen, please pass me the green beans, please?" John needed to speak to her even if it was simple table talk. Anyone could see she was a nervous wreck about the bishop's invitation of the familye to his home tonacht.

Kristen lifted the bowl next to her and passed it over Anna to John. She said nothing.

"Don't you want any?"

"No, thank you. I'm not that hungry."

Great! This attempt at conversation was not working. Best he just eat his dinner and not prod any further before his desperate efforts become obvious to the others.

"Aunt Miriam, will you be coming to the bishop's house too?"

"Jah, Kristen. We'll all be with you. No need for getting *naerfich*."

"I can't help being nervous, if that's what naerfich means."

"You're starting to learn Pennsylvania Dutch, gut, niece." Aunt Miriam smiled at her.

John kept his eyes on his plate of food as he spooned mashed potatoes into his mouth and listened to the conversation.

Daniel told about the projects he'd completed at the store and Mary about the batch of under-sweetened ruined pies at the diner. Mamm and Daed nodded with a few comments now and then while Anna interjected every few minutes with a question.

Everyone seemed to be stalling to get dinner finished and go off to the Bishop's place. John was going regardless of how

Kristen felt about it. They were going as a family.

"Vell, we best be getting ready for our visit with Bishop Ebersol." Daed stood and pushed his chair in.

John glanced at Kristen and her eyes met his. He wanted to say many things to her. Wanted to calm her nerves. But all he could think to do was fold his hands in a gesture of prayer to remind her that God was with her. He wished he could point to his heart, too, but Daed didn't miss a thing.

Kristen remained in her chair looking at him for a moment, her expression serious and pensive. She nodded, folded her hands in the same prayerful gesture back to him, smiled, and stood to go.

The bishop introduced his wife, Madeline, to Kristen before they all took a seat at the long table laden with several pies and plates of iced cookies. Madeline let Anna and her young daughter, Susanne, take a few cookies, and then go off into another room.

A knock at the door, followed by Madeline's voice and approaching footsteps, brought in two other guests.

Kristen jerked up straight, surprised at the two people who joined them at the table.

Jacob Mast gave her and her family a nod,

but his sister, Katie, sat down and kept her eyes on the bishop. She acknowledged no one. Why was she here?

John gave Kristen a glance, his hands on the table. He touched his two index fingers together.

Pray. She knew that's what he was silently telling her to do. And she also knew that he was doing exactly that. For her.

OK, then. I'll pray to You, God. But I have no words to say, except please help me get through this, no matter what happens here. And if you can hear me, Mom, I wish you'd told me whatever it is you wrote in your letters. Then none of this would be happening now.

Madeline came in with a pot of coffee and invited everyone to partake in the desserts sitting before them.

Kristen nibbled on a cookie to be polite. She couldn't stand to swallow a thing with her stomach churning so hard.

Onkle Jonas took a piece of blueberry pie as did Jacob Mast, while the others reached for the cookies.

Bishop Ebersol finished off his snack then cleared his throat after a final gulp of coffee. Everyone looked up as he unfolded three sheets of paper. Mom's letter.

"Emily Esh wrote this letter to be given to

the presiding bishop of this district in the event of her death to be read to her familye. Since I am your bishop at this time, it is my duty to see fit to carry out her final wish. Here is what she writes . . .

My dear family and friends,
I have lived with a hurt and a lie in my heart for many years, thinking at first, that it was my only choice to give my dear dochter, Kristen, a respectable gut life. If I knew then what I came to know now, I would have chosen a different path. I would be the Amish frau and mamm I was meant to be. But instead, I panicked and took a live-in help position with an Englischer I'd befriended at the Amish Country Commons Store. I didn't consider that he might have had feelings for me which could have been why he'd made the offer to take me into his home. My heart was only for one man. Jacob Mast, the father of my dochter, Kristen, and my eheman . . . my husband.

Gasps sounded one after the other, and Kristen's vision blurred. She could barely keep her ragged breath from choking her throat closed. Aunt Elizabeth put an arm around her. She heard murmuring now but didn't dare look up at Jacob. Her . . . her . . . biological father and Mom's husband? How could that be when her mother had been married to her father? This was him? And he'd abandoned her? She braced herself for more.

Jacob and I didn't want to slip up and take our love too far too soon. We did not want to sin in the eyes of God and the church. But we so wanted to be together, and it was a long wait until autumn for a young couple in lieb. So, we went to the next county to an Amish settlement and got married by the new bishop there. We told him that Jacob had to leave for work in Pennsylvania, and we'd already come too close to acting like man and wife and wanted to love one another fully the right way, in the eyes of God, before he left. We promised to tell our bishop and family and have a small wedding celebration once Jacob returned from helping his onkle repair the insides of the haus and barn since it was not sufficient to keep the bitter cold out. It would only be a few weeks, but to us it seemed forever.

Jacob promised he'd send a letter for

me to give to Mamm and Daed when I decided to tell them our news. He also said he'd send for me after I told them so that we could spend a night or two together. I had no idea that I'd never hear from him again. By the end of February, I knew I was with child.

The bishop paused to take a sip of water. Not a sound was heard other than his swallow. He cleared his throat and resumed.

Katie went with Jacob to Pennsylvania to help with the cooking. I figured he'd told his sister of our marriage, so I decided to use our phone shanty to call there and ask about my unanswered letters.

Jacob gave me the number in case of an emergency. Said they kept a phone in the shed since his onkle took ill. Katie answered. She told me that Jacob was already out in one of the buildings working on the insulation. So, I asked her if my letters had been received, and she said they had. Since Jacob never responded, I'd assumed that he panicked after we married and then all the more when he'd read that I was carrying his child. Maybe he feared people would think our marriage was due to being in the family way instead of our desire to love one another as God intended. I didn't know what to think.

Kristen closed her eyes. Maybe the next time she opened them, she'd awake to another reality.

The bishop kept reading.

She wanted to plug her ears.

Ross came regularly to buy preserves and pies at my little counter in the store. Each Saturday he was there bright and early as March came in, even with the harsh cold winds and occasional snow squalls. We'd speak a bit and by season's end, we became casual friends. I needed to relate my situation to someone. All I'd wanted was a little advice and a sympathetic ear. Maybe some information about one of those places where unwed mothers go for help and shelter before my condition became obvious. But what he offered was much more than that. A job cleaning and cooking, along with a home for me and my child. A new life where I could forget the memories of Jacob. I knew I'd never be given such a chance again. But before I decided, I had to try to find Jacob. Make sure he no longer wanted me to be his frau. So, I booked a bus ticket to Lancaster for that Monday and told my family that I was making a day visit to Katie. Which was, in fact, part of the truth.

When I got there, bright and early the next day, Katie seemed shocked to see me. She ushered me inside the warm haus as if I were something not to be seen or heard. When we were seated at the kitchen table she told me Jacob wasn't there. That she had no idea where he'd gone. It'd been weeks, she said. And she'd been caring for his onkle all the while. I asked about my letters — if any of them had arrived before he left. She said they had. After he'd gone, she'd saved the rest for whenever he'd be back. I could barely get down the pie and tea she set before me. I called a taxi and headed for the next bus back home. I knew what I had to do."

Katie's shoulders shook; her face and eyes downward.

Kristen felt like whopping her behind the head. How could she do that? The bishop went on.

My sister, Miriam, ran into us at the Amish Country Commons a couple times, so I ended up telling her that I was with child, and that I'd be going away to work for Ross in the Englisch world. I know she assumed Ross Maddok was the father, and I left it at that. It was less complicated, and I didn't want to hurt Jacob's reputation if he ever returned to Palatine. She promised never to tell a soul that I was with child when I left.

Jacob had his head down with closed eyes as he listened.

Aunt Miriam's hand covered her mouth.

Kristen couldn't stop her bottom lip from trembling. *No more, Mom. I don't want to hear it!* But the words kept coming.

17

The bishop turned the page. No one stirred. It was as if everyone was listening to the reading of a good novel. But this was about her mother.

Aunt Elizabeth squeezed her hand.

Kristen turned to her in silent gratitude.

Since Jacob never contacted me, not even once, I had two choices. I could be on my own without a father for my child and be the speculation of the community for years to come. Or I could go away and work for Ross Maddok with a roof over my head and save face for all of us. I decided on the latter.

Katie sobbed.

Kristen didn't know whether to take pity on her or give her a good piece of her mind. She looked away and remained silent, praying that this letter would come to its end. Now.

I told Ross straight away, that I belonged to Jacob Mast and would always love him. He understood that we would live as employer and employee. He accepted my terms when he took me to his haus by the ocean in Bradley Beach, New Jersey. When Kristen was born, he asked if I would consider an annulment of my marriage to marry him, but I explained that Amish marry for life. It was the only time he'd asked or made any show of affection toward me. But Ross continued to be kind even though he was away from home more often from that time on. He treated Kristen as if she were his own. I bear no grudge in my heart for Ross's long ongoing relationship with Mattie Cook. He needed a woman to love him, and I would never be that for him.

Kristen glanced up at surprised faces. Somehow this didn't really shock her. She'd rarely see Ross around on weekends. And he and her mom acted like friends, never more than that, despite her wishes otherwise.

"He consulted me on the terms of his will because he wanted to leave the bulk of his estate to me and Kristen. Said he had no real family to speak of. I insisted that he not do that. Ross gave us everything we needed while he lived. I am glad that he has Kristen's admiration. I want her to know that he cares for her very much and planned to leave her nearly everything he has. She needs to know this if I should pass on before Ross. This way when his time comes, Kristen will understand why there is no inheritance from him.

May God lead my dear dochter in the path that best suits His Will for her.

Finally, if Katie Mast has survived me, I want her to know that I am grateful for her contrition and the truth she let me know after so many years. Reading the letters that she'd kept from me, so long ago, has only affirmed my love for Jacob all the more. He would never abandon me or his child. I understand the deep fear that drove Katie to keep us apart. And I am sorry for all of us because of it. She has my forgiveness.

With all my love and gratitude,
Emily Esh."

The room was completely quiet save for a few sniffles.

Kristen wondered if the heavy quick beating of her heart could be heard. She wanted to disappear.

But maybe not as much as Katie wanted to. She sat there with downcast eyes, as tears dripped from them onto her gray dress.

Kristen dared to glance in Jacob's direction. Both hands covered his face as he silently wept. She could barely watch him . . . her father, in such distress. Then she looked to John. His eyes were closed and his lips moved quietly. He was praying. He surely practiced what he preached. She needed just one glance, one little gesture from him to steady her nerves.

Everything felt so surreal she hoped she'd wake up any minute now. But this was no dream. She kept her eyes on John. Then she prayed, too. *Please God, help me get through this. Help me not to feel so deceived. I was raised with a secret all of my life. How can I trust anyone ever again?*

No sooner had the words gone to God, John opened his eyes and stared right into Kristen's. For a brief instant, a kind smile grazed his lips, and he nodded his head, as if to say, "Everything will be fine." She nodded back to him and felt a large measure of relief wash through her. Here was her answer to prayer. She could trust someone again. She could trust John.

"Please, if anyone needs to get some air or wants kaffee, go ahead," the bishop said. "I'll ask Madeline for a fresh pot." He stood and headed toward the kitchen.

Aunt Elizabeth gave Kristen a tissue, and Daniel and Uncle Jonas headed outside.

Aunt Miriam got up and came over to Kristen.

"Maybe we can get Madeline to make you a cup of chamomile tea." She wiped a stray tear off of Kristen's cheek.

Kristen didn't know whether to cry more or to laugh. She seemed to do both. "Not everything can be fixed with chamomile tea." Tears ran into her smiling mouth.

"Come. Let's get us some fresh air." Aunt Miriam took Kristen's arm and practically lifted her out of the chair.

Aunt Elizabeth followed as they headed to the front porch.

John stood before them as they leaned against the porch railing. He didn't seem fazed if his mother or aunt heard what he had to say.

"Remember when you told me that you heard some of the ladies at our haus on Church Sunday talk about the scripture passage of how the truth shall set us free?"

Kristen nodded.

"Vell, here it is. The truth. And it will set you free, Kristen."

Kristen nodded again.

"This is the time for the truth in your life, Kristen. Look at it as a gift from both Gott and your mamm. You had Ross Maddok's support and care while you grew up, and now you will have your vadder's, Jacob Mast's."

"But I'm not any man's daughter, really. Only my mom's. I never knew Jacob, and Ross was not my father as much as he pretended to be at times. Right now, I belong to no one."

Aunt Elizabeth gave Kristen's arm a squeeze while Aunt Miriam blew her nose.

"First and foremost, you are a child of Gott, and He has a plan for all of us. Seems to me that He's leading you to that plan. You had nothing to do with the decisions Katie or your mamm made. It's all part of His plan. Just place yourself in His care," John said.

Kristen wanted to sob like a child but held her tears long enough to say, "And in yours, too?"

Without any secret gestures or quiet motions, John openly replied, "For sure and for certain, Kristen."

When everyone had settled back into their chairs at the table, Katie stood at her place.

The bishop gave her a nod, and she took in a breath and began to speak.

Kristen didn't think she could hear any more of the secrets that surrounded her mother's former life, but she endured, hindering on John's scripture reminder earlier. This was the time and place to learn the truth . . . all of it.

"My time of reckoning has come. I ask forgiveness to the Esh and Wagler families for my deceitfulness all those years ago. And I will ask it of the entire community on Sunday in a kneeling confession. My punishment for this transgression is that I've had to live with the unhappiness it's caused my dear brudder and Emily. And the knowledge that it's tainted the lives of Ross Maddok and Kristen. I have no excuses for the damage I've caused, but I will at least try to explain why I behaved so foolishly."

Kristen forced herself to look at Katie and to listen.

"I was already fifteen when Jacob was born and our mamm died birthing him. The span of years between us brought no other kinner. I raised Jacob like he was my own, and our daed was all too glad for it, not able to take care of an infant, or later, a toddler, with all the carpentry work he had back then.

"When Jacob was three years old, our daed died from severe diabetes, leaving me and Jacob. I was scared out of my wits as to how I would manage to pay for things without our daed's carpentry business. But Daed left us well off to get by for a couple years or so on our own.

"When the money was gone, I had to come up with a plan to continue on. This is not to say that the community did not offer their help. They did. Our haus was painted as needed, and the fencing repaired. I got help with the canning whenever I was not up to it myself. And I got many a ride to the doctor free of charge even by my Englisch neighbor. Gott was very gut to us in our time of need.

"But I knew I didn't want to depend on the generosity and time of the community forever. I was nearly eighteen by then." She sighed and went on, a faraway look on her face.

"Most Plain women would have found a gut husband and that would solve the problem all around. But I was not fit for marrying, and word got out to most eligible suitors. I too have diabetes and my chances for a healthy full life at that time seemed questionable. Never mind bringing a boppli into the world. Complications were always a big risk, especially nearly twenty years ago.

"So the men of our district stayed clear of me. I went to no singings and had no one waiting to take me home, and no one to talk with me after the common meal that followed Preaching.

"Jacob was my whole life. I had managed to make a meager living with my sewing crafts, and the little wooden Amish figurines Daed had taught me to make. Those were big sellers with the Englisch at the small stores around here. By the time Jacob was sixteen, he'd become quite the carpenter and the jobs he began to acquire kept us without money worries from that time on." A faint smile crossed her face.

"Years later, when I received the mail one day while in Pennsylvania with Jacob, a letter addressed to him was partially torn open. Must have happened at the post office but it brought me the temptation to read it, especially when I saw the return address of Emily Esh.

"Jacob never spoke about Emily to me, or of any maidle, so I was curious and opened the letter. What I read shocked me. My

Jacob was married to Emily. She wanted him to join her in Stone Arabia so they could tell our bishop of their marriage and have their celebration. She suggested that afterward, they could move to Chautauqua County, where they'd been married. Said they could visit me every month or so." Katie paused to gather her emotions.

Jacob offered her his glass of water.

She shook her head and went on.

"I was to be left behind. Alone. And it scared me more than the day our daed died. I'd come up with a plan to survive back then, and I decided I had to come up with a plan again. So, I folded the letter, put it in the envelope and into my dress pocket. Each day I'd check the mailbox for any letter to Emily that Jacob would leave to be picked up, and for letters that came for him from Emily. I'm sorry to say that I took them all but never read any more of them, and so I never knew about their boppli on the way. No wonder she came to Pennsylvania seeking out Jacob that day.

"When we got back home, I'd heard that Emily had gone off with the Englischer. I was surprised but also relieved. But poor Jacob was beside himself with grief and shock. He became listless.

"Miriam Esh, not knowing he was married to Emily, tried to befriend Jacob after Preaching and with invites for supper. She'd always seemed sweet on Jacob. Naturally, she figured he was a single man since he hadn't grown a beard, what with keeping their marriage hush hush. And his rejection of her and any other interested maidle soon became a topic of gossip."

Katie dabbed at her eyes.

Kristen kept her gaze on her unable to feel a twinge of remorse. Then she turned to Aunt Miriam beside her and saw a crimson face.

"A few weeks later, Jacob came in from the carpentry shop one day and announced that he was leaving. I could understand his reasons with all the secrecy here and all. But to my great disappointment he wanted to go alone to start a hardware business in Lowville where our mamm and daed had been born. He said he'd send me money to get by on and asked that I stay and keep up our haus here in Stone Arabia. He didn't want to part with it just yet. I tried to convince him to take me along, to cook and clean for him, but he insisted I not go. He said he needed the time by himself.

"When he first moved there he lived in a little room in the back of the store he'd opened. The moment I learned of that, I came to realize that my selfishness and fear had ruined my dear brudder's life, and in the end, I was alone anyway. He lived that way for years before he moved in with our cousin, Margaret and her familye.

"Year after year, it was harder for me to live with what I had done, so about three years ago I went on a search to locate Emily. I remembered the name of the Englischer and his general whereabouts from a mention of it from Miriam when Jacob had inquired about her after Preaching one Sunday. I went to the local library and asked the librarian to help me locate such a one.

"We found only the one name in New Jersey and an address to go with it. I mailed Emily all the letters Jacob had written to her that I'd kept. I included a note with my deepest apologies and also to please return them if I had sent them to the wrong party. They never came back, so I assumed Emily had received them. I couldn't work up the courage to tell Jacob. I kept telling myself each day that I'd do it tomorrow. Vell, today is that tomorrow."

Katie bent down and retrieved a brown bag from the floor and placed it on the table. "And now I turn over all the letters that Emily had written to Jacob. Please forgive me, brudder."

Jacob nodded, and then looked away.

"What about the notes left at our haus?" Onkle Jonas asked.

Kristen sat erect now. She'd almost forgotten about those.

"That would be me." Jacob's voice filled the quiet room. "I asked an Englisch neighbor to help me, and he drove me here. We stayed at The Budget Motel for a couple weeks. He drove me over to the Waglers to leave the first two notes. Then I borrowed a friend's buggy. Old man Goff's, not far from The Price Chopper."

A few heads nodded.

"Vell, it was a gut long ride, but I figured the car got enough attention. That's how I left the last note, and then my Englisch neighbor drove us both back home."

"But why? You didn't even know that Kristen was your dochter yet." Onkle Jonas's brows furrowed.

"Nee, but I knew that she was Emily's dochter, and I remember how some folks spoke ill of Emily for leaving me for the Englischer even though they did not know we were married. She left the church and was automatically shunned. I was just looking out for what was Emily's. I had no idea why she left me and kept our marriage to myself all these years, but I knew if anyone

251

found out, she'd be further scorned and her dochter a reminder of her wrongdoing. I meant no harm, and I'm sorry if I scared any of you."

He paused and let out a deep sigh. "I tried my best not to make those notes sound like threats. Surely they weren't. Had Kristen gone back, she wouldn't be going through all of this."

"The truth needs to be told, Jacob. No matter how painful it is. Kristen has the right to know these things. Would you not want her to know that you are her vadder?" The bishop looked upon Jacob with compassionate eyes.

"Because of that very fact, Bishop, I'm feeling nearly sick with grief for what she's hearing and feeling right now."

Kristen stared at Jacob.

The man her mother had loved and married. The man who'd lived the past seventeen and three quarter years unaware that she'd even existed. Did this man, her real father, truly care about her?

18

After everyone had left, John decided to stay with Jacob a bit longer. He seemed so stunned and forlorn as he sat on a rocker on Bishop Ebersol's porch, the bag of his aentie Emily's letters on his lap.

"So you'll be staying a few more days, jah, Jacob?"

"Nee. I hope to leave first thing after breakfast by taxi. Doesn't seem likely I'll get to speak to Kristen just yet." Jacob quickly brushed tears from the crinkled bag and tried to compose himself.

The screen door creaked opened. "Can't sleep?" The bishop stood between the partially opened door and the porch. He gave a slight nod to John, and John acknowledged it.

"Nee. Too much going around in my mind. Might as well sit out here in the summer breeze for a spell."

"Much was revealed to you this day,

Jacob. With time and Gott's grace, you'll be able to come to peace with it all."

"I'm not worried about that for me, but for my dochter, Kristen. Foolish as I now know it was, that's why I sent those anonymous notes. I had a feeling her staying here would unravel things, but I never expected this." Jacob kept his gaze ahead toward the fields.

"Why not stay an extra day and go see Kristen at the Wagler haus tomorrow?"

"I thought of that, but I don't want to intrude on her new life."

John opened his mouth to intercede.

The bishop put up his hand. "But you are part of her new life, Jacob. You're the vadder she's never known. These are the facts. Pray about it tonacht, jah?"

"Jah, I will, Bishop. Best I head up for bed now." He turned to John. "Gut nacht, John. Denki for sitting with me. I wasn't the best company."

John wished he could feel anger toward Katie, but he didn't. He'd heard how Katie had suffered loneliness and subtle rejection all of her life. Jacob had reaped the benefits of a mother's loving care from her at the onset of his life. Poor Katie lived her entire existence for him and for him alone. She hadn't known how to let go when the time had come for her to do so.

She must have seen it as the end of her life, and her actions changed the destiny meant for Jacob and Aenti Emily.

And for dear Kristen.

Kristen had just washed the last dish from breakfast and was sponging off the counter when she heard the sound of an approaching horse and buggy. She went through the motions as if today were no different than yesterday. But on the inside, her heart was bursting with all she now knew. "Expecting company, Aunt Elizabeth?"

"Nee. I plan to make a load of church peanut butter to bring to the store later."

"Oh, yeah. I nearly forgot with all that's happened."

"Ach, that's understandable, niece. John will return on his lunch break to drive you to the store so you can help arrange some of the boxed items on the shelves. He and Daniel left before sunup."

"Who could blame them? Monday is opening day." Kristen went to the screened door.

Jacob Mast walked toward the house.

"Oh, no. I have to go upstairs."

Aunt Elizabeth looked out and then hurried to her side. "Kristen, that won't do. He is your vadder, and this must be as hard for him as it is for you. The gut Lord brought this truth to us for a reason. Let's see it through, jah?"

"Please stay with me, Aunt Elizabeth. I don't know what to say or how to act with him."

"Not to worry, child. Shhh, here he is now."

Kristen smoothed out her apron and stood by her aunt as she opened the screened door for Jacob. "Goede Mariye to you, Jacob. This is a nice surprise."

"I thought I'd come by for a proper visit with Kristen if she is up for it. I brought some cinnamon buns that the bishop's frau, Madeline, baked this morgen."

"Ach, how nice. I'll put on a fresh pot of kaffee. We've already had our breakfast, but who can resist a taste of those sweet, delicious buns? Come. Have a seat."

Aunt Elizabeth took Jacob's straw hat. Kristen was glued to the spot and couldn't seem to move or utter a word. Now she understood why Jacob must've been staring at her that day. She couldn't take her eyes off him. He had the same dimple in his cheek as she did. His eyes were dark like hers and his fingers long. She'd always been told she had piano playing fingers. Her mom didn't have long fingers.

"Kristen, come sit and have a bun." Aunt Elizabeth placed a dish for her by the empty chair next to Jacob.

He smiled and nodded.

She did the same, and then sat beside him.

"I'll just have half a bun. I'm still full from the corn mush we had." Kristen didn't think she could swallow one bite.

"We'll split it." Jacob took the bun, cut it in half, and placed one half in her plate and the other in his. "My stomach is churning in a big way for eating much."

Kristen turned to him and their eyes met. He had to be as nervous as she was. For some reason that made her relax a bit. "I'm sorry if I'm acting strange toward you, but I'm still trying to take in all that was said last night." She handed Jacob a napkin.

He took it with a weak smile. "And I, too, Kristen. To learn that I have had a dochter all these years is quite a shock. I cannot say it is an unhappy one, though. I am honored to have such a fine young maidle as my child."

Heat spread across Kristen's face. How could he say that? He barely knew her.

"I know you have decisions to make down the road. But I hope we can get to know one another better while you are here."

Kristen nodded as she picked off a small piece from the cinnamon bun. It was beyond weird to suddenly have a father. Especially since she'd been considering looking for her real dad the last year or so.

Aunt Elizabeth placed the pot of fresh coffee on the table.

The screened door opened.

Aunt Miriam stopped in her tracks and stared at Jacob. "Ach, I didn't realize you had company. I'll come by later." She spoke so quickly that her words nearly tumbled one into the other.

"Miriam, stay and have a cup of kaffee with us. We have delicious cinnamon buns that Madeline sent over with Jacob."

Aunt Miriam stood motionless for a moment as if she didn't know what to do.

Kristen had never seen her aunt so ruffled. If she wasn't so shaky herself, she might have openly chuckled.

"Nee, I was thinking of going over to the store to help and stopped by to see if you wanted me to take anything there." She remained motionless by the door.

"Vell, maybe Jacob and Kristen would like to go with you. Then you can drop them back here for dinner. Jacob, please join us. I'm making a gut beef vegetable garden soup. Miriam's recipe."

Jacob looked at Kristen the exact same time that she looked at him. Then they both smiled.

"Jah, if you're sure it isn't any trouble," he said, looking as if he didn't know where to focus his gaze.

"Ach, no trouble at all. Miriam, of course, you'll stay for dinner too, jah?" Aunt Elizabeth turned and faced her.

"If Aunt Miriam is going to take us to the store in her buggy and then back again, it doesn't make sense for her not to have dinner with us." Kristen stood and walked over to her aunt and took the two pies she held in her arms.

"Jah, vell, I suppose that'll be fine. Denki." Was that a tremor in her voice?

Kristen then realized that Aunt Miriam was still sweet as could be on Jacob. She was like a tongue-tied teenager in his presence.

"Shall we go? There's lots of work to be done, I hear." Aunt Miriam was trying to sound like her usual brisk self, but the tremor was still there.

Jacob stood. "If we're going in Miriam's buggy, then I have to unhitch the horse from the bishop's buggy. He said he won't be needing it today. I'll ride back home in it after dinner."

"OK. We'll meet you outside. See you later, Aunt Elizabeth. Have fun making the church peanut butter."

"Jah, I always do. I eat many a spoonful now and again as I go along. Ach, Jacob. I'll make you a jar to take back with you."

"Denki, Elizabeth. Margaret and Eli love it as much as I do."

Aunt Miriam led them out the door, and Kristen turned to wave to Aunt Elizabeth. Her aunt stood at the door watching them with a smile peeking out from under the hand that covered her mouth, and the other on her chest. She looked overcome by emotion.

This was one of those good memories in the making.

John loaded sacks of flour onto a pallet in the corner of the store where bulk goods would be sold. He turned when he heard the jingle of the door and thought he was hallucinating. What was Jacob still doing here? He'd thought he'd headed out first thing this morgen.

By the look on Aenti Miriam's and Kristen's faces, this was a gut thing. *And we know that in all things God works for the good in those who love him, who have been called according to his purpose.* John always kept

260

Romans 8:28 in his heart, and especially during the meeting at the bishop's haus last nacht. The revelation of secrets and deception seem headed in a direction of healing.

He put the last sack of flour down, brushed off the powdery white that had gotten on his hands and walked over them. "Goede Mariye. This is a surprise." John extended his hand to Jacob and then locked eyes with Kristen.

She seemed nervous but not fearful or unhappy. "Aunt Miriam was on her way to the store, so we came along. Now you won't have to go back to the house to get me, and my, er, well, Jacob, could see the store."

"This is gut, Jacob. You have experience with running a store. Maybe you can look around and give us a few pointers. We never got to that with all that's happened."

Jacob walked slowly around the store with John. He stopped several times to suggest a different arrangement of the tools. John respected his opinion greatly, with Jacob running his own store all these years.

"You don't have any brooms?" Jacob turned to look in all directions.

"We'll be getting them tomorrow."

"You can put the ones used for inside the haus in a barrel on display. The barrel makes a gut holder."

"That's a great idea. Denki."

"Starting a business was a lot of work, but it gave me a new purpose at that time. Eli is learning the business gut nowadays. That means I can come for more visits if Kristen chooses to stay on here. I'm hoping she does."

"I'm hoping she stays, too."

Jacob looked at John with a glint in his eye. "Vell, then. Let's hope that she stays for the both of us."

John gave his familye's long time friend a wide smile. "I'll be praying on that." He felt a satisfied relief that if the time came, it would be Jacob he'd be asking about courting Kristen more so than his daed. Although by now, he was pretty sure that Daed knew he'd be moving forward with this. But did Kristen?

Kristen walked over with a bin of bagged clothespins. "Where should I put these?"

"Those would go where we sell the clotheslines," John said.

Kristen looked at Jacob for a long moment, opened her mouth to say something, and then paused again.

"Something wrong, Kristen?" John couldn't refrain from asking, even with Jacob standing right there.

Kristen hung her head, took in a breath

and lifted her eyes to Jacob. "This is awkward. I just realized I don't know what to call you."

Jacob glanced at John then returned his gaze to Kristen. It seemed that she trusted John enough to say this in his presence.

"Most folks call me Jacob. A few call me Jake. But no one has ever called me Daed." He smiled and a red tinge peeped from under his bearded face.

"So, uh, you want me to call you, Daed?"

"If you feel all right about it."

"I guess I'm OK with that."

"Kristen, I know that we are practically strangers, so if calling me that makes you feel out of sorts, Jacob is right fine."

Kristen looked away from him and placed the basket of clothespins on the floor. Her gaze remained on the basket until she answered. "I'll always love and miss my mom. And now it looks like God has given me my other parent. Isn't that something?" She looked at John, and then to Jacob . . . her daed, where she rested her gaze.

Two similar sets of dark eyes searched each other's faces.

John smiled to himself then quietly walked away.

It was time for Kristen to get to know her daed.

19

"Would you like to come outside for a short walk?" Jacob's gaze held steady into Kristen's.

"Sure. I can put the clothespins out later." The tremor in her hands nearly caused her to drop the basketful before she set it down.

Jacob went ahead of her toward the front of the store and held the door open.

When they got outside, the sun had faded into the clouds and the breeze picked up.

"I'm not used to this mountain weather." She looked up at the sky. "It seems to change from one minute to the next some days."

"Jah, it does. Farmers around here have a short growing season. Seems to me that the Waglers have the right idea opening a store. Should do gut, no matter the weather. Folks need the kind of items sold here."

"I hope so. They've worked so hard getting it all ready. How is your store in Lowville doing?"

"It's gut. Some weeks are slow. Then it picks up. But it's a living and for that I'm grateful."

Kristen didn't know what else to talk about with her newfound daed, as they walked along the side of the road.

A horse and buggy went past and the driver tipped his hat.

Jacob did the same as dust rose from the ground.

Then a car passed and turned into the driveway up ahead.

"The homes around here all look alike, even the Englisch ones." Kristen hoped her attempt at conversation wasn't boring him.

"All you have to do is look at the electric poles." Jacob pointed ahead to one.

"What do you mean?" Kristen looked at the pole they approached.

"If there aren't any wires running from the pole to the haus, then they're Amish."

She stopped walking. There were wires going from the pole to the house that the car had just pulled into. But none at the next pole. She smiled. The conversation definitely wasn't boring. At least not for her. "I never would have noticed that."

Jacob smiled back. "When you grow up around here, it's something everyone comes to know."

"This is a silly question. But if you'd been hiding the fact that you and my mom got married in secret, why do you wear a beard? Seems only the married men around here grow them. Right?"

"Vell, every married man must grow a beard. But unmarried men can also wear a beard. Not having a beard, though, is a sure sign of an unmarried man because married men cannot shave."

Kristen smirked. "So all the ladies around here know that John and Daniel are unmarried. It's like an advertisement."

"It tells their marital status mainly to those who are new in the area. Or if John and Daniel were to visit another community. In our tight-knit communities, word has it who is married and who is not, even the bearded ones."

"Hmmm, OK. Um, how do you like living in Lowville?" As long as she kept the conversation going, the awkwardness seemed to lessen.

"I am content there. It's not so different than here as far as the weather and folks go. We just have a few more stores in town, like the Wal-Mart."

"Yes, I remember. In New Jersey we have stores one on top of the other in the malls there. And so many fast food places, too."

"*It wonders me* how they all stay in business?"

"There are enough people to go around to all of them. At Christmas time, you can't get near the stores. They're jammed packed. Mom never liked to shop in the crowds." Kristen almost hushed herself. She hadn't intended on mentioning her mother to Jacob. It was too awkward.

"Jah. Your mamm liked peace and quiet. It's gut that she lived near the ocean all those years."

"It's not that quiet compared to here. Especially in summer when all the city people come to the beach on the weekends. I guess she adjusted."

"I hope she did. How about you? Have you adjusted to the Plain life?"

"Me? I guess so. I just wish the dresses had buttons and that we had a shower and . . ."

"Kristen, I'm not talking about things. I'm talking about inside yourself. Most Englisch folk think the Plain life is all about what we go without, because that's what they see from the outside. But really, it's about what we become on the inside."

"Really? Like what?"

"Vell . . . a steadfast heart for one. An

267

uncluttered mind. And always a joyful spirit in doing all our work for the Lord and His people. A simple life gives those things to us on the inside."

Kristen wanted all of that. She longed for it. A tear escaped with the unexpected surge of emotions that assaulted her.

Jacob stopped walking. "What is it, Kristen? What did I say to upset you?"

"You made me realize that I haven't adjusted to the Plain life on the inside, like you say. I've only done it on the outside, with how I dress and what I've given up. My cell phone, television, and long hot showers. I don't have a steadfast heart or an uncluttered mind.

"And I definitely don't get much of a chance these days to have a joyful spirit because every time I begin to, God throws something else at me to deal with. Like you!" Her hand shot up to her mouth. She was surprised and frightened by the sudden anger that shook her very core. "I'm sorry," she said as the breeze cooled her hot cheeks. "I better not talk anymore. Can we head back to the store now?"

Jacob nodded.

They walked down the long road in silence. So much for their father-daughter talk.

Kristen had to hold back the onslaught of tears that threatened to gush forth. She'd hurt Jacob. Her daed. And she knew that if she didn't have an Amish heart on the inside, as Jacob described, then she would never be able to join her heart with John's.

As they approached the store, John was out front shaking out the welcome mat. He looked up, placed the mat down and with arms crossed over his chest, gave Kristen and Jacob a big smile.

Jacob stopped walking just before they got in ear shot of John. He turned to Kristen. "Seems you have a big admirer. John is a gut man."

"It doesn't really matter, does it? Seems that I've inherited all my traits from what the Plain people call, *the outside.*"

"Kristen, that is not what I was trying to say to you. I —"

"Everyone knows I was born of Amish parents but raised in the Englisch world. Inside, that's who I am." She held out her apron in front of her. "This is just a costume. What was that word we last learned in English class? Oh yes, a *facade.* I'm sorry to disappoint you. Daed." She let go of her apron and rushed past Jacob, then John, and went into the store.

■ ■ ■ ■

When Jacob reached John, he appeared worn and troubled.

"What happened, Jacob?"

"Kristen's not feeling the peace and joy that I told her being Plain can bring to us on the inside. And because of that, she thinks she's just going through the motions in what she wears and what she no longer does. She feels that she doesn't have the ability to be Amish. And it's all my doing, John."

"Nee. She's had a rough time since her mamm was killed. It's been one thing after the other. She's had little time to let our ways heal her wounds and renew her life. I guess my daed is right."

"What do you mean?"

"When he noticed that my feelings for Kristen were growing, he advised me to back off. At least for now. He said she has a lot to work out and doesn't need me to complicate things even more." John kicked a rock and sighed. "And it just came to me, that maybe he's thinking that the whole reason for Kristen trying to be Plain is because of me."

Jacob looked into John's eyes. "Ach, John,

nee. Kristen was born Amish and Gott has sent her back here to be who she was born to be. I truly believe that her mamm knew this too."

"Jah, maybe you are right. And I know she wants to be part of this familye. She has led a very lonely life in the Englisch world. Amish or not, she is part of us all now."

Jacob patted John on the shoulder, and in that moment he felt sure Kristen wouldn't ever experience that loneliness again.

At 6:00 PM, John arrived back home with Daniel and Daed.

The bishop's buggy was hitched to the pole.

Apparently Jacob was still at the haus and would stay for dinner.

When John opened the screened door, he nearly dropped his hat when he entered the kitchen. He looked at his mamm. She merely looked back with saddened eyes.

Jacob was seated at the table looking down into his iced tea, swirling the ice with the spoon. He raised his head just long enough to motion a greeting.

Aunt Miriam was setting the table with a heavy hand and a tight-lipped scrowl.

There stood Kristen by the stove in the same exact clothes she'd worn when she'd first arrived to Stone Arabia. No kapp, her dark hair in a ponytail with a red crunchy thing that matched the striped t-shirt she wore with blue denim jeans. Her eyes met his. "Something the matter?"

"Maybe I should be asking you that question." He hung his hat on the peg and walked to his seat at the table.

Daed and Daniel joined him but remained quiet. They both looked as if they were waiting for some kind of a show to begin.

"Nothing the matter with me at all." She turned to the counter and placed baked biscuits into a basket.

John didn't like her snippy attitude. Yes, she was hurting, but she had no cause to take it out on him and to cause poor Jacob such heartache. "We don't play games here, Kristen. You're being cruel."

She whirled around, nearly knocking the basket of biscuits off the counter. "I'm being cruel? No, I think you have it backward, John. Here I was making a complete fool of myself, thinking I could fit in just because I wore Plain clothes, used my cell phone out of the house, or whatever. Well, the joke's on me, isn't it?"

"I have no idea what you're talking about. Where is all of this coming from? Jacob feels mighty awkward, and he's our guest here."

She turned her gaze on Jacob. "I'm sorry if I'm making you uncomfortable and for anything unkind that I've said. I know that you were only being honest. Besides, I'm not really a Mast, am I? I don't even bear the name. I was raised Englisch. One hundred percent inside and out."

Aenti Miriam turned to Kristen with her hands on her hips. "You're an Esh, Kristen," she said in a firm voice. "Same as me. Same as your Aenti Elizabeth before she married your Onkle Jonas. And same as our elder brudder, Matthew, who lives way out in Indiana with his frau, Ruth, and their three kinner."

By this time Mary and Anna had taken their seats at the table. They looked on with expressions of surprise and puzzlement.

Kristen gave them a nod, placed the basket of biscuits on the table, and headed for the porch.

"Aren't you having dinner with us?" Mamm asked. The sadness in her eyes more pronounced now.

"No, thank you. I'm not hungry. Angela is picking me up to go to the library. It closes at 8:00 PM. I need to use the computer there to search the job market."

"A job? You'd have to travel quite a bit around here to get to and from any job that pays enough to be worth your while." Daed acted as if pursuing a job was totally unrealistic.

"I never said I was looking for a job around here." She grabbed a biscuit and walked out the screened door.

Jacob's face turned ashen.

John had lost his patience now. He excused himself and followed after her.

Kristen stood by the mailbox at the edge of the property, waiting for Angela.

"Hold on there, Kristen. Listen to me. And listen gut. You can do whatever you like. Become baptized to our way of life or walk away from it once you turn eighteen. You can get a job with the Englisch, or in an Amish establishment nearby. It's your life. But please, never be so cruel and arrogant to our familye again. It's disrespectful. They don't deserve that, especially Jacob. He's in as much shock over all of this as you are. They care for you."

She turned and glared at him with fiery wet eyes. "You mean, only if I'm Amish, through and through. But I'm not. And I might never be able to be that for . . . for . . ." She placed her head in her hands and sobbed.

John walked nearer to her. He longed to embrace her, but that was too risky being in open view. He got as close as he could. "For me?" he whispered.

Without lifting her head, she nodded.

His heart nearly melted. "Loyalty and a gut heart are great blessings. You have always had those, Englisch or Amish. You don't need to conform to anything but Gott's will for you. Just trust in Him to lead you to the life you are meant to live."

Kristen lifted her head and wiped at her eyes with the backs of her hands. "What if God's will is not what I want?"

John whisked away a stray tear from her cheek with his thumb. "Gott's will for us could never be bad. He seems to be putting your life together piece by piece, like a puzzle, jah?"

Kristen laughed through new tears. "This is a difficult puzzle to finish. Like one of those with a thousand pieces."

"Ach, but the finished puzzle picture will be perfect," he assured her.

Kristen smiled.

John relaxed and reluctantly stepped back.

A car came down the road.

"That must be Angela. We'll see you later. Mamm will have a plate waiting for you."

"John?"

"Jah?"

"Can you please tell Jacob good-bye for me?"

20

Kristen came down to help with breakfast wearing a denim skirt and a simple white cotton blouse. Again, no bun, no kapp, no apron. Not until what she felt on the inside was genuine, could she dress the part.

Aunt Elizabeth came in and glanced at her attire for the briefest moment. "Goede Mariye, Kristen. I think some dippy eggs might make a nice change from the corn mush today."

"Does that mean eggs you can dip into? Sunnyside up?"

"Jah, it does. We have enough of the bread I baked yesterday for that."

"Will we cook up some bacon, too?"

"Bacon will be gut."

As Kristen went to retrieve the bacon from the ice chest, Anna came running in, smiled at her, and then went straight to the stove to make the coffee. Not a minute later, Mary strolled in. The three of them made quick work of breakfast.

Kristen had her own part in the preparations each morning. When did that happen? Seemed she'd always made the bacon or the mush and placed the butter and jams on the table. They worked as a team. It was one of the things she liked about the Plain life. Being a part of things.

The screen door opened and Kristen had a smile ready for John. But it quickly froze on her face when it was Jacob who came through the door.

"Goede Mariye, all."

Aunt Elizabeth wiped her hands on a dish towel and went over to him.

"Goede Mariye, Jacob. Such a nice surprise. Take yourself a seat and join us for breakfast. I didn't hear you pull the buggy in."

"Denki, Elizabeth. I didn't come by buggy. I had the taxi driver who was scheduled to come take me to Lowville, drive me here instead. I postponed my trip back home 'til after the opening of your store. I know that Monday is the big day. I'll be staying at Katie's haus."

"Ach, that is awful nice of you, Jacob. Jonas and the boys will be so very happy to have you with them."

278

Kristen brought sliced grain bread to the table.

Jacob had his eyes fixed on her much like he did the very first day she'd met him. Maybe he thought she'd switch back into her Plain apparel today. Nope. Not 'til it rang true for her. If that ever happened.

"Will you be coming to Preaching tomorrow, Kristen?"

She was about to answer Jacob when Uncle Jonas, John, and Daniel came in.

"Jacob! Thought you'd be half way to Lowville by now." Uncle Jonas patted Jacob's shoulder and sat next to him.

"Nee, I'm staying for the grand opening of your store."

"That's gut news. We could always use your opinion seeing how you've had your own store for all these years now."

Jacob nodded. He no longer kept his gaze on Kristen.

She breathed a sigh of relief.

John gave her a quick glance and his expression was hard to read. Maybe he'd given up on her. Just as well. He'd be better off with a nice, genuine Amish girl.

Aunt Elizabeth brought the dippy eggs to the table.

They all paused for the silent prayer, but this time Kristen didn't say the Lord's

Prayer. She merely uttered a silent, *help me be who I'm supposed to be. Amen.*

While the platter of eggs and bread were passed, Kristen observed Jacob. Her father. She wasn't sure she'd ever get used to referring to him that way. He seemed a gentle, kind man, and despite the fact that his life hadn't gone the way he'd planned with her mom, he still had happiness about him. Must be that inner joy he spoke about yesterday. The joy Kristen couldn't feel.

"Aren't you eating, Kristen? It's the first time I've made dippy eggs since you've been here." Aunt Elizabeth fixed her eyes on Kristen's plate.

"I'm sure they're good, but I'm not hungry. I'll just have some juice for now."

John glanced at her with a solemn look. Or was it irritation she saw there? What business was it of his whether she ate or not? She looked at Aunt Elizabeth and saw the disappointment on her face. She'd messed up again. She'd hurt her aunt's feelings with her refusal to eat the eggs. Most likely considered selfish and rude. "Well, maybe I'll have just one egg with half a slice of bread."

Aunt Elizabeth's eyes brightened, and she quickly passed the platter to Kristen while Anna tore a piece of bread in half and placed it on her plate.

She wanted to sneak a glance back at John to see if his irritation had softened, but she kept her eyes on her food instead. She hadn't accepted the egg and bread for him. She did it for her aunt.

"I'm glad you're planning on coming to the store with us, Jacob," Uncle Jonas said while buttering his bread.

"Jah, I'll try not to be in the way."

"Nee. We're getting a big delivery today and your help would sure be appreciated. Kristen and Anna are going to load up the candy counter, and Mary and Lizzie will be going over all the things the maidles are interested in buying."

"Jah, we were thrilled when we received a basket of Edna Lucille soaps from my sister-in-law, Ruth, all the way in Ohio where they're made. There's not an Amish girl around who doesn't love that soap. She sent us four bars each of Jasmine, Honeysuckle, Peach Ginger, Lilac, and Citrus Grove." Aunt Elizabeth counted each scent on her fingers. "Five different kinds. That makes twenty bars. But there might be one bar missing because I think we ladies should treat ourselves to a bar of the honeysuckle. Just for the smelling, of course."

Kristen cocked her head. "Only to smell?"

"Vell, we make our own soap and don't use the fancy kind. But we enjoy the scent."

Kristen rolled her eyes.

John's frown deepened.

Right now, she didn't care.

"Honeysuckle is my favorite, too," Mary said. "Kristen, you'll have to take a whiff of it. I think there is an ocean scented one that is made, too. Wish we had one of those for you. Next order we'll include a few so you can be reminded of your ocean."

Kristen forced a smile. Once again, John was right. Her family cared for her, despite the silly soap smell-but-don't-use rule. But that didn't mean she was worthy. Or that she could care for them in the same unselfish way with all the little thoughtful things they did. She was so wrapped up in herself with the saga of her upturned life that she had little thought for anyone else.

At least she might be able to be of some help at the store . . . with her father. She needed to show him her nicer side if she hadn't yet lost it completely.

Jacob was so busy helping the men unload the delivered supplies and setting everything in its proper place, he wasn't able to focus too much on Kristen.

She was part glad and part disappointed.

She'd finished helping Anna set out the fudge and now she'd stay by the kaffee counter to help Aunt Miriam.

"Jacob, would you like some instant kaffee or tea? We're trying our propane urn today. It boils five gallons of water and keeps it nice and hot."

"Jah, that would be gut. Denki, Miriam."

"I brought a blueberry pie. Just have to slice it. Kristen can you do that?"

Kristen nodded, unwrapped the foil from the pie, and began her task.

"I think it would be a gut idea to have a plate of cookies and free kaffee and tea here for the customers. We can put out disposable hot cups, a jar of sugar, and some powdered milk." Miriam dished out a slice of pie that Kristen had cut and placed it on a paper plate for Jacob. Then she filled a mug with hot water. "Instant kaffee or tea?"

"Kaffee is gut, denki. Blueberry pie is my favorite."

"Jah, I know how much you liked blueberry ice cream, too." Aunt Miriam's face took on a hue of pink. "Um, because Emily told us a funny story about how much of it you ate at a singing at Ann Zook's haus."

"Jah, I remember that nacht. I was a complete *wutz*. Wonders me how Ann's mamm didn't put me out for hardly leaving much for anyone else?"

"Ach, we were *lobbich* in our youth at times."

"Very silly. For sure and for certain." Jacob gave out a short laugh at the memory.

Aunt Miriam watched him with a smile on her flushed face.

Jacob took a bite of the pie then looked back up at her. "You still live in the same haus you grew up in?"

"Jah. When everyone went off and married, they let me stay there. Elizabeth invited me many a time to come live with them, but I love that haus and am grateful to the Lord that I can live there. I feel a certain comfort being surrounded with the things of our familye. Daed's rocker, Grossmammi's special quilt given to our mamm, the small gardens we all tended together. And the same peaceful view out the windows I've seen since I've been a kind. That's what I mean."

Kristen never heard Aunt Miriam so talkative and unguarded before.

"That's important, Miriam. I'm happy for you." Jacob sipped his coffee in silence.

"Are you all right, Jacob?"

"Ach, jah. I was just thinking about how gut it is to have a home like that. I hope Kristen can one day feel the same way.

Wherever she chooses to live." He turned and gave her a quick smile.

Aunt Miriam cut a thin slice of pie for herself, and then looked at him with complete seriousness, the smile gone. "You sound worried."

He looked toward Kristen again but said nothing.

Hearing him say that with her standing right there was strange and the time had come to change the topic of this conversation.

"Aunt Miriam, is there electric lighting here in the store because the owner is Englisch? Like why there's also a sink?"

"Jah, that's right."

"So how come Plain people can use these modern things here if they don't at home?"

"It's allowed to be used here because it came with the store and your onkle and aenti don't own this place; they rent it. Electricity is not permitted if we own the business. Just like with our homes. Many Amish stands at the markets of larger communities have electricity because it comes with the stands they rent there."

"Interesting." Kristen eyed the blueberry pie.

"Go ahead, have yourself a piece." Aunt Miriam handed Kristen a paper plate.

"Is it OK if I take it with me? Angela is coming any minute to drive me to the mall. Anna and I finished up setting up the candy counter. I want to get doilies to place under some of the candies in the plastic bins, and a few things I need for myself."

"Sure, take a slice for Angela, too." Aunt Miriam wrapped two pieces in waxed paper.

"Do you need money to buy whatever you need?"

Kristen didn't expect Jacob to ask her that.

"I am your vadder, so if you need anything you can come to me."

"Oh no, thank you. I still have some money that I saved in my own account."

Jacob nodded. He looked uncomfortable.

"You tell Angela to come to the store on Monday, if she can, *jah*? It's a special day around here." Aunt Miriam was quick to ease the tension as if she could sense his uneasiness.

"OK, I'll tell her. Will you be here . . . Jacob?"

"Jah, I'll be here. Would be a shame if I missed such a special day for my gut friends."

"So, you'll be at Preaching tomorrow at the bishop's, too, then?"

"I will."

Kristen looked at him with a pensive

expression. "I'm glad." With that she took the wrapped pie slices and walked off.

When Kristen entered the kitchen to help with breakfast the next morning, neither Aunt Elizabeth or Mary made much of a fuss over her long, light green dress and darker green bandana. Although she did notice them exchange the quickest glances.

"Green suits you vell. I've been looking for a nice shade of green to make Anna a new school dress." Mary touched the fabric, smiled, and then went about her breakfast tasks.

"Mary, I don't want you to think I don't like the dresses you made for me. I'm just not ready to wear them yet." Kristen didn't want to do anything more to hurt the feelings of any member of the family.

"Ach, they're not going anywhere. Don'tcha worry yourself none at all."

Kristen smiled and went to the stove to make the corn mush. A tug on her dress caused her to spin around.

Anna stood next to her. "You look nice, Kristen."

"Oh, thank you, Anna. So do you."

"Does that mean you're coming to Preaching with us?"

"Yes, I think I'll come, if there's room."

"We'll take the familye buggy, so there'll be room."

Kristen turned to the deep familiar voice she'd come to know so well.

John was at the screened door looking at her, a smirk on his lips. He was handsome in his black trousers topped with a black vest over a white shirt. His blond thick hair was soft and shiny. Kristen was tempted to touch it. He held his black broad-rim hat in his hand.

"OK, good." Kristen figured the less she said the better. Bad enough she was going to Preaching in a conservative, solid long dress instead of the appropriate Plain dress with the white apron that was always worn to church services.

Still, it took her over an hour at the mall, with Angela's help, to find three solid colored dresses that were simple and long enough to be considered modest to Amish eyes.

She'd come up with an excuse as to why she needed to sit in the back rather than with the family. She preferred not to cause them any embarrassment.

It would be so much easier to go upstairs and change into one of Mary's homemade dresses, kapp, and apron. But would it, really? On the inside, she'd still be torn.

21

Kristen sat in the large Ebersol barn during her second church service. Could it be possible that she'd been with her Amish family for one full month already? Then again, sometimes it felt like nearly a year with all that had happened. And much longer than that since her mom's accident. She missed her so much.

Looking ahead at the women on the benches before her, she wondered what she had in common with them. Other than being related to three of them, and little Anna, not much.

With her background, how could she fit in? She was all wrong from the very beginning. Born of an Amish mother in the Englisch world because her mom assumed Jacob had abandoned them.

She was the daughter of a shunned church member. Kristen doubted that any of these women present today had a past like hers.

John didn't need a girl with a past.

What had she been thinking?

None of the women sat near her.

Aunt Miriam kept turning around and would then whisper something to Aunt Elizabeth.

Had Kristen simply worn the proper attire, she'd blend in, and no one would be leery of her. More than likely, these people never heard the expression, 'Don't judge a book by its cover.' Then again, she herself had no idea what was under her outer appearance. How could she expect anyone else to? That was the whole confusing problem. To them, she was a stranger from the Englisch world. And in her heart, she was a stranger to her very self.

The barn grew quiet.

Kristen looked up.

Katie Mast had walked in.

This wasn't the first time John had seen the hush-hush reaction from the congregation toward a penitent who would be meeting with the bishop at a member meeting after the service to confess his or her transgressions. Word got around fast about such matters. According to Daed, public confession was a gut thing. The person is made right with Gott, the church, and the community again. Poor Katie Mast. She needed all three in a big way.

Despite the busy morgen and afternoon of worship and communal mingling, John hoped for an opportune time to talk with Kristen. He couldn't help notice how lovely she looked in her light green dress and the green bandana. Her attire was more in the Mennonite fashion than in the Amish, still, he respected her efforts to go out of her way to get something modest to wear while going through her identity crisis.

How could he hope for a chance to speak with her during the common meal being at the table with all the men? Maybe Kristen would be one of the maidles who brought out the food to them. After eating half his meal, he knew she wouldn't be. When he and the other men finished eating, the women and children ate.

John busied himself with small talk to the other men about the upcoming opening of the Wagler store.

Finally, the women began clearing the tables.

Katie was among them, looking relaxed now.

Then Kristen came out to help.

He made his way over to her as she approached one of the tables to help clear it of leftovers. But the moment he drew near, Katie had approached her, too.

Then Jacob appeared with Aenti Miriam, and at one point, Bishop Ebersol and his frau were among them.

Judging by Kristen's smile, she was happy and felt at ease, despite her changed apparel from one church service to the other.

John was relieved. He'd been worried that a few staunch old timers might let Kristen know in their own subtle way that they did not approve of her change of dress.

But if the bishop and his frau stopped to chat with her, that was a big deal, an outward gesture to the others that Kristen was to be treated as one of them.

The bishop was a wise man, and John figured that he had a gut sense of the struggles within Kristen's heart and soul just now. He didn't want to lead her away from the faith and fold by being too hard on her, but toward it, with kindness. John was grateful.

Shortly before they were to leave, Kristen stepped onto the Ebersols' porch with a glass of lemonade in her hand. For the moment, no one else was around.

John made wide strides from under the shade tree to the porch and ran up the six wooden steps two at a time.

"John! Where did you come from? I haven't seen you all day."

"I know. The menfolk were interested in hearing about the opening of the store tomorrow, and I noticed you were busy after the meal." If only she knew how he'd been waiting for a chance to be with her all afternoon.

"Yeah. It was so nice of Jacob's sister to talk with me, especially after her ordeal following the service. And then to have the bishop and his wife come over to say hello. I'd thought since no one sat next to me at Preaching, well, it doesn't matter."

"You thought you'd gotten the cold shoulder for not wearing Plain clothes like you wore at the last church service?"

"Hmm. I shouldn't be surprised at how you pick up on things, but I always am."

"I pick up on things, as you call it, about you, because I want to see you happy and at peace here." He looked around. They were still alone, so he took a step closer to her. "Kristen, no one sat next to you because you sat in the very last bench and most folks want to sit up front to hear the sermons better. Families with kinner avoid the last bench if it's near the opened barn doors because the outside sounds distract the little ones. And that's the truth of it."

Kristen looked up at him. He could smell the slightest scent of honeysuckle on her, probably the Edna Lucille soap Mamm and Mary were so excited about. He wished he could remove her bandana and bury his face in her soft dark hair. He shook the thought from his mind.

"I hope I acted all right with Katie. I tried my best to be nice to her, but a part of me is so angry about what she did to Jacob and my mother. I would've been raised here from the very start had she not done that. I wouldn't have these mixed up feelings about who I am."

"Vell, Katie had to answer to Gott and the church for her mistakes, and once that's done, we don't speak on it further. It's forgiven. Try to keep in mind that her actions were borne of loneliness. Not that I condone any of it, but you understand about loneliness, jah?"

Kristen nodded. She looked into her glass of lemonade, put it down on the step next to her, and then fixed her eyes on his. "John Wagler. I know I've said this once before, but I'm convinced that one day you'll be a deacon or even the bishop around here. Wait and see."

"If that's what Gott ordains, Kristen, then I hope you are here by my side." John could hardly believe his thought surfaced right out of his mouth that way. But there it was, hanging in the air between them.

A smile began to claim Kristen's lips. Then as quick as a flash of lightening, it vanished, and so did she.

Kristen wished she hadn't let her emotions get the best of her. But had she stayed on the porch in John's presence another second longer, she'd have burst into tears. No sense in talking about a future with him. He was so wise and had such a deep faith. Compared to him she was a scared child full of doubt, anger, and confusion.

Even though they were born of parents from the same background, they came from different worlds. How could she become all that she had never been here in Stone Arabia?

"I'll be seeing you tomorrow at the store, then?" Jacob's voice startled her.

She didn't expect anyone to come behind the barn.

Aunt Miriam was beside him. Again. Smiling.

"Uh, yes, I'll be there. I'm looking forward to when Anna puts the 'open' sign on the door. She's been talking about it for days," Kristen said.

"Jah, she's so excited. I think we all are." Aunt Miriam clasped her hands to emphasize the point.

Jacob smiled and nodded. Then he turned his attention back to Kristen. "It's gut that we were all able to attend Preaching together. Best we get some rest before the big opening in the morgen."

"Uh-huh. I'll go see if Uncle Jonas is ready to go home. I was back here looking at the mountains." Not entirely a lie. She'd noticed them as soon as she ended up behind the barn in her attempt to spare John her trauma. And in noticing them, she thought of him all the more.

He'd been trying to show her the beauty of this place, and she'd just now seen what he meant for her to see. She'd felt what he'd felt. She was tempted to run off to tell him, to let him know that maybe there was hope for her after all.

For supper, Aunt Elizabeth served hamburger noodle casserole, the Wagler family favorite.

Kristen never thought that hamburger meat mixed with brown sugar, tomato soup and cream of celery soup baked with noodles could taste so good. She held out her plate for seconds.

"Kristen, would you be interested in a part time job at the Farm Style Diner?" Mary asked.

"A job? Where you work?"

"Jah, I gave up my morgen hours there so I could help out at the store. I was thinking that maybe you would like to take those hours, and then when I go to work at the diner in the afternoon, you can come to the store."

"I've never worked as a waitress before."

"Ach, breakfast is an easy shift. Folks order eggs, pie, or a doughnut with kaffee or tea. And Mrs. Kraus, the owner, is very nice. The morgen shift starts at 7:30."

"I guess I could give it a try. But how will I get there?"

"I could take you when I take Mary to the store with me each morgen," John was quick to say. "The diner is only a few minutes away. We open at 8:00 AM, so after we drop you off, we'll have some time to get things ready at the store for the day." His offer was kind but his expression didn't match it, as he scooped up the last of his casserole with a slice of bread.

"OK, thanks. When would I start, Mary?"

"I took tomorrow off for our opening, and I begin my part-time hours on Tuesday. I told Mrs. Kraus that I'd bring you with me to meet her then if you were interested."

"When did you come up with the idea of me working there?"

"Only yesterday. I took a walk to the diner from the store to pick up my pay. I was in such a rush on Friday that I forgot all about it. When Mrs. Kraus said she'd be putting a Help Wanted notice up, I thought of you. Ach, I hope you don't mind me telling her that you might be interested. If you're really not, it's fine, you know."

"It's OK, Mary. I could use some job experience. Thanks for thinking of me."

John pushed his plate away and stood. "I'll start milking the cows for you, Daniel."

Now Kristen was sure she wasn't imagining John's irritation.

It hadn't gone unnoticed by Mary either.

"Did I say something to bother you, brudder?"

"Nee, nothing you said. It's what you went ahead and done." The screen door opened and then closed again. He'd vanished as fast as vapor.

John heard the screen door as he got to the barn. He should have known that Kristen wouldn't let his comment go. And she had every right not to. He immediately regretted it.

Mary was only doing what she thought was a favor to Kristen. His sister was a kind and gentle person, and he could only imagine the sting she felt from his words. He'd have to apologize before going to bed.

And as soon as Kristen entered the barn to confront him, he'd apologize to her, too. He had no right to be angry about which direction her life would go. It was in Gott's hands. Not his. Although he'd hoped his input might sway her to stay in Stone Arabia. Near him. If she got some job experience here, she could up and work in another diner or restaurant somewhere else. Even back in New Jersey.

Kristen should have been here by now.

John turned and looked out the barn door toward the haus.

Kristen stood halfway to the barn on her cell phone. Had she come out to speak to him and then gotten a call? Or had she come out to make a call and not for him at all?

Her back was turned to him so he continued to watch her. She listened intently, and to his surprise, jumped up and down and raised her free arm up to the sky. Then she began to pace back and forth as she continued to talk until she hung up. He couldn't move and she spied him standing there watching her. She ran over.

"John. John. I can't believe the news I just got from Riley Gallagher. I really can't believe it!" She was breathless and unable to stand still.

"What news, Kristen?" Did he really want to know?

"Mattie Cook wants to transfer the title of Ross's house over to me. She said that Ross had always wanted me to have the house, and she could never feel right about taking it, especially after what her son had done. So, I'll have a home back in New Jersey! Can you believe it?"

John was sure his knees would buckle. He forced a smile. "That is gut news, Kristen. Will you be moving back there then?" He had to know. Now.

Kristen's smile disappeared. "I . . . I haven't even thought of that. I was so happy to hear that the house I grew up in will be mine. My room, the ocean, and the memory of my mom are all part of that house. I need to think about this. Yeah, I'll think about it for a while. The house isn't going anywhere, right?"

John shook his head. "And neither am I, Kristen."

Kristen looked into John's deep blue eyes.

What was he trying to tell her? That he'd always be there for her? As a friend? Or that he'd wait for her to settle down in Stone Arabia. With him?

Her heart swelled with love. Yes, she loved John Wagler. She also loved her Amish family and always having them around. She enjoyed eating meals with them, going to church together, and now helping out in their store. Coming here had helped Kristen forget the long lonely times. Had her mother foreseen all of this?

If she moved back to the house at the Jersey Shore she'd be alone again. Sure, she'd see Cindy, but things had changed between them, and in September, Cindy was going off to college at Princeton. As far as Derick was concerned, she didn't even consider him a friend. He'd abandoned and betrayed her in her greatest time of need.

Other than the house itself, what did she have to go back to? Modern conveniences? Things? Her beloved ocean was all she really missed there.

"John, if . . . if . . . I stay here. Would it be a problem if I went back to the ocean a few times each summer?"

"The ocean?"

"Yes, the ocean. Can I go see the ocean a few times each summer if I live here?"

"I see no problem with that, so long as you are accompanied by a familye member."

"I might ask Jacob to come with me to the house, so he can see where I grew up and the area where I lived. It might help him to know me better. What do you think?"

"I think he would be very pleased."

"Then I'll ask him tomorrow. I have to go back soon to meet with Riley and Mattie Cook to sign the title for the house. I'll announce this to the family before I go, of course. If it's not a church Sunday in Lowville and Jacob can come next weekend, would you like to come too?"

"Ach, Kristen. You know I would. But I have to tend to the store each Saturday and I think you and your daed need some time alone together."

She nodded. "OK. Well, I came out here to say that I'm sorry if Mary trying to get me the job at the diner upset you. Although, I can't understand why?"

"I felt threatened that you'd learn how to do a job that you can also do away from here."

"You mean, you really want me to stay?"

"Jah, I do. I guess I kept throwing hints but never came right out and said it to you. I didn't think the timing was right for me to be asking you to think of me. Daed said . . .

Ach, never mind."

"Your daed? What did he say?"

"He figures you have enough to think about without adding me to the mix. I tried to respect his wishes the best I could."

"John, is it because I'm all confused about being Plain? Because of my mixed up background? Maybe your daed feels you and me should always be like cousins, even though we aren't related. Most likely you'd be better off that way. I'm not in your league in the Plain world."

"My league? Kristen, there aren't any leagues in the Plain world. We all strive for the same gut life: service to the Lord and to one another, but no one is viewed better than anyone else. Putting people in leagues is the complete opposite of our beliefs." He moved closer to her. "But I wouldn't mind having you in my corner of the world."

Kristen smiled, and then crooked her pointer finger and motioned for him to bend forward as if she were going to tell him a secret.

He leaned down close.

With her breath warm in his ear, she whispered, "I'm already in your corner, John. I just need to get better at being me." She quickly planted a kiss on his cheek, light and soft, and walked off toward the house.

A peek over her shoulder had John still standing there with his hand to his cheek where her lips had been.

22

On the morning of the store's opening day, Kristen hurried along with Mary and Aunt Elizabeth to get fresh fruit, corn mush, and buttered sliced grain bread on the table.

Anna had the coffee ready minutes after, and by the time they all sat down to eat, Kristen was revved up from all the rush. She'd skip the coffee and have milk instead.

After the silent prayer, John looked over at her with a smile. A reminder in the midst of this new busy day, that the words spoken between them the night before were not imagined. She smiled back.

Uncle Jonas looked up right at that very moment and caught their exchange. If he disapproved, he didn't show it as he spooned fresh berries over his corn mush.

At least no one looked at her with disapproval for another day not dressed Plain. Today she wore a blue version of the long green dress and matching bandana that she'd worn for Preaching.

"Ach, I'm so excited to get to the store. I wonder who will stop by?" Aunt Elizabeth spoke with widened eyes as she sprinkled sugar on her berries.

"Calm down, Lizzie. As long as we are there, that's all that matters," Uncle Jonas said with a chuckle. "Word gets around right quick about these things. I figure that the same folks who come to Preaching will show up to wish us well."

"I hope you're right, Daed. I made a lot of fudge," Anna said, stirring her mush. "And we have the cookies that Aenti Miriam baked for the customers who want kaffee or tea."

"Don't go worrying about the fudge or cookies, Anna. I think John and me can finish them off if not enough folks take to them," Daniel assured her with a laugh.

"That's for sure and for certain." John gave Anna a gentle poke to the nose.

Everyone laughed.

So far, it looked like it would be a good day.

When they arrived at the store, Aunt Elizabeth recruited Kristen to figure out a way to get the small price sign for the Edna Lucille soaps to stand up.

Kristen went to the supply drawer near the cash register and got a roll of tape. While she taped the sign to the basket of soaps, Mary and Aunt Elizabeth refolded the pretty hand embroidered handkerchiefs that Mary had made, and set them on the same table with the scented soaps.

"Vell, I best go check to be sure John and Daniel didn't move my canned preserves from the shelf I put them on to make room for more of their manly things." Aunt Elizabeth walked off while Mary folded the last of the handkerchiefs.

"I wish I had something I'd made to sell. Everyone brought something except me." Kristen's comment was louder than she'd planned, and Aunt Elizabeth turned around and walked back to her.

"Ach, that's not true, niece. John tells me that you were a big help around here with figuring out the best way to arrange things. Didn't you set out these tables for the soaps, handkerchiefs, and candles?"

Kristen nodded.

"And you went out and got us the paper plates, kaffee cups and doilies. Seems like you brought more than you know." Aunt Elizabeth patted her on the shoulder. "And if you didn't do a single thing except pray for Gott's blessing on our store, that would be more than enough, jah?"

"Jah." Kristen smiled, grateful for such a kind and doting aunt.

Minutes later, the hands of the clock settled on the eight and the eleven. Five minutes to opening time.

Kristen felt Anna's excitement when she watched her run from the candy counter to the back for Uncle Jonas and her brothers.

"Come, it's almost time to open." Anna had Uncle Jonas by the hand, pulling him along to the door with Daniel and John close behind.

When they'd all gathered by the door, they paused for a silent prayer.

Then Uncle Jonas lifted Anna so she could hang the OPEN sign on the suction hook at the upper part of the glass door.

"Wagler's is open for business," Uncle Jonas announced.

Anna clapped.

A minute later the door jangled open.

Jacob and Katie stood there with Aunt Miriam.

Katie held out a covered basket to Aunt Elizabeth.

"I better get the water urn going." Aunt Miriam rushed over to the counter with her cookies.

"Sorry we made Miriam late," Jacob said.

"Yesterday I suggested we pick her up so we could all come together. No sense in bringing another buggy if the three of us fit in Katie's."

"Jah, but my biscuits took longer than I'd planned. So sorry." Katie avoided looking at anyone in the face.

Kristen could imagine Katie's awkwardness well, and her anger toward her aunt softened.

"Here, I'll take those." Kristen took Katie's basket of biscuits from Aunt Elizabeth. "Let's set some of these out." Kristen led the way to the counter and handed Katie a paper plate lined with a doilie. Her Aunt Katie.

While they set biscuits onto a paper plate, Katie's gray blue eyes met Kristen's and she gave her a small smile. "Denki, Kristen Mast." Before Kristen could respond, Katie hurried away.

The store's door jangled again and when Kristen turned to see who it was, she did a double take.

What was she doing here? There stood Sadie Krantz and her mother, Lucy.

Aunt Elizabeth rushed over to greet them.

Kristen decided to forego a greeting as long as she could. She walked away from the water urn, cookies, and biscuits, in case they headed there next. She needed to get herself together. This was, after all, the woman that John had almost married.

Sure enough, Aunt Elizabeth and the two women walked over to get some coffee and chat.

Kristen went to see how Anna was doing at the candy counter while she tried to keep one eye on Sadie. She breathed a sigh of relief. Maybe John would miss Sadie's visit. Her relief was short lived.

There he was, walking tall toward Sadie and her mother.

Unable to fully hear what was being said, Kristen could only hope that Sadie was talking about her new life in Pennsylvania. Was she engaged? Or did she move back to Stone Arabia?

"Kristen. Want a sample of fudge?"

Kristen could barely take her eyes off of Sadie and John. "Uh, sure, Anna. Which should I try? The vanilla or maple walnut?"

"Try both!"

Kristen took a sample of each onto a small napkin. When she looked back at John and Sadie they were walking out the door. Together.

Panic mounted on top of panic, and Kristen's throat closed up. She nearly gagged on the fudge. A fit of coughing overtook her.

"Kristen. Are you OK? Did you choke on a piece of walnut?" Anna's voice pealed through the store.

Jacob was the first to run to her. He began to pat her on the back. "Katie, come. Do whatever it is you do when someone is choking." Jacob waved his sister over.

Katie was about to intervene when Kristen swallowed the piece of fudge lodged in her throat. She held up her hand. "I'm OK. I had a piece of fudge stuck in my throat."

Anna stared with scared eyes.

"I ate so fast, I hardly chewed," Kristen was quick to add. She didn't want Anna to think it'd been her fault in any way. "Now, I better try a piece again, and chew it this time."

Anna kept her eyes fixed on Kristen's mouth as she chewed and slowly swallowed. "Umm, that's really good, Anna. I'm sorry if I scared you. I have to learn not to eat so fast, OK?"

Anna nodded, then with a new smile she asked, "Which do you like better?"

Kristen laughed along with Jacob and Katie.

"Ach, Kristen, you gave me a gut scare for sure." Jacob faced her now.

"I'm sorry. Thanks for coming to my rescue. And you too . . . Aunt Katie."

Katie smiled and nodded.

"So, do you like the way we set things up?" Kristen didn't know what to talk about with her new father and new aunt. She wished that Aunt Elizabeth or Aunt Miriam would come over, but they were talking with Sadie's mother, Lucy. Which meant that Sadie and John were still outside somewhere, alone together.

"I like it fine. Makes me realize how much I need to change some things around in my own store. My cousin doesn't always keep things organized. Different tools end up in the same crate and the rakes with the shovels."

"It probably don't matter much, Jacob. Because it's a store mostly for men folk, and men don't notice things like that, so long as they can get what they need," Katie teased in a soft voice.

"Jah, Cousin Margaret sometimes comes to mop the dirt she says we missed on the plank floors after we've swept up at the end of the day. We don't know what dirt she sees that we don't. Poor Margaret. She has her work cut out for her, jah?" Jacob laughed at his own words, and Katie shook her head with a smile.

"Aunt Elizabeth will probably be the same way. She has the floors at the house gleaming, even with the dirt that gets dragged in from the fields, especially on rainy days."

"I put out a rubber runner at my store on days it *makes wet.* It helps with the muddy boots and all."

"I'll have to tell that to Uncle Jonas," Kristen said.

"Tell me what, Niece?" Uncle Jonas startled her from behind.

"Oh! About Jacob's suggestion of putting a rubber runner by the door so customers won't drag in mud all over the place."

"I think that's a right gut idea. Denki, Jacob."

"I'll bring you one from the hardware store next time I visit." Jacob looked over at Kristen with a smile. "I'll be comin' more regular now."

"We'll be glad to see you back here any time." Uncle Jonas slapped Jacob on the back. Then he turned to Kristen. "Do you know where John is?"

Why was he asking her? "Um, well, no. No, I don't." She wasn't lying. She had no idea where John went. She only knew who he'd stepped out the door with. Kristen tried to sound nonchalant but her eyes began to burn as tears threatened.

Uncle Jonas hesitated. Did he notice her eyes filling up?

"I best go fetch him. Seems many of our church neighbors have arrived, and it would be gut if all of us were here to greet them."

The door jangled and Kristen recognized some of the faces from Preaching, although she didn't know them by name.

The women immediately gravitated toward the table displaying the Edna Lucille soaps and Mary's handkerchiefs.

Aunt Elizabeth rushed over to greet them.

The men shook hands with Uncle Jonas and Daniel then they all headed toward the back to the tools and bulk items.

No sign of John. Or Sadie.

John's anxiety mounted as Sadie went on with her litany of complaints about caring for her onkle in Lancaster. He had to get back to the store. Surely by now his absence was obvious. This was not the proper time or place for this, but Sadie had reasoned it was her only day in Stone Arabia and that John already knew the facts regarding her move to Pennsylvania. So, he gave her his ear.

"If I do one thing not to his liking, Onkle Samuel holds the farm and haus over my head as a threat in his own subtle way. Ach, it's terrible. David doesn't want me wearin' myself out trying to please my onkle after

314

we're married and ready to start a familye."

"I can't really tell you what to do about your onkle's attitude and difficult disposition, Sadie. But being that your beau feels the same about all of this, if I were him, I'd offer to buy the place and pay your onkle a little at a time once you're married. This way, carin' for him won't be done as some kind of trade for his haus and farm one day."

"But that was my onkle's idea right from the start."

John hadn't felt comfortable with her onkle's offer when she'd first proposed it to him while they were courting. Hearing how it was turning out made him all the more sure he'd made the right choice to part ways and stay in Stone Arabia.

"Maybe he felt he had no other choice, Sadie. 'Tis a sad thing to trade care for things. Especially in the Plain life. Just doesn't seem right, ain't so?"

Sadie glared at him. Her lips formed into the thin line he'd always hated whenever she got angry.

"Denki, John. We best be going now. My mamm must be wonderin' what became of me." She turned and quickly walked back to the store.

John picked up his pace behind her. How long had they been gone? Maybe Daed hadn't missed him much with all the folks comin' and going.

Kristen! Did she see him step outside with Sadie? What must she be thinking?

John didn't have long to wait for the ramifications of his absence. He spotted the bishop right off, standing with Daed by the counter where the kaffee and tea were served.

Madeline, the bishop's frau, stood with Mamm by the shelves where her homemade preserves were displayed.

He hadn't been there to greet them alongside the rest of the familye. John wondered what excuse Daed made for him.

He paused to summon his courage.

Kristen and Mary stood by the table of soaps and womenfolk items, talking with an Englisch lady who held a bar of soap in her hand.

Other neighbors wandered around the store taking a look at this and that.

But it was Anna who spotted him first.

"John! Come see how much fudge I sold already." Her excited voice rang through the store.

With that, all heads turned.

John walked to the candy counter as calm as he could. He knew that Daed's and Kristen's gazes were on him now and could only hope that Kristen didn't notice that he and Sadie were back at the same time. He'd explain it all to her later. For the time being he had better get himself over to where Daed, Daniel, and the bishop stood.

"Anna, your fudge is very popular. Save me a piece of the maple walnut for after supper tonacht, jah?"

Anna nodded enthusiastically to John.

He headed toward the kaffee and tea counter.

"Goede Mariye, Bishop. I'm sorry I was out back when you arrived." John reached out to shake the bishop's hand.

Daed took a sip of his kaffee at the same time Daniel did.

Fact is, he was out back; he just left out the part that he'd been there talking with Sadie.

"Vell, I'm glad you came when you did so I could extend my gut wishes to you with the store. I need to get back. I have another stop to make." The bishop took a cookie and walked off toward his frau.

Daed held his tongue 'til the door jangled behind the two of them as they left. "What were you doing out back for so long? You knew people would come to wish us vell. Of all times not to be here. The bishop is a busy man, and I'm sure he stayed longer than he'd intended waitin' on you. I told him you were around somewhere." Daed's eyes were fixed on John's face.

"Sadie wanted to talk with me about some trouble she's having in Lancaster. Said today was the only day she'd be here. I didn't intend to be gone for more than a few minutes."

"It was a half hour or more," Daed said as he refilled his cup with hot water.

"Jah, I know. Sorry."

"Ach, it's all right. At least you came in time to greet the bishop. Best you walk around and greet a few others who came while you were gone."

"OK, Daed." John turned to go when Daed put a hand on his shoulder.

"Is Sadie thinking of comin' back here, *sohn*?" His eyes had a twinkle in them.

"Nee. She's to be married soon to a farmer there. Just some trouble living with her onkle."

Was it his imagination or did Daed's face fall?

Sadie was a fine woman, and even though they'd known each other as kinner, they just didn't think alike. More than that, John didn't love her. He loved Kristen. And he had to explain his and Sadie's absence to her. Now.

John was back. And so was Sadie Krantz. Why did they go off together? Did he still feel something for her that he hadn't realized 'til he saw her today?

Sadie was the perfect example of a good Amish woman. Born into the community, raised here all of her life, and baptized into the faith. Everyone knew her family, and she could do all the things that many Amish women did so well: sew, cook, can, and of course, speak their Pennsylvania Dutch language. Sadie would be the perfect wife for any Amish man.

Unlike herself. She was like a quilt with mismatched patches. Maybe John's attraction to Kristen was just that. An attraction. She was all wrong for him. Probably all wrong for this life, too. If only God would give her a sign to keep going. To keep trying.

Jacob's voice broke through her thoughts. Her biological father. Her daed. Shouldn't that be enough of a sign? She *was* Amish. But the blood in her veins did not control the state of her heart and thoughts, and all that she was. Could that really be changed?

"Kristen, Katie and I will be going now. I hope to be seein' you again soon. Meantime,

Katie would velkum a visit from you if you'd like every now and again. She lives only a mile off from here."

"Um, sure. I'll come visit when I can," Kristen said, her eyes going from Jacob to Katie, who stood beside him. Then she remembered her idea about going to the Shore with Jacob for a weekend. "I was wondering if you'd want to come with me to New Jersey for a weekend to the house that I grew up in. Angela would be glad to drive us to the train."

Aunt Katie put her head down.

"Oh, and you can come too, Aunt Katie."

Katie smiled and shook her head.

"Nee, if Jacob can go, it would be gut for the two of you to get to know one another. As father and dochter, jah?"

Kristen nodded.

Aunt Katie was trying hard to make amends.

"Jah. I would like that very much, Kristen. This weekend?"

"Yes, if you don't have church on Sunday. We don't here."

"It's an off Sunday for us in Lowville, too. We can leave first thing Saturday morgen for whatever time you arrange with Angela. I'll come from Loweville to Katie's on Friday night so we'll be ready as early as

320

you like."

"That's great. I'll see if there's a train around 9:00 AM. Then I'll call Riley. He's the attorney in charge of the estate. He has the keys to the house. We'll stop at his office on the way to pick them up. He's only ten minutes from the house. Well, actually, from my house. It's legally mine now."

Kristen realized that no one else knew this just yet, except for John. She'd only found out the night before, and with the rush this morning to get to the store on time, she'd had no chance at breakfast to tell the whole family.

"Vell, then. You must be happy about that." Jacob showed no feelings about it one way or another. His smile remained intact, and his eyes held her gaze with the same steady warmth and kindness.

Kristen nodded. She wasn't sure how she felt about it either. All she could think of was John with Sadie.

"Katie, we best be seein' if Miriam wants a ride back with us or if she plans on stayin'." Jacob placed a hand under his sister's elbow.

"OK, then. I'll see you soon . . . Daed. Bye, Aunt Katie."

Jacob and Katie headed for the door as John walked toward her.

23

By the look on Kristen's face, John had to be careful how he worded his explanation of why he'd been with Sadie. Maybe he should just act as if nothing was wrong. Because, in truth, nothing was. He hadn't gone looking to spend time alone with Sadie. She'd sought him out and there wasn't a warm moment between them.

"John."

John stopped short at the familiar voice that called his name. There stood Sadie.

"I just want to say gut-bye. I'll be passing along your words to David about Onkle Samuel." Sadie smiled at him, and then turned to Kristen. "Sorry I didn't get a chance to visit with you, but I needed a friend's opinion about my onkle's stiff-fisted attitude and bent John's ear about it. Now I'll be off to bend the ear of David, my beau. I have a feeling that men think alike. John's suggestion might very vell give David a way to tame Onkle Samuel's stubbornness a bit."

"Oh, I hope so. Thanks for coming to see the store." Kristen's face brightened considerably.

John breathed a sigh of relief. In hindsight, Sadie probably realized that their chat together alone might have caused some uneasiness.

But what made her think she had to explain anything to Kristen? He'd never even been in Sadie's presence while with Kristen. Well, not since he'd been courting Sadie and the three of them had pizza together a few times. Were his feelings for Kristen apparent even then? Either way, he and Sadie wouldn't have lasted as a couple. He was glad that she had a new beau now.

"I bought my mamm a bar of the Edna Lucille soap in lavender." Sadie held the bar up to show them. "It's hard to find around here."

"What is it about that Edna Lucille soap you ladies love so much?" John shook his head and laughed, glad for the change of topic.

"It's one of those things men folk don't understand. Ain't so, Kristen?"

"Sooo true. I hope we can get more of them. We only have five left."

"I hear that they sell them online now, so

you can place an order that-a-way. This district allows the use of a computer for business orders and such," Sadie said, as she held the wrapped bar to her nose for a whiff.

"Are we finished with the soaps now?" John purposely crossed his arms and tilted his head in a show of impatience. Things had lightened up and a silly mood had come over him.

"Jah. We're finished. Mamm is waiting to go." Sadie bid her farewell and walked toward her mother.

Lucy caught John's gaze and waved.

He waved back, and then turned to Kristen.

She looked at him with a playful smile.

Maybe his silliness was contagious.

"What are you smiling at?" John asked.

"You. Me. Us. We make quite a pair."

"How so?"

"The whole Sadie thing. I saw how worried you looked when you first came over here."

"Vell, I figured you might've taken it the wrong way. I mean, with Sadie and me stepping outside alone for longer than I'd intended."

"I had my moments."

"Why, Kristen? You needn't doubt how I

feel for you. Don'tcha know that yet?"

Kristen fidgeted, and John wished he could give her a long deep kiss to prove his words and quell all of her misgivings. But of course, he couldn't. The Amish didn't kiss or hug in public. From the corner of his eye, he saw Mamm watching them.

Then the door jangled and in walked Angela.

"Hi, guys. I had to stop in on opening day to wish you luck. The place looks fabulous!"

"Denki, Angela. There's hot water for kaffee and tea, if you like. Mamm is over there by her preserves," John pointed in that direction. "Ach, Anna is waving frantically behind you from her candy counter. I think it would be a gut idea to visit her first."

Angela turned and waved at Anna.

"Oh, before you go. Are you free to drive me and Jacob Mast to the train station on Saturday morning around 8:00 AM?" Kristen asked.

"I'm pretty sure my slot is open then. I have to drive Mrs. Stolfus to the doctor that day at one o'clock, but that gives us plenty of time."

"Thanks, Angela. You'd better get going. Anna is waving again to get your attention."

Angela laughed and walked toward the candy counter.

John focused his attention back to Kristen.

She rubbed her hands together and chewed her bottom lip. "You agreed that it was a good idea for me to show Jacob where I grew up, right?"

"Very gut. Now I only wish you'd take my advice about not doubting me."

"John, I don't doubt you. I doubt myself. My life. Who I am. What I can and cannot do. My faith, too."

"Kristen, look how much Gott has revealed to you already about your life. An Amish familye you never knew about. Jacob being your daed. And now the haus at the beach being yours as it was intended to be. Pray and let it all unfold."

"I hadn't looked at it that way because everything happened so fast. I haven't had much of a chance to think with a clear head, let alone pray. And maybe I'm still a little mad at God."

"Best to count our blessings than our misfortunes, jah?"

"Jah, yourself! There's that preacher talk again." She gave John a playful punch in the arm.

"Ach, nee. I'm just telling you what helps me in tough times. Seriously, Kristen. Make time to pray and to be grateful for all the blessings coming into your life."

Kristen nodded.

John hoped she considered him one of her blessings. He thanked Gott every day for bringing her to Stone Arabia.

"I got my candy and a couple of jars of strawberry preserves, too," Angela said, walking toward them munching on a hunk of fudge. "Which reminds me, Kristen. Your Aunt Elizabeth asked if I'd drive you home to pick up the sandwiches she forgot this morning."

"OK. Sure. Should I bring a package of cheese for you, John?"

John grinned, glad that Kristen was in a happy teasing mood. Her face radiated joy straight to his heart. "Nee. Just bring back that smile you're wearing."

Kristen waited for Jacob before going inside the house. He stood before her with a generous smile.

"Vell, it's so long for now, dochter. I have to return the bishop's horse and buggy and join him and his family for dinner. It was gut being here for the opening of the store."

"Yes. An exciting day. OK, then. See you on Saturday."

"Jah. Saturday."

That night Kristen and Mary helped Aunt

Elizabeth put together a quick supper of cold meats, bread, pickles, and a slaw. It'd been a long day at the store and a simple meal was in order.

She wasn't sure if this was the right time to share her news with the family. They were tired and so was she. But she needed to tell them tonight about a decision she'd made as she'd helped set out the food.

When the silent prayer was over, Kristen took a few slices of ham from the plate passed to her, reached for a piece of bread, and spooned some relish onto it to make an open sandwich. She couldn't eat until she'd said what needed to be told. John was the only one she'd told, and she knew he wouldn't share the news until she announced it.

"I have two things I need to tell everyone tonight. I know we're all exhausted, but I'll make it as short as I can."

"Sure, Niece. Go ahead. Listening doesn't take much work." Uncle Jonas folded his hands in front of him and waited.

The others now focused on her instead of the food before them.

"OK. Um, the first thing is that I received a call from Riley Gallagher to let me know that Mattie Cook transferred the deed of Ross's house to me. She said she didn't feel right taking what she knew Ross wanted me to have."

"That's gut news, Kristen," Uncle Jonas said as Aunt Elizabeth nodded in agreement.

"Does that mean you're moving back there?" Anna put her sandwich down and became very serious.

"No, Anna. But it does mean that I can't take the job at the Farm Style Diner." Kristen turned her gaze to Mary. "I'm sorry, Mary. I'll tell Mrs. Kraus when we go tomorrow morning. But I haven't left her high and dry. On the way back to getting the sandwiches for lunch this afternoon, I had Angela stop at Katie Mast's house. She seems so lonely and all. I decided to ask her if she'd like to apply for the job. She loved the idea."

"Denki, Kristen. I'm sure it will be fine with Mrs. Kraus. But why won't you be able to work there?"

"I want to spend some time at the house to clean it out and decide what I want to keep, and what I can sell or donate. It might take two weeks or so to get it all done."

"I thought you were going there with Jacob for the weekend?" John got ahead of her.

She should have told him this before they

left the store earlier, but he was busy with Daniel in the back rearranging things.

"Yes, I am. But I got to thinking . . . I'll probably need time to go through everything. I won't be able to do much with Jacob there, so I'm thinking a week, maybe two to get it all together. Jacob will take a train back here on Sunday afternoon, and Angela will drive him back to Katie's. He can then go back to Lowville whenever he wants."

"Is it safe to stay there alone?" Aunt Elizabeth fiddled with her kapp strings. Uh-oh, she was nervous.

"I've stayed there alone more often than not. I'll call Angela every day so she can tell you what I'm up to." Kristen smiled, hoping to disarm the worry that had etched onto everyone's faces.

John's held more than worry. There was a distinct trace of sadness there too.

"You'll all be glad to be rid of me for a while," Kristen teased.

John pushed his plate away and stood. "I'll be eating later."

"John!" Onkle Jonas's voice rang out clear and loud.

John turned and waited for him on the porch.

Aunt Elizabeth motioned for everyone to

eat again by lifting the platter of ham out and waiting for someone to take it in the fog of tension that now hovered among them.

24

"I don't know what is going on between you and Kristen. But it would be best if you kept your head in the presence of others, jah?"

"I'm sorry, Daed. It bothers me that Kristen doesn't yet feel that we care about her. That comment about us being glad to be rid of her got to me."

"John, Kristen's mamm was broken and I *s'pect* she did her best to raise her, but it doesn't surprise me that Kristen turned out broken, too. It takes time to fix what's broke, jah?" Daed gave John a pat on the shoulder and turned to go.

"Daed, I'm trying to fix her."

"Jah, I can see that. But some things only the Lord can fix. You'll need more patience. She'll soon have time to sort things out. Meanwhile, we'll keep her in our prayers."

Sort what out? Plain or Englisch. Kristen was caught in-between. Her half Plain, half Englisch clothes practically called out for a decision.

John sighed as his daed went back to finish his supper. While he was frustrated with Kristen, he also felt sorry for her confused state of heart, mind, and soul. *Please, Lord, let her find herself. And let me be a help and not a hindrance to her.*

"John. John." Anna ran toward him.

"You said to save you a piece of the maple walnut fudge. It's waiting on your plate inside." She was breathless from running.

"Ach, Anna. Denki for remembering. I guess I better finish off my sandwich first."

"Jah. Mamm left it on the table. Said you'd be back soon enough." Anna grabbed his hand. "Come."

"Is Kristen still at the table?"

"Jah, but she's done with supper. She's waiting to help me make more fudge for tomorrow. It's easy. Wanna watch?"

"I'll watch while I finish my supper." It would be Kristen he'd be watching more than the making of fudge. But when they walked into the kitchen, Mary was at the counter getting the ingredients for fudge ready.

"Where'd Kristen go, Mary?" Anna's face immediately fell.

"She went off to bed with a headache, Anna. Told me to tell you gut nacht. I'll help with the fudge for a bit."

Anna frowned.

John shared her sentiment as he took a seat to finish his sandwich. Daed and Mamm were probably in bed, too. It'd been a big day. He wished he hadn't left the table during supper in such a huff and hoped he wasn't the cause of Kristen's headache.

Mary put down the sugar and turned to John and Anna with her hands on her hips. "Vell, I don't feel too appreciated right now."

"Sorry, Mary. I wanted to teach Kristen how to make the fudge. She said she had a lot to learn about making desserts." Anna opened the ice box and got out some butter.

"How about I stay and learn?" John asked.

Anna giggled. "Menfolk don't make fudge."

Mary turned to John with a mischievous smile. "Ach, I think you want to learn so you can teach Kristen. Ain't so, Brudder?"

His reaction earlier in front of his family revealed more than he'd intended. "I won't be denying that, Sister." He returned her smile and they got to work.

The next morgen when John entered the kitchen with Daed and Daniel, Anna was filling a basket with wrapped fudge, while Mamm and Mary placed breakfast on the table. Where was Kristen?

When they took their seats, he could stand it no longer. "Is Kristen still feeling grank?"

"Nee. She asked us before bed last nacht if she could go to the haus a few days early. She wants to *redd up* the place before Jacob's visit. Angela picked her up half an hour ago. Jacob will go as planned over the weekend." Daed ended his words with a slow nod, his gesture of approval on the matter.

So, that was why she went up to bed so quick. Probably called Angela on her cell phone to arrange for a ride, and then talked it over with Mamm and Daed. Couldn't she have waited a little longer to say good-bye? Had he driven her off? Was she staying longer than two weeks?

"What about Kristen going to talk with Mrs. Kraus at the diner this morgen about Katie?" Maybe he could get more details if he prodded with sensible questions.

"Ach, Mrs. Kraus won't mind once I tell her that Katie will be coming today to apply for the job. So long as she can get someone to work the morgen hours." Mary seemed perfectly fine with it too.

In fact, everyone seemed fine with Kristen's earlier departure. Except him. He decided to prod a little further. "Did you get to say gut-bye to Kristen, Anna?"

Daed let out an impatient sigh.

"Jah. I gave her some fudge to bring to her beach haus. She said she'd bring me back salt water taffy."

"That sounds gut." John's insides finally unfurled.

Kristen would be back. Of course she would.

The first thing Kristen had to do when she arrived in Bradley Beach was to meet with Mattie Cook and Riley to finalize Mattie's wishes for the house. She decided to have the taxi drop her at Riley's office for their appointment before heading for the house. After all, it wasn't hers . . . yet.

Even though Kristin had met Mattie many times over the years she was still unsettled about seeing her. Maybe deep inside, she blamed her relationship with Ross for the ultimate demise of her mom.

When Kristen entered Riley's office, Mattie sat at his desk. Red curls framed her freckled tanned face and the 'I Love Boating' tee revealed well defined muscles. As always, her love of the outdoors emanated from her rugged yet simple demeanor.

Kristen nodded and sat in the chair next to Mattie facing Riley behind his large, gleaming mahogany desk. While she was grateful for Mattie's generous action of transferring the title to her name, it was awkward being in the same room with Alex's mother. Of course, the logical part of her knew that it wasn't Mattie's fault that her son was unstable.

Riley told them each where to sign.

There was a tremor in Mattie's hand.

"Are you sure you want me to have the house? Ross left it to you, not to me. So you have nothing to feel guilty about." Kristen's words hung in the air before Mattie nodded and her pen touched down.

She signed and dotted the 'i' in her name then slid the paper over to Kristen and handed her the pen. After Kristen had signed it, Mattie turned to her and held out her hand.

"Many blessings, Kristen. And I'm so sorry."

"Sorry?"

"If it hadn't been for my boy, your mom would be alive now. I feel I should apologize for him. He's too crazed to have remorse, I think."

Kristen blinked back the sting of tears in her eyes. She'd lost her mom, and Mattie had lost Ross and her chance for a happy marriage to him. Now all she had was a very disturbed, angry son.

"It wasn't your fault, Ross's, or Mom's. It was Alex . . ." Kristen let her words trail off.

"Yes, my Alex had his own ideas about us. He despised Ross just because he wasn't his father. If only I'd known what he was capable of doing. I'm so sorry." This time Mattie's eyes filled with tears. But she quickly swiped them away and stood to go.

All the while, Riley had sat there, quiet, listening to the sad account of the demise of his two good friends. He quickly got on with things. Professional as ever. "Thank you, ladies. All I have to do is file this with the county, and we're all set. Kristen, once you're of legal age you can live in the house again, if you like. Here are the keys." Riley held them out to Kristen.

Now it was her hand that held a tremor.

"Hold on a sec. I forgot all about that letter you found for Kristen, Mattie."

"Oh, yes. It was under the kitchen table when I'd gone to the house to . . . pray, as soon as I'd heard that Ross had left the place to me. I went over, sat in the living room chair I always sat in when invited to the house, and prayed for him and your mother. And for you. I came away with my decision right then and there. Anyway, on my way out the back door I spotted an envelope on the kitchen floor with your name on it. I gave it to Riley to safe keep for you." Mattie cast Kristen a timid smile.

Mattie prayed for them? In her time of shock and grief, she'd prayed? Was God trying to get a message through to her?

"Thank you." Kristen took the envelope from Riley and glanced at it. *To: Kristen. From: Mom.* A shiver ran through her.

Friday was already here, and Kristen's unoccupied chair across from John continued to match the emptiness in his heart. He ate his meals quicker than usual to make short of his pain and to avoid any conversation that might lead to the topic of Kristen at her beach haus.

So far, whenever Angela stopped by to tell Mamm of Kristen's latest news, he'd been at the store. While he wanted to know that she was all right, he feared any news that might hint of her former world claiming her for its own. The only word he wanted to hear was that Kristen was coming back. To stay. With him.

John was about to go hitch the buggy to Old Faithful and begin another day at the store with Mary and Daed, when Aenti Miriam opened the screened door.

"Goede Mariye, John. I came to help your mamm catch up on some bread and pie baking before we go to the store this afternoon."

"That's gut. Hope there's a cherry pie in the batch." John smiled and turned to go.

"Hold on a minute." Aenti Miriam stepped inside and handed John a shopping bag. "Here, I made a cherry and a blueberry pie last nacht for the kaffee counter. Now you'll have your cherry pie."

"Denki, Aenti. I'll ask Mary to slice it as soon as we get there. She's upstairs getting her bag."

"I visited with Katie yesterday. Jacob will be on the train to New Jersey first thing tomorrow morgen. He's looking forward to learning about Kristen's life and seeing her again. It's such a blessing, ain't so?"

"Jah. That it is." John opened the screen door to go. He wasn't up for this conversation. He missed Kristen too much to speak about her.

"Did you talk to her on Angela's phone when she called?" Aenti Miriam pressed on.

"Nee, I've been at the store." John leaned against the opened screen door.

"Maybe Angela can say a hullo for you to

Kristen." Aenti Miriam kept on the topic.

Mary came down the stairs. "I'd like her to say hullo from me, too. Can you tell Angela that later, Mamm?" Mary waited for Mamm's nod then walked outside.

John said nothing. Finally, he closed the screened door behind him.

When Mary and Daed were settled in the buggy, John flicked the reins and Old Faithful trotted toward the road.

"You know, I'm not one for meddling in anyone's business. But this time I just have to tell you, Brudder, you're acting like a pouting little boy. Not even a hullo to Kristen. It wonders me, John. It really wonders me."

" 'Tis not a matter for you to be wondering about," he said as he flicked the reins again to hurry Old Faithful along. The sooner they got to the store, the better. In his whole life, Mary had never voiced her disapproval of anything that John had done. He must be acting like a real dummkopf for her to speak out that way to him.

Daed kept silent. At least for the time being.

After tending to several customers with a pasted smile on his face, John decided to take heed to Mary's admonition.

She was a quiet but observant young

woman, and her spoken words held much introspection behind them.

He walked over to where his sister stood by Mamm's cherry preserves and church peanut butter. She'd just opened a box of the blueberry ready to be added to the shelves.

"Don't we sell letter writing paper?"

Mary turned from the jars with a brightened face.

"Jah, we do. We have the plain white kind, some yellow with the state bird on it, and the light blue." She led him to the end of the aisle where the school supplies were kept. "There," she pointed.

John remembered when Kristen had measured all these shelves and suggested the items that would best go on each of them.

"I don't s'pose you have the address of Kristen's place at the beach handy, do you?"

Why would Kristen want to come back to him if she thought he didn't care enough to even ask how she was? He couldn't let his own fear of what she might say in regard to her former world cut her off dry until she said the only words he longed to hear. It was downright foolish indeed.

"Nee, not here. It's at the haus. I think I'll write Kristen a letter, too. We'll address the letters at home when Mamm, Aenti Miriam, and Anna come to relieve us at lunch time. I'll have Anna write something at the end of my letter. She'll be thrilled about doing that, jah?"

"Listen, Mary. I'm sorry about being snippy with you on the way over here. I'm not myself lately, is all." John was tempted to tell her more. He wanted a woman's opinion on what he should do while waiting to see if the girl he loved would come back to Stone Arabia for always.

"Ach, I was just being sensitive. You remember when I was courting David Schultz and how he never wrote to me even once whenever he'd go back to Pennsylvania to visit his brudder?"

John nodded.

Mary had been crazy in love with David Schultz two years back.

"It wondered me how he didn't yearn to pick up a paper and pencil and write his thoughts to me. Vell, now I see why the gut Lord made sure we didn't stay a couple for too long."

"Truth be told, Mary, I'm not sure I want to hear Kristen's thoughts about New Jersey and her beloved ocean and haus there. I want to hear that she misses us and our way of life here."

"Kristen can be fond of a place and its

things and still miss us and her life here, ain't so?"

"She'll always be caught in the middle of both worlds unless she misses one more than the other." John took a sheet of the yellow paper with the bluebird on it and a matching envelope.

"Seems to me that it's not so much about places and things as it is about people. Her familye is here now. And you're here, John. She needs time to make peace with her memories, is all. But she can't make a life out of them there."

"How'd I get such a *schmart* sister?"

"Ach, go on! Write your letter back here while I tend to the customer who just came in." Mary leaned around the shelves and peered down the aisle to see who jingled the door. "Ach, it's just big Ben from the farm down the road. Probably wants to have a gab session with Daed by the tool bin." Mary pulled out a sheet of white paper from the shelf and headed up front.

John took a composition book and walked to the next aisle where the wooden stools that Daniel made were displayed. He grabbed one to sit on, placed his paper on the composition book and began to write to Kristen.

Mary had said that it wondered her how

David hadn't yearned to write his thoughts to her. John's yearning for Kristen went beyond mere letter writing. He longed to see her face, hear her voice, and have her presence across from him at the table again. That was the truth of it and that's what he wanted to write in his letter to her.

Dear Kristen . . .

25

Kristen did a good job eliminating the musty smell that had taken residence in the house since it'd been closed up. But that wasn't unusual for a place only a block from the ocean. She'd left the windows opened the last few days to give it a good airing out. Now it smelled clean and fresh like the ocean.

The fridge had been emptied and turned off the night before she'd left to stay with Cindy and her family. She shuddered at the memory. She'd been so scared and bewildered. Felt so alone. Things had certainly changed since then. Tomorrow her Amish father was coming to visit and see the place where she'd grown up.

She wore Englisch clothes while here. Shorts and a t-shirt today. A skirt and quarter sleeved t-shirts for the weekend. Not Plain by any means, but not too shocking for Jacob.

Kristen wanted everything in the house to sparkle, be neat, and welcoming. She straightened out all the magazines that were on the coffee table, went over the wooden floors with a damp mop, cleaned the kitchen counter, sink, and placemats on the table with a soapy sponge. Then she uncluttered the guest room and made up the bed with clean sheets.

Later that afternoon, she walked to Del-Ponte's on Main Street for rolls and Danish for breakfast, and cookies and pastries for dessert as a special treat for Jacob. If he was open for Italian food for supper, she'd order in from Citricos. She had just enough money from her meager bank account to cover it all, but she expected to have more once she sold some of the odds and ends that her mom had accumulated as gifts from guests at the hotel. There was also a load of books in Ross's office on business topics that she could sell on eBay.

So far, she hadn't seen Cindy or any of her other beach girlfriends. She had no intention of seeing Derick, and she wasn't too keen on running into any of the parents of her friends either. Undoubtedly, they didn't even want her there with all that had happened and the ongoing investigation of the accident.

As she walked back from Main Street she thought of how many times in her life she'd walked up and down these same blocks. She detoured to Brinely Avenue and passed Ascension Catholic Church. She remembered the time she'd stopped in as a young teenager to see what it looked like inside. It was dark, quiet, and had a smell of candle wax. She'd sat down and felt very at peace in those moments. Neither her mom nor Ross had been church goers, so she'd never gone to services.

Kristen stopped in front of the church. John's encouraging words to pray echoed in her mind. She climbed the steps and tried the door. It was open.

Quietly, she stepped inside. The scent of candle wax was no longer there. Instead, there were electric candles. The quiet and peacefulness was unchanged. She took a seat in one of the pews midway into the church and closed her eyes.

She jumped at a sound. Someone putting change in the poor box. She'd fallen asleep. For how long? She took out her cell phone. Four o'clock. She'd dozed off for little over a half hour. *Guess I needed the rest, Lord. I also need You to show me what to do with my life. Let me know if You truly intend for me to be Plain or to come back here and start anew.*

And . . . if there is some way you can work John into the picture, I'd be forever grateful. I don't think I could be in either world without him. Even though he acted like a total jerk at the table Monday night. Well, maybe not a total jerk. More like, fed up with my comments. I left without saying good-bye, so I could get back at him. Sorry, Lord. I'll call Angela and ask her to say hello to John for me. I miss him so much. Why did I wait four days?

The first of August promised to be a beautiful day, and John was happy that Jacob would have such fine weather for his visit to the beach. He only wished he could be there, too. But this was Kristen's time with her daed. Not his. Not yet.

Daed had dumped out the last bucket of sweet corn into the wheel barrow. "That should be enough to sell outside in front of the store. We got a good harvest this year."

"Jah, I bet we'll be having lots of corn fritters and corn puddin' for supper the next couple weeks. Mamm has lots of corn recipes on hand."

Daed nodded. "John, before we head out to the store, I want to remind you that in order to court a young lady in our district, both have to be baptized before going public together on buggy rides and to singings and what not."

"I know that, Daed. I used to court Sadie, remember?"

"Jah, that I do. But Sadie is baptized."

"This is about Kristen, ain't so?"

"Just want to be respectful of Jacob. He's her daed, after all."

"Jah, I know that too, Daed. And I'm right sure that Jacob approves of my feelins' for Kristen."

"Just the same. There's an order to how things are done in the Plain life, and you need to abide by it. If Kristen comes back same as she left, you'll both need to be thinking on matters."

John knew exactly the matters Daed was referring to. It wouldn't be long before the bishop started to question Kristen's intentions regarding her faith. Her eighteenth birthday was soon approaching, and she'd be of legal age to do as she pleased, regarding which life she chose. If she wanted to stay here, she'd need to show a steadfast desire to live Plain and then be approved for instructions. If she didn't, John couldn't court her without risk to his own future in Stone Arabia.

"I know, Daed. I know."

John grabbed the large bucket and walked off toward Old Faithful and the buggy. He took out the large sack in the backseat that was to be filled with the corn that Daed pushed along in the wheel barrow.

"Daed. I won't do anything to shame you or Jacob. And neither would Kristen. I can tell you that."

Daed nodded then began to place the corn into the sack that John held open.

There was nothing more that John could say. His and Kristen's fate was in Gott's hands. He had to take the advice he'd given Kristen. Trust in the Lord's plan. *Trust.* That was the key word. *Help me, Lord. I'm grateful that I never told her it'd be easy. It isn't, is it?*

Kristen paced back and forth on the front wooden porch waiting for Jacob's arrival. She knew that when he gazed out the window of the taxi as it headed out from the train station to the house, he'd see all that was part of his beloved Emily's life and that of his only child's.

The groups of stores that would flash by. The various eateries, ice cream shops, and bait and tackle stores. The tree-lined blocks tucked in from the main road, and the large homes that graced each corner with wrap around porches and beautiful flowers.

He'd most likely see young women wearing flip-flops, halter tops and shorts, walking dogs and riding bikes. There'd be shirt-less men here and there, hosing off their shiny cars or watering the front gardens. This was the Englisch world. Kristen's world.

When the taxi pulled up to the house, Kristen ran down from the porch to greet Jacob.

"Hullo, Kristen."

"Hi, Jacob. Did you have a good trip?"

She took his small overnight bag and the shopping bag that held his black vest and straw hat. She smiled when she noticed he'd worn navy jeans, a white shirt and baseball cap. He looked like a combo folk singer lumberjack guy.

"Jah, it was very gut. Denki." He paid the taxi driver and followed Kristen up the porch steps of the beach house.

She bid him to take a seat on one of the two Adirondack white wooden chairs.

He gazed at the ice bucket on the small round table between them.

"I thought you might like a cold drink before I take you on a tour of the house and the area." She reached under the ice and retrieved two lemonade Snapples and poured each of them a cupful.

"Denki. I could use a cool drink. Pink lemonade. I haven't had this in a while."

"I like it because it's pink. Do you think it tastes different than the regular lemonade?"

"Your aenti Katie used cherry syrup when she made it for me as a kind. It gave it a sweeter flavor."

"I buy this brand because they use natural ingredients. Let's see . . . the label says that the coloring is from vegetable juices. No artificial coloring."

"You made a gut choice then. It's very tasty."

"Oh! Are you hungry? I can order sandwiches if you want to eat now. I have cookies in the meantime. It's eleven o'clock. A long while since you've eaten breakfast," she rambled.

Jacob smiled. "Not any longer than any other day. We usually eat around noon. I'm fine. Denki. We'll eat whenever you like."

"Um, OK. I'll phone for the sandwiches from the deli at noon. Do you like turkey?"

"Jah. I do. I pretty much eat nearly everything, although I've never taken a liking to rhubarb pie, even with strawberries."

Kristen laughed. "Well, I'm glad I didn't get us rhubarb pie for dessert tonight. I never had it, but it doesn't look very appetizing. Reminds me of red celery." She laughed again, and Jacob joined her. Relief weaved itself into her laughter. So far, their small talk was going well.

"Would you like to see the house now? Then maybe we can take a walk to the beach after lunch."

"Jah. That sounds gut."

Kristen stood and held the screened door open for Jacob. He entered the home that Emily, Kristen, and Ross had lived in for nearly eighteen years. A home that was only four hours from Stone Arabia, but a world apart in every other aspect.

"It's not a big house, but it was big enough for us." Kristen assumed that Ross's house appeared small to Jacob in comparison to some of the Amish homes that housed large families. Like the Waglers' home.

John flashed into her mind, and she had to refocus.

"It's a nice size from what I can see," Jacob told her, his eyes darting about.

"The bedrooms are upstairs. I have the guest room all ready for you." She motioned to the stairs. "I'll show you where you'll be sleeping." Kristen walked up, turned and waited for Jacob to reach the landing. "Down the hall, there." She pointed and led the way.

"This is a nice room, Kristen. Denki for making it up for me."

Now that she looked at it, her effort at preparing it for him was a bit obvious. The furniture gleamed, as did the window panes. There was still a slight scent of the lemon polish she'd used. The local newspapers sat neatly in a magazine holder next to the bed, as well as a Bible on the night stand. The wildflowers in the small glass vase on the bureau were noticeably fresh. If Jacob could see all the clutter she'd moved out of the room into the basement maybe he'd find it humorous.

"I'm glad you like it. There's a bathroom down the hall with a sink and shower. No outhouse here." Oops! Did she sound as if she was poking fun at that?

"Jah. I know that the Englisch have indoor plumbing. Some Amish communities have it, too. Did you know that a few haushalds in your district have special permission for it due to health reasons?"

"No. I didn't know there were exceptions to the rule. Not having indoor plumbing is the thing I find hardest to get used to in Stone Arabia. I hope one day they'll change the rule about that."

Jacob laughed. "Being born without indoor plumbing makes it easier I s'pose. I can see how the opposite can make it hard to take."

"I guess anyone can get used to anything if they have to. Some things about this place aren't easy to take if you come from Stone Arabia."

"Jah? What things might those be?" Jacob cocked back his head with a curious blink.

"Traffic for one thing. Look outside. The parking spots are nearly all taken already by those who come from other areas to go to the beach. And being so close to the ocean can make it very damp here at times, and it feels as if it goes right through your bones. When there's a storm in the forecast, we have to listen to the news to see if we'll be evacuated due to flooding. So far, we've only been flooded here once. The basement got two feet of water that time. Ross had to rent a water pump and then get a dehumidifier to keep mold from forming. Things like that."

"I never thought of the problems with living so near to the ocean. I guess every place has its gut and not-so-gut things, jah?"

Jacob had a good point. Bradley beach had its problems along with its beauty. As does living Plain in Stone Arabia. Her mom once told her that there was no perfect place on earth. That only Heaven was perfect. She'd nearly forgotten those words.

"Heaven, according to my mom, is the

only perfect place. Well, let's go downstairs, and I'll order us some sandwiches."

Jacob didn't move. He looked at Kristen with surprise again. "Your mamm told you that?"

"Uh huh. Why?"

"I used to tell your mamm that. She'd get mad at me for it sometimes. Vell, not really mad. Just pretended to be mad, is all." Jacob looked sad all of a sudden. He must have loved Mom a lot.

Kristen wondered what her life would have been like had they stayed together. Would she still have met John?

"How long did you know my mom before you courted her?"

"Ach, our whole life. We grew up in the same district so went to the same Preaching services and school. Then later we attended the same classes for German and for baptism instructions. After that we started going to singings together, and before you know it, we were a couple."

"You look so happy talking about her. I hope one day someone will look as happy when they talk about me," Kristen said, leading them both down the stairs.

"Someone already does," Jacob told her as they entered the kitchen.

Kristen picked up Sonny's Deli take-out

menu, but her gaze focused on Jacob instead of the sandwich choices. "Really? Who?"

"The Waglers. All of them care a great deal for you, Kristen. Little Anna's eyes light up at the mention of your name. And I could say the very same thing about John."

"John?" Kristen cleared her throat at the high pitch sound of her own voice. "He's a good friend, but I think I'm more of a pain in the neck to him than anything else, especially since I'm nearly four years younger than he is. He's been my sounding board from day one about all of my problems. I came with a lot of baggage, as they say. It's not really fair to him. Or to any of the Waglers."

"Doesn't seem like a matter of fair or unfair. Seems more like a matter of situations beyond your control. Beyond the control of any of us."

"Maybe. But I've been more trouble than anything else to that family."

"Your familye," Jacob emphasized.

Kristen sighed. "Well, yes, that's true. But I'm different than all of them. I didn't grow up Plain like they did. Like you. I'm the oddball because of that. Even if I was baptized, people will probably not think of me as being Plain."

"Kristen. Each of us is who Gott made us

to be. We're on a journey of doing Gott's will from the moment we enter the world. You were born of Plain parents. But Gott placed you on a different path. Who can question His ways?"

Kristen laughed. "Now you sound like John. I guess it's an Amish thing. I'll try not to question God's will, even though I don't understand it at all." She picked up the phone to call in their lunch order, and Jacob took a seat at the table. Who would've ever thought that she had an Amish father? And that he'd be sitting at her kitchen table? Before June, she'd never even given a thought to the Amish. Hadn't ever seen a Plain person. Little did she know.

After lunch Jacob walked to the beach with Kristen. She asked him to wait while she got them each a pass for the day. Then she waved him on and they walked onto the crowded beach.

Colored towels and blankets were strewn about most of the sand. Beach chairs and umbrellas occupied nearly every other spot on the beach.

"It's always packed like this on weekends during the summer. But once Labor Day comes, all the bennies are gone."

"Bennies?"

"Yes. That's what the locals here at the shore call the outsiders who come here to soak up the *beneficial* rays. Bennies. Get it?"

Jacob laughed. "Jah. I get it. The Amish use nicknames, too, you know. Like we call, Ben Gaber, Big Ben, and Ben Zook, Skinny Ben."

"That's right, I forgot about that. Imagine the nickname they'd have for me?"

Jacob stopped walking to look at her. "Beautiful Kristen." He averted his eyes. "Jah, that's a gut nickname for you, dochter. You have a beautiful heart."

26

Kristen was unable to sleep. She focused on the sound of the ocean through the open window. It soothed her some, but she worried about what Jacob thought after seeing the world she'd lived in all of her life. Did he have doubts as to whether she could conform to life in Stone Arabia? Would he trample down his doubts just because she had no other family and had been born to Amish parents?

Dawn was only a short time away. She turned to find a more comfortable position when she heard her mom's bedroom door creak. She snapped up, got out of bed, slipped into her terry robe and walked toward what had been her mom's room.

The door was ajar. She tiptoed closer and looked inside.

Jacob stood before the framed photos on the bureau. He picked up the one of her mom holding her as an infant. Ross stood behind them smiling. He stared at it without a flinch.

"I was a month old when that photo was taken."

Jacob swung around nearly dropping the framed photo.

"I accidentally opened this door instead of the bathroom. And I saw the photos."

Kristen nodded and walked over to stand next to him. He was family, and she was not about to enforce trespassing rules.

"And in this one, I was eight." She handed him another framed photo of a young girl on the beach holding a pail full of water, wearing a big smile.

"You were a happy kind, jah?"

"At the beach, I was always happy," she said, studying the photo.

"Only at the beach?"

"Well, no. It's just that I was lonely a lot not having any siblings, with my mother working so much. But when she was home with me, we had nice times. I need to remember those more than the lonesome ones."

"Jah, that would be best. Who is the woman in this photo?" Jacob handed Kristen another framed photo. She was with a blonde haired, older woman sitting on a bench on the boardwalk.

"Oh. That's Sylvia. When I was in grammar school, she picked me up each day and stayed with me 'til Mom came home. She was very nice and made me great ice cream sodas. She doesn't live too far from here."

"What about playmates? Didn't you have any kinner to play games with?"

Kristen's mind went back down the years. Images flashed in her mind like so many photos. "Sure, I had some friends. We played together mostly during lunch time in the schoolyard. And on the weekends, I'd go to the movies or on the boardwalk with them. But after school, most of us stayed at home. The difference was that my friends had brothers and sisters, and they did their homework together. Like Cindy and her brother."

"And that's why you felt lonely, jah?"

"Partly. Not having family over on holidays like my friends did, made me feel lonely, too. Sometimes, my mom had to work at the hotel on Christmas and Ross would be away on business. I'd be sent over to Cindy's house to be with her family. I loved sitting at their dinner table and secretly wished they were my family."

Jacob placed the framed photo back on the bureau.

She didn't see pity when he looked at her.

She saw a quiet understanding.

"Vell, had you grown up Plain, you would've been too tired from chores to play with the other kinner for very long."

Even though his words were meant to lighten the topic, they were also very true. From her short time with the Amish, she noted how children had their chores cut out for them at an early age. But for the most part, the children, like Anna, seemed anxious to please and no complaints were heard.

"Anna never seems tired. At least not compared to me." Kristen told him with a laugh.

"Jah, she is full of energy. Maybe it's that fudge she likes so much," Jacob teased.

Kristen laughed again. She was now fully at ease with Jacob . . . her father.

"Probably all that sugar revs her up. Well, while you get yourself washed up, I'll go make us some breakfast to rev us up, OK?"

"Sounds gut to me."

They left the bedroom, and Kristen went downstairs as Jacob entered the bathroom. She heard him turn on the water in the sink and realized she'd forgotten the clean towels in the dryer.

She retrieved a couple and ran upstairs to give them to him when she heard him talking. She stood back from the partially closed door.

"Jacob Mast, it should have been you standing behind Emily and Kristen all those years ago."

Kristen stepped closer. She had to strain to hear him.

"Ach! Katie. How I wish you hadn't done what you did."

Tears welled in Kristen's eyes but she stood perfectly still. She knew she should walk away, but she wanted to give him the towels and would wait until the talking stopped.

He continued. "Jacob Mast, you will take up where Emily Esh left off. Kristen is your dochter. The gut Lord brought you both together at last. It is truly a blessing for sure and for certain." He stopped.

She waited a few more seconds to be sure and then knocked on the door. "I forgot to give you towels . . . Daed."

He took them and gazed into her misted eyes. He probably realized that she'd heard what was said. Yet his wide smile conveyed only affection and joy. And even though the Amish did not encourage much physical affection, she leaned over and kissed him on the cheek then scurried back downstairs to fix them both a tasty breakfast made with the love that was bursting from her heart.

While they ate, Kristen was pleased that Jacob took a second helping of the scrambled eggs she'd served at the table right from the pan. She realized that this was the first time she'd ever cooked for anyone all on her own, except for herself.

"Tell me. Did you grow up Christian, dochter?"

The question surprised her.

"Uh-huh. Catholic, actually. It's the church closet to us, and Mom said she had me baptized there. She wasn't a church goer and so I only attended Masses there with Cindy and her family for Christmas and Easter. Sometimes I'd stop in for a while by myself."

"So, being in Stone Arabia is your first experience with a church community then."

Jacob put his fork down for a moment and looked at her with a frown and raised brows. She couldn't tell if it was sorrow, compassion, or both that she saw in his eyes.

"Well . . . yes. I didn't know any of the parishioners at the church here because I wasn't there regularly."

Jacob resumed eating.

"To be honest, the best part about church services in Stone Arabia is the gathering and the food afterwards," she said.

He chuckled at her comment and she laughed with him.

"Jah, that is always gut. I am sure many others will agree with you on that."

"But seriously . . . Daed. I like not being alone and anonymous anymore."

Jacob nodded. He gazed at her with a quiet understanding. No more frown, no sanctimonious words.

Kristen smiled and her father smiled back as they resumed eating their eggs and toast. She basked in the ease between them now.

#

After Kristen waved good-bye to Jacob as his taxi departed, she went to her room to begin the arduous task of cleaning out her closet and drawers. She decided to tackle one room at a time during her two-week stay. Then she'd have time to touch up some of the white paint that had chipped off from the molding, and give attention to more detailed things. The house had surely been neglected.

She'd filled a large black plastic bag and as she tied it closed her cell phone rang. She'd clipped it onto the waistband of her jeans, and quickly saw the caller ID as Angela's. "Hi, Angela. What's up?"

"I have a few messages for you. Mary asked me to say hello, as did Anna, your aunt and uncle, and John. Then later on I saw your aunt Miriam, and she also asked me to give you her best."

John was the only name Kristen focused on. Not that she didn't appreciate greetings from the others, but Angela never mentioned John in any of her previous daily calls.

"So, John is added to the greeting list, I see. That's nice to hear. Did you get the voice mail message I left for you to say hello to him? I guess he's just saying hello back." She tried to sound calm considering how hard her heart pounded inside her chest.

"Yes, I got the message, but John asked me to say hello before I got a chance to listen to it. I'll tell him you said hello in a little while when I pass the house. They should be home relaxing on an off-Sunday."

"OK, that's great. Thanks." Kristen had a dozen questions, but she didn't want to sound overly curious about John, although Angela was no dummy and surely noticed something between Kristen and him.

"So, did Jacob leave today?"

"Yes. We had breakfast first and took a short walk on the boardwalk before his taxi came. I think he had a nice weekend here."

"Who wouldn't have a nice weekend at the shore on a sunny weekend in August? Which, uh, reminds me of something else."

"Oh? What's that?"

"I think you'll need to learn how to drive a horse and buggy soon."

"I wanted to learn but never got a chance yet. Why?"

"It's frowned upon if you hire a driver too often for things that are not really considered important. Like going off to swim in a lake too far for a buggy to get to."

"Oh. I planned on asking you to drive me back to that huge lake where we had the picnic. Why was it OK for you to drive us that time?"

"The Waglers only do that once or twice a year, and they have the bishop's permission. It's a family outing on an off-Sunday."

"Did someone say something to you?" Kristen remembered Onkle Jonas forbidding her to ask Angela for such rides after that night she'd come home so late from taking Cindy back to the shore.

"No. I just know from experience. I've been a driver for a few Amish families here for several years now, and I hear things. I thought it better if I tell you before anyone else does."

"Thanks, Angela. Uncle Jonas already

spelled that out for me, but I figured it was only because he'd been upset when we came home late from our drive here and back."

"Maybe. But he would have said something sooner or later anyway. I'm only supposed to drive you to doctors, weddings, funerals, the mall when necessary, places that are too far to get to by horse and buggy, and the occasional family picnic."

Kristen sighed.

"Of course, this doesn't mean you can't go swimming. You'll have to get yourself to a closer place by buggy."

"I better get all the swimming in that I can while I'm here, then. We have a family-size buggy, and a two person open buggy that Uncle Jonas got for John when he started to court Sadie. But someone almost always has both of them out now that they have the store. One more thing to deal with."

"I'm sure they'll make a way for you to have a buggy. It should be fun learning to drive a horse and buggy. Bet you never thought you'd be doing that."

True. She also never thought she'd have to swim in a dress, wash with hand pumped water, use kerosene and battery lamps, and most of all, fall in love with an Amish man. A very handsome, protective, strong, Amish man. Then again, she was born of Amish parents. She kept forgetting that.

Monday morning when Kristen got back from her swim she was surprised to see mail in between the screen and storm door. She'd thought the mail was still going to Riley's office. And if not, why wasn't it in the mailbox? Then she saw a note under the rubber band that held the mail together.

Stopped by to say hello, but you were out. Figured you'd want your mail while there. We can talk about the bills I have here another time. –Riley Gallagher

The only way she could pay the bills is with the inheritance from her mother or if she rented the house as soon as possible. But everything hinged on her turning eighteen, according to Riley. Her mom had willed her all of her savings but at the age of eighteen . . . and the house would not be legally hers until that time, even though Mattie had signed it over to her. Two and a half more months. She could make peace with that.

In the meantime, she had to make more progress on cleaning it out as the Realtor requested. She'd get to it in a little while. Right now, she wanted to open the two letters that bore the same return address of

371

Stone Arabia and postmarked Palatine, N.Y.

She went into the kitchen and sat at the table. She could tell by the handwriting and stationery that one was feminine and the other masculine. Both return addresses simply said Wagler with the Dillenback address.

She opened the yellow envelope with the bluebird on it. It was from Mary. She told of how things were at the store and that Katie was doing well at her job at the diner and enjoyed it very much. Anna had written a few lines on the very bottom. She'd made a new flavor fudge and couldn't wait for Kristen to try it. She ended it with an "I miss you."

Kristen smiled and put the letter aside. Then she opened the blue one. Curious, her eyes quickly scanned to the end for the signature. *Yours, John.*

Her heart sped up and a sweat dampened her brow. She wasn't expecting a letter from John. She didn't even think men wrote letters much these days. Well, at least not in her world with e-mails and texting.

She took a deep breath and read . . .

Dear Kristen,

I hope this letter finds you well and that your time with Jacob was enjoyable.

I know you have a lot of work to do there at the house. I wish I could be there to help. But the store takes all of my time and of course, I could not come alone.

Things are good here. Everyone is fine and sends their best to you.

You are missed. It is not the same without you sitting across from me at the table for meals. Who will point out all the cheese I eat?

Take care. With prayers and good thoughts.

Yours, John

Kristen read the letter again. "You are missed." Those three words made her heart reel. She got up and paced the length of the kitchen back and forth. She was so excited she wanted to jump up and down. But before she got to thinking much more about it, the doorbell rang. No one except Riley and Mattie Cook knew she was back at Bradley Beach.

Kristen peeked out from the window.

What was Cindy thinking?

27

Kristen opened the door with reluctance.

"Hi, Cindy. Hello, Derick."

"Why didn't you tell me you were here? My parents drove down the block last night and said they saw lights on in more than one window. I thought I'd come by and see what was up," Cindy said all in one breath.

"I had to come and get the house cleaned out so I could rent it. I've been here since Tuesday."

"Tuesday? That's almost a week, and you didn't even call me?" Cindy looked highly insulted. Or was it surprised?

Kristen shrugged. "I had too much to do. Sorry."

"Well, forget it, then. Derick and I are on our way for a swim. Want to come?"

Kristen looked at Derick. She'd been avoiding his fixed glance. He continued to stare.

"No, I'll pass. I had a swim before. I'm

still cleaning."

"Maybe we can help." Derick's dark eyes, glued to her face, awaited her response.

"No. But thanks, anyway. Some of the stuff is personal, and it's sort of an emotional private time. My mother's things and all. You know?"

Derick nodded, and she thought she saw a hint of disappointment before he finally looked away. Kristen chose to ignore it.

Cindy reached for her hand. "I'm sorry you have to go through all of this, Kris. There hasn't been any more news about Alex Cook. I guess it takes time to investigate those types of things. I have a feeling he didn't do anything. I mean, we've known him all of our lives."

"That's true. But sometimes you think you know someone, and you really don't." Kristen couldn't help but focus her eyes on Derick as she spoke the words.

He kept his gaze downward.

"Well, we'd better get going. Lena, Susan, Mike, and a few others are meeting us." Cindy obviously got the dig and nudged Derick before he could respond.

Kristen hadn't seen or heard from those friends since graduation. As she gazed at Cindy and Derick standing there with thwarted expressions, she realized that she no longer had anything in common with either of them. Nothing to share or talk about. Things had definitely changed. Or could it be that it was she who'd changed and no longer clicked with them?

"OK, have a nice time. Thanks for stopping over. Bye." Kristen's words nearly collided, and she quickly closed the door. *Phew! Don't I ever get a break? Are You testing every emotion and nerve I have in me, God? Are You even there? Am I talking to the air?* She made a wide gesture with her arms and then walked into the living room and flopped onto the sofa. She was tired and wound up all at once.

Then she remembered John's letter on the kitchen table. She smiled and stood, retrieved the letter and sat back on the sofa. She reread it again and sighed.

I want to go home.

And right then and there, she knew that this house, and the Jersey Shore, wasn't it.

"It's a full week that our Kristen is in New Jersey, jah?" Mary asked John as he opened the store door.

"Jah. She left last Tuesday." John kept his voice as monotone as he could manage while his sister stepped inside. He turned the CLOSED sign over to OPEN and wondered if Kristen had received his letter and if she'd write back.

Mary removed two pies from her bag and set them on the kaffee counter. Then she began to fill the urn with water.

"Doesn't Aenti Miriam do that?" John picked up a knife and cut himself a hearty piece of cherry pie. Anna was under the weather with a stomachache, and he'd skipped breakfast to clean out the chicken coop and wash some eggs for her.

"Jah, but Aenti Miriam is home baking more pie to bring to Katie's this afternoon when she helps her redd up the haus for Jacob when he comes tomorrow."

"Jacob is coming for another visit?" Why would Jacob come again before Kristen got back?

"Nee, not exactly a visit. He'll be setting up his carpentry shop. He's moving back to Stone Arabia. Ach! Katie is so happy."

Did this mean that Kristen was coming back to stay for gut? What else would prompt Jacob to make such a move? He was all set up in Lowville.

"What about Jacob's hardware business?"

"His cousin, Eli, Margaret's sohn, will run it. Jacob taught him all he needs to know." Mary began to set slices of pie onto paper plates.

"How did you come to know all of this?"

"Aenti Miriam told us when she came by during breakfast to drop off the pies. You were still out doing chores."

"Do you think Kristen knows?" Surely Jacob must have discussed this with her over the weekend at the shore.

"Aenti Miriam didn't say much else. Ach, I better put the mat by the door, it's *making down* hard! It didn't feel like rain at all."

John finished off his pie and waited for the urn water to heat up to make a cup of kaffee. He didn't know quite what to make of this latest news. His first reaction was to assume Jacob was coming to live closer to his dochter. But then again, he could be doing it for Katie, too, now that he knew how lonely she'd been most of her life.

The next day at noon when Mamm and Daniel came with the other buggy to relieve Mary and bring lunch for John, Mamm had a funny look in her eyes.

John had been working full days at the store while Daed tended the fields now.

Daed announced that it would be him, instead of John, who'd work outdoors in the afternoons on gut weather days, rather than being cooped up in the store jabbering most of the time. Daniel still helped Daed in the morgens. This was fine by John. He preferred to focus all his time on getting the store underway.

"A letter came for you." Mamm handed John a white envelope. The return address was Bradley Beach, New Jersey. That explained the look in her eyes. Mamm had to know it was from Kristen, but she said nothing more.

"Denki."

Mamm smiled then started toward the preserves and canned items where she usually spent most of her time. She turned back for a moment.

"Did we sell some preserves today, John?"

"I don't know. Mary was there most of the morgen while I was in the back."

Mary turned when she heard her name. "What's that?"

"Preserves. Did we sell any this morgen?" Mamm repeated.

"Jah. Four jars. Two strawberry and two orange. The Englisch woman, Julie, down the road a piece from here bought them."

"I don't think I've met her. I'll have to bring four more tomorrow to replace those." Mamm moved some of the jars around on the shelf to fill the spaces where the bought preserves had been.

While Mamm and Mary talked over the

canned items, John stole away to read Kristen's letter. Daniel was in the back where the tools and feed were kept, so he slipped into the school supply and stationery aisle. Seemed to be the most private place in the store this time of day. He opened the envelope and unfolded the loose leaf paper Kristen had written on.

Dear John,

Jacob and I had a nice visit here. He enjoyed the beach and seeing the area where I grew up. It was more crowded than I'd have liked on a Saturday, but we got to walk on the boardwalk early on Sunday before he left. The beach was empty at that time, and he got to see it at its best.

I've been busy cleaning things out, so I can rent the house in a couple of months and pay the bills that are accumulating. So far, I have three big trash bags full to donate to the church.

I hope everyone there is fine. I was happy to hear from you, and from Mary and Anna. Please tell your parents and Aunt Miriam that I send my best and am thinking of them.

I miss seeing you at the table across from me, too. Here, I eat on the move, while I'm doing something else. For breakfast, I buy a bagel (no cheese) and a small container of orange juice and have it while I walk on the boardwalk each morning. When I get home I begin the cleaning again. In between, I order a sandwich or some pizza. By eight o'clock I'm tired and in bed. I guess I've gotten used to waking up and going to bed early.

I should be back by next Tuesday. By then I hope to have the place in tip top shape. The real estate office will take the keys, but I have a second set for myself.

Angela told me I have to learn to ride a buggy because Amish aren't supposed to hire a driver so much for things (like swimming) other than going to doctors, weddings, funerals and faraway stores. Maybe you can teach me? That way I can get around without calling Angela all the time. I think Old Faithful will be a better choice than Rusty.

I hope the store is doing well and that Anna's new flavor of fudge is a big hit. Please tell her I can't wait to try it.

See you soon.

Love, Kristen

Love? She'd signed it, *Love, Kristen.* Is

that how the Englisch generally signed letters to friends, or was this a special closure . . . just for him? She was coming back next Tuesday. Coming back to Stone Arabia. To stay? If she planned to rent the haus, then she can't very well go back there to live. His heart started a hard pounding.

"John? John? Are you in here?" Daniel's voice got John to his feet. He tucked the letter in his pants pocket and walked out of his new private place. "Jah, here I am. What is it, Daniel?"

"Daed thinks it would be neighborly to assist Jacob to restore the old carpenter shop building he has behind Katie's haus. Mamm and Mary agreed to stay here all day on Saturday while you, me, and Daed help Jacob get the place together. Katie, Aenti Miriam, and Rachel will be making us food and cold drinks."

"Rachel, huh?" John gave his younger brudder a sly smile.

"Ach! Don't go making a big deal out of it. Aenti Miriam is friends with Rachel's mamm and that's how Rachel found out about it. If Kristen were here she'd want to help, too, especially since it's her daed's shop we'll be working on."

"That is true. I think Rachel and Kristen could be gut friends, ain't so? Maybe even sister-in-laws." John elbowed his brudder.

"Vell, there goes your secret!" Daniel said with a wink.

Before John had a chance to answer, Daniel walked off.

John shook his head with a huge grin and went to get himself a cup of kaffee. The caffeine didn't empty his mind of questions.

Would Kristen want to be approved for baptism instructions and accepted into the church? John couldn't ask to court her otherwise. But that didn't mean he couldn't woo her in his own way. Then again, this all depended on Kristen's choice. A choice not solely influenced by her feelings for him, but for everything such a life entailed. A calling that would come from deep within her from the Lord Himself.

There were now four large plastic bags lined up in the hallway. Three for the church and one for the trash. Kristen had put aside the fancy unused tablecloths, crystal candy dishes, and wine glasses, gifted to Ross from various clients. She hoped to sell them on eBay.

She'd saved her mother's bedroom for last. Emotionally, it would be the hardest to clean out.

When she opened the top bureau drawer,

the first thing she found was a pair of beautiful women's tan leather gloves, never worn and still in the box. Most likely another gift. Then she came upon small boxes of jewelry. One contained a dainty silver chain link bracelet. Another a pair of jade earrings, and three others with rhinestone brooches. All of them appeared never worn. If only she had something of her mother's as a keepsake.

The Internet FiOS connection would be a big draw for potential tenants requiring high speed Internet service. Still, she should have had Riley cancel it while the house had been empty, but she'd been in no shape to even think one coherent thought back then.

Kristen went to her room and turned on the computer. As far as she could tell, all was in working order. It'd been so long since she'd logged on to her e-mail. Back then, she was pretty near addicted to checking e-mail messages on a daily basis. There were four hundred twenty six messages. She scrolled down and scanned them. Most were spam mail. She picked out the messages from her friends and deleted the rest. Derick and Cindy were her most frequent contacts, followed by Lena, Michael, and the others in their little group. The messages were dated June except for a few early

July dates.

"Why read them now? Whatever we had back then is over." She clicked DELETE and stared at the screen. Seemed as if she'd deleted her entire past life away. Funny. It didn't feel too bad at all. In fact, it felt kind of liberating.

She shut the computer off and headed back to her mom's bedroom. The closet needed to be emptied. She'd do that next. She opened the door and stared at the contents.

The musical jingle of Kristen's cell phone snapped her back to attention. She glanced at the number. Riley Gallagher.

"Hi, Riley. I meant to call and thank you for stopping by with my mail."

"Hi, Kristen. No problem. In fact, I'm calling to let you know you have a few more pieces of mail that came today. A few bills and one letter postmarked, Lowville."

Jacob. Kristen smiled.

"Oh, and there's one with no return address. Looks like a letter, too."

"Thanks, Riley. I'll be heading out to get something to eat, so I can pass by and pick them up."

"Tell you what. I'm stopping by The Fish Fry for some shrimp and fries. I can get you something and drop it off with the mail.

What would you like?"

"Oh, wow! I'd love the same as you with a Coke."

"You got it."

A half hour later, Riley rang the bell with mail and a seafood lunch. They sat on the front porch to eat, but Kristen sorted through the mail before she sampled the crispy shrimp.

"What? Oh no! This better be a joke. And I have a feeling I know exactly who wrote this." Her hands were shaking as she handed a letter to Riley.

You're a tramp same as your mother. The seed doesn't fall far from the tree . . . offspring of a woman who lived in sin unmarried to that pervert, Ross Maddok. You're most likely their illegitimate daughter. One tramp down, one to go.

"This has to be from Alex Cook. He's still being held in jail. Mattie refused to bail him out." Riley folded the letter and slipped it into his pocket.

"I suppose it isn't a joke then. He despises me just as he did my mother and Ross. What a difference from Jacob's notes. He anonymously left notes for me to go back to where I came from out of concern. Alex's note was

386

out of pure hatred. But why even warn me with a threat?"

"Because he's bullying you. He wants you just as scared as he is now. You're safe here, nonetheless." He excused himself and was back in what seemed less than a minute.

Kristen and Riley ate in silence. She only picked at her shrimp; her appetite gone. Just as they'd finished, a police car pulled up to the house. They stepped onto the porch with friendly greetings.

"Officers, thanks for being willing to watch the house until Kristen Esh is finished cleaning it out. Maybe another day or two?"

Kristen nodded to Riley. She'd leave immediately if she'd emptied her mom's closet sooner.

A half hour later, Riley and the police were gone except for a patrol car parked outside. Kristen debated whether to tell the Waglers about this. It'd worry them so, especially John, who'd gotten quite upset when she'd arrived late from accompanying Cindy home. He seemed convinced that Alex wanted to harm her. And he might be right. She'd tell the family after she was back in Palatine safe and sound.

With the assurance of the police on guard, Kristen turned her attention to the first black plastic bag she came upon in her mom's closet. When she opened it, the scent of cedar teased her nostrils. It contained a quilt. She pulled it from the bag and opened it out onto the floor. There were patches that had roses, pineapples, and hearts on them, all in subdued colors of greens, burgundy, and blues with a touch of brown.

"How pretty!" Why would her mom keep this hidden away? It would have looked beautiful on the bed. When Kristen turned it over, there was a piece of yellowed paper under it. She read the words: Our Wedding Quilt.

Wedding quilt? Had Mom and Jacob used this on their wedding night? She ran her hand over it with reverence, wondering if her mom had made it or if it was a gift.

She folded the quilt and laid it across the rocker. It was definitely going back with her to Palatine. Maybe Aunt Elizabeth could tell her something about the design.

Then she turned her attention to the smaller of two worn suitcases. The material of it was faded and the zipper got stuck midway in opening it. She gave the zipper a forceful pull. It separated into a split, which meant it was now useless, but at least she'd gotten access to its contents.

"What's this?" She removed the white tissue paper and uncovered a white kapp, a brown bonnet, and then a blue Plain dress with a matching apron, a brown apron and a cape. Under those was a pair of black stockings. She held them up, one at a time. They were in perfect condition. Carefully, she laid them on the bed beside her. She removed more tissue. A doll. The same kind that Anna had in her room. One without a face.

Kristen had been tempted to draw two eyes and a smile on it but thought better of it after Aunt Elizabeth explained that all Plain dolls were made that way to avoid a graven image.

"Was this Mom's doll?" She lifted it out of the suitcase and hugged it. Mom must have played with this very doll when she'd been a little girl. Chills ran up Kristen's spine. She had her keepsake.

She set the doll aside and took out a black book with the word, JOURNAL, across the front in simple silver letters. Under that was a piece of aluminum foil. She carefully unfolded it to find dried white daisies wrapped in waxed paper.

The first entry in the journal was dated, February 6, 1999. *Wow! A little over seventeen years ago.* She flipped through the pages, counting each date. The entire journal had only thirteen entries.

The closet could wait a tad longer. The police weren't going anywhere so there was nothing to fear.

Kristen sat cross-legged on the floor next to the bed and began to read. She gasped at the first line.

Feb. 6, 1997

Dearest Lord,
   It is with great joy and fear that I welcome the new life within me . . .

28

The words blurred, but Kristen read on. Her heart pulsed quicker and it took all of her willpower to keep her hands steady enough to hold the journal on her lap.

I am waiting for my news to arrive to Jacob. I think it will be a couple of days, maybe three at most. I wouldn't think to ask him to leave his uncle in a fix, so it will be best if I go to Pennsylvania. We could publicly announce our marriage there and have our wedding celebration in autumn. We'll stay until after the autumn harvest. By then his uncle will be set for winter.

Kristen turned to the next entry.

March 16, 1997

Dearest Lord

It wonders me why Jacob hasn't written me back. Best I write another letter in case the first one got lost in the mail somehow. These things happen.

I haven't told a soul about the marriage or the boppli yet. If Daed comes to know, he'll summon Jacob right back. Soon the whole district would learn of it. But that's not as bad as it could be for a girl in my condition in an unmarried state. We did not sin in the eyes of God. That is a far worse fate. I shudder to think on it and am glad we married before such a fate befell us.

Kristen got up to stretch her legs and get a tissue from the box on the night stand. She peeked out the window. The police hadn't moved. Then she sat back on the floor and continued to read.

March 23, 1997

Dearest Lord,

I am starting to panic now. Still no word from Jacob. I hope he is all right. Surely, someone would contact us here if something was wrong.

I had a bit of nausea this morning at the Amish Commons. Ross Maddok, the Englischer who always comes by each Saturday, had me sit down. He said I went pale in the face. I told him I hadn't eaten much for breakfast, which is the truth. I am too nervous to eat these days.

Off I go now to write another letter. I might take this one to the post office rather than leave it in the mailbox here. I want the postal clerk to check that I have the proper zip code for the address of Jacob's uncle.

Kristen couldn't put the journal down. She turned the page.

March 30, 1997

Dearest Lord,

Today I had nausea for nearly the whole day, but it isn't a sick feeling to me. It is a special reminder that our boppli is there inside me, growing. Truth be told, my joy would be overflowing if only I had heard back from Jacob with a happy response.

If I don't hear back soon, I'll make it my business to put a call through to his uncle's phone shed from the phone shanty up the road here.

Kristen read more quickly now and turned to the next entry.

April 6, 1997

Dearest Lord,
This morning I was in such a bad way that I told Ross Maddok of my situation. He often stays to chat for a while after he makes his purchase. He told me he has a friend who owns a vacation house in the next county. This friend is in Europe for six months, and so Mr. Maddok is free to use the house whenever he likes. Mostly, he comes for the mountain air during weekends from his home in New Jersey. It's a big house, he said and could use someone to clean it regular. He was mighty surprised that I'd never seen the ocean after he told me the location of his home.

Right in the middle of our conversation I burst into tears. I wanted to run and hide. But Mr. Maddok was very kind, and it didn't take much prodding for me to tell him the whole of it. I think I was busting to say something to someone. I wanted so much for Jacob to be the first to know. Does he know, Lord? Has he received my letters? Why doesn't he write back? It's been one month today since I sent word of my news. Three letters ago.

Kristen wasn't about to stop reading now.

April 13, 1998

Dearest Lord,
I got to the phone shanty just at sunup to call Jacob at his onkle's place. I figured I'd catch him before he started the day. But Katie said that she'd just finished the breakfast dishes when she heard the ringing of the phone in the shed next to the house. Jacob had already gone out to work on building repairs. I asked if my letters had gotten there. She said that they had. My question made it obvious that her brother wasn't writing me back. I was too upset to talk much more and hung up after asking Katie to let Jacob know that I called.

Just as Aunt Katie had told it.
Kristen turned another page.

April 20, 1998

Dearest Lord,

Ross Maddok came by again this morning for some fresh pie. He said he was going to cook up a shrimp boil. I gave him another surprise by never hearing of such a dish.

After our culinary chat, he asked if things had gotten any better with my situation. I didn't have to say a word. I guess the strained look on my face from keeping back the tears gave him his answer.

I was completely shocked when he offered me a new life in New Jersey as his live-in help. He confided that he'd been eating in fast food places and that the house was a mess ever since he'd bought it several years back when he'd expected to live there with his fiancé. They parted ways a few weeks after the house was purchased. Seems he'd had his share of heartbreak, too. He asked me to think on the job offer. I hardly had a chance to say a word when Miriam showed up with the mini pies I'd forgotten.

I introduced them. Miriam gave me a funny look. I suppose it wondered her why I knew the Englischer by name.

Please let Jacob contact me. How can he leave me at such a time? It's just not like him. Not like him at all.

"Oh, Aunt Katie. You must have been really scared to death of being alone to do this!" Kristen didn't even want to get up for another tissue. She read on.

April 27, 1998

Dearest Lord,

Each morning I awake to the disbelief that my dear Jacob has abandoned me and our unborn boppli. Katie said that the letters had gotten there OK, so he has to know the situation. I hope she told Jacob I called. It isn't fitting for me to go visit him there without a proper invitation because no one knows we are married.

Ross Maddok came along late to The Amish Commons today. I began to feel nervous about it. I've accepted the fact that I must leave. With him. He wouldn't hear of me going to one of those places for unwed mothers. Said I was entitled to vacation time, and he'd give me a few weeks when the time came. Part of me is glad for it.

Ross said he was later than usual because it had taken him time to heat up some of the leftover shrimp boil he'd brought in a thermal lunch container. Said it'd still be warm for me to have for lunch. It was. And tasty, too, despite the nausea. His kindness makes me less afraid.

April 28, 1998

Time is running out. I need to give Jacob one last chance. Proper or not, I will make the trip to Pennsylvania tomorrow by bus. Let him explain things to me face to face. Once I leave Stone Arabia, my family will no longer speak my name since the meidung will be placed upon me. I will miss them all so much. Therefore, I better make sure that I know what I am doing and why.

April 29, 1998

Dearest Lord,
It seems that Jacob has just up and left. Katie had no idea where or for how long. Or even if he'd ever be back again. Did our hasty marriage and the news of a boppli on the way scare him off? Where

could he begin anew as a married man in any Amish community? I was so shocked and humiliated that I nearly gulped down the tea Katie gave me and left the pie so I could hurry to catch the next bus out. I suppose sending me to work in the Englisch world for a kind man who lives by the ocean, is Your way of coming to my aid.

I hardly know the man, yet he has opened his home to me. Lord, you know that I can never love anyone other than Jacob Mast. I made it clear to Ross that I am a married woman and will always be so. Perhaps one day Jacob will be back in my life if it is Your will. I'll tell Miriam where I'll be if he ever returns to Stone Arabia and expresses a desire to find me . . . find us.

"Two people in love thinking that each had abandoned the other. All because of Katie Mast. I guess if Mom and Dad can forgive her, then I'll have to try harder to do the same. Real hard." Kristen's words echoed in the room and a deep sense of loneliness overtook her.

She'd continue the rest of the journal later. Her legs hurt from sitting on the floor and her stomach growled, even though she hadn't regained her appetite after the shock of Alex's foul note.

There was still the letter Mom had left for her. She hadn't had the courage to read it yet. It was in her room in the drawer of her night table. *Later, Mom. I promise.*

When John and Daniel arrived at Jacob's place to begin repairs on Jacob's carpentry shop, John was glad that it wasn't as warm as it had been.

Katie invited them inside for some kaffee and blueberry pie before they got started.

Jacob was at the table eating a hearty piece and motioned for them to sit down. "Ach, I can hardly talk with such a mouthful of this gut pie. Go ahead, eat yourselves full. We'll need the energy for the big job ahead out there. It's been years since I took a hammer or a paint brush to that shop. I'm amazed the structure held up so vell."

"Must be the location. The wind doesn't wear away at it in that spot as much. We'll have it in gut shape in no time." John nodded in agreement with Daniel's opinion. His brudder knew what he was talking about when it came to carpentry. He could probably do the whole job on his own in a day.

John and Jacob would more than likely be

his helpers while he took on the bulk of the repairs.

"Kristen is coming back on Tuesday. I want to get this done before then. This will be a big surprise for her, for sure and for certain. I didn't tell her I was moving back to Stone Arabia." Jacob wore a huge smile as he reached for his cup of kaffee.

"She'll be pleased about it, no doubt," John agreed as Katie sat to join them.

That Katie Mast was more than happy over the whole thing was more than obvious. Her whole demeanor had changed.

It dawned on John that he'd never seen Katie smile in all these years that Jacob had been in Lowville. He'd always felt sorry for her going to Preaching alone. No familye to sit with. Now that would change. She had her brudder here again and also a niece in Kristen.

Maybe one day he and Kristen could expand on that — give Katie more nieces and nephews. Only time, circumstances, and of course, Gott's plan, would tell. It was a prayer he never tired of each nacht at day's end and each morgen at day's start.

"Have you heard from her again, brudder?" Katie asked Jacob.

"Nee. She has much to do there before she comes back. I sent off a letter a day or so after I left there. Wanted to say denki for the visit. The haus is in a nice location being so near the ocean. I think she'll have a tenant when everything is settled."

"So, it looks like the north will be her home, then." Katie patted Jacob's arm, her smile, sure and confident.

John wished he felt that same assurance. What more did he need? She wrote that she'd be back on Tuesday and that she'd missed him too. Her haus would be up for rent. Jacob had moved back, and she'd now have her Amish vadder nearby. She had no familye there in New Jersey. She was, in fact, Amish by birth, so folks wouldn't consider her an outsider trying to fit in. Or would they? Did it matter?

It did to him. For Kristen's sake. He wanted her to feel velkummed and at home in their community. Maybe that's the thing that bothered him most. What if Kristen never felt that this was her home? Would she forever be stuck between her former life and this one? "An unsettled soul is a restless one," his grossmammi would say.

The kitchen door opened, and Aenti Miriam walked in. "Goede Mariye, all. I came to help make some refreshments and lunch for our hard workers." Her smile went directly to Jacob, who promptly returned it.

"Vell, vell, vell. Aenti Miriam sparked the interest of Jacob Mast after all these years," John whispered to Daniel.

They both chuckled.

"Something amusing, boys?" Aenti Miriam had her hands on her hips.

"Nee, just glad to see everyone so happy this morgen," John said, keeping a straight face.

Aenti Miriam squinted her eyes at him, and then walked to the counter to help Katie.

When John looked over at Jacob and Daniel, the two of them quickly stood wearing wide grins. John repressed another chuckle until they got outside to begin a day of work.

He'd never seen Aenti Miriam smitten before.

When Kristen turned on the lamp atop the night stand to read the remainder of Mom's journal, Mom's letter was at the forefront of her mind. Why had she put off reading it? What could be more shocking than the letters the bishop read and these journal entries?

She'd read it right after she finished Mom's journal as a closure to it all. Yes, that made sense. Kristen turned to the last entry she'd bookmarked and turned the page.

May 2, 1998

My Dearest Lord,

There is no doubt now that Jacob will not be in touch with me. I have to go away and leave behind my family and beautiful upstate, New York. Ross said that Bradley Beach is beautiful, too, in a different way. Here, we have the mountains and streams. There, they have the ocean and beaches.

I had to tell at least one person of my plan or my family will think something awful bad happened. I chose to tell Miriam, my eldest sister. She came by The Amish Commons again today. And again, Ross was there with me. I think she suspected something before I said a word. I told her that I was with child, which would surely show had I not let out my dress, and had to go away to New Jersey. She didn't ask many questions, and I didn't have the chance to give details. We had to talk quickly while Ross was speaking to another Englischer who came to buy fruit preserves, and I had a few free moments. It is not easy to talk privately at home, and there is no more time. I am leaving tonight. I repeated the words: New Jersey, to Miriam, so she'd remember where I was . . . just in case. I added: Bradley Beach, but am not sure she heard as she turned to go.

I wrote a letter for Miriam to give to Mamm and Daed after I am gone. I told her where to find it. Miriam was not for the idea at all, but she agreed to do me this special favor. I know she thinks that Ross is the father of my boppli. Just as well. Jacob knows the truth of it, and that's all that matters to me.

I ask for blessings for this new path I will take. And please watch over this unborn innocent life I carry within me. How sad I am to take this boppli away from all that I have come to love. Especially, Jacob Mast.

"Mom! Oh, Mom! This is crazy. Just plain crazy! You should have told your father the truth about marrying Jacob. He'd made sure that Jacob was found. And then Katie would have had to confess back then. Shoulda, woulda, coulda. I guess what's done is done."

The date of the next entry surprised Kristen. It was only two and a half years ago.

October 4, 2014

Dearest Lord,

I haven't written in this journal for many long years. But tonight my usual Our Father and the few favorite psalms I've come to read will not do. My heart is both broken and relieved.

Jacob Mast never abandoned me and Kristen. His letters reached me after all this time.

I am so ashamed for doubting him. But the situation back then brought panic and humiliation so great that I couldn't think of anything else to do, other than go away.

In so doing, I've hurt Jacob and denied him a happy life and kinner. I've hurt Ross by never loving him as I sensed he'd hoped I would at the beginning before he met Mattie. Still, the great kindness and generosity he showed me and Kristen never wavered. I've hurt Mamm, Daed, and my sisters and brother, for the shame I brought upon them by leaving the faith and being placed under the Bann. And I've hurt my very own daughter by denying her the life she should have been born to; a peaceful, simple life with two parents and siblings to grow up with and sit at the dinner table with. I fear that my choice has done harm to her. Still, she turned out to be a good girl. Smart, responsible, and kind. Ross was always there for advice — a father-figure for sure.

I can easily harbor deep anger toward Katie Mast for keeping Jacob and me apart. But her apology and words of deep regret are ones I truly understand. Fear prompted both of us to our fate. Grant us mercy.

There was one more page left to read. Kristen turned to the final entry, dated May with no year. It had a completely different feel to it. Mom's words were . . . happy.

29

My dearest Lord,

After much prayer and rereading of Jacob's letters, I've come to realize that You are giving me a second chance. Maybe I can make things right after all.

First, I need to tell Kristen who she is. Ross and I had a long discussion about it, and he is in agreement. He'll soon be marrying Mattie Cook, and she will live here, which means he'll have much less need of my cleaning and cooking, and more need of privacy.

I will be forever grateful for his generosity and care for us all these years. I can work at a hotel or keep house anywhere. Which brings me to the third thing . . .

I'm thinking of moving with Kristen to Palatine. I know I'm shunned and cannot see or speak to my family or the friends I'd had, including Jacob. But I still plan to see the bishop to tell of the situation which led me to my choices back then. Maybe he will pave the way for Kristen to have no stigma placed upon her due to my actions. It's the one thing I will ask of Katie Mast. To stand by me in my testimony. She is, after all, repentant. I know that once the truth is out, that my family will accept and love Kristen as one of their own. How nice it would be for her to have aenties, onkles, and cousins in her life. And eventually, dear Jacob.

I so much want Kristen to experience the Plain life, even if just for a period of time. I know that not all communities are perfect, but we are blessed without much troubles. I want her to know the simplicity, the sense of family and community, to gaze at the fields, farms, mountains, and streams. If she is drawn to such a life, she'll surely know it. May You bless the journey to her roots, Lord.

Kristen ran her hand over her mom's last entry. One of hopes, dreams, and second chances.

"It was almost your happy-ever-after, Mom," Kristen whispered with a sob. She closed the book and set it aside. For the moment all she could do was sit and weep into her hands.

The late afternoon sun had begun to set, and the room flooded with a golden light. This was Kristen's favorite part of the day, and she'd often walked on the beach at this time.

Now that she'd finished reading the journal, her mother's letter beckoned. The beach! Yes, the beach was the perfect place for reading the letter. But how could she go if the police were keeping an eye on the house? And wouldn't it be risky?

No, Alex Cook would not intimidate her. She'd go out the back, under the backyard fence, with a baseball cap and her hair tucked under it. She knew how to go from yard to yard until she got to the corner of the block. Away from the police car.

Kristen wiped away the tears, put on her hat disguise, and made it through the backyards in no time. Several had no fencing between them, which made it much easier.

She hurried down Fourth Avenue toward the beach and got a whiff of someone's barbecue. A few children were headed her way back from a day of sand and ocean, carrying small coolers and towels. She smiled at them and quickly walked onward.

Traffic hadn't yet crowded Ocean Avenue, as it would in a couple of hours when the Friday night dinner crowd headed out in droves and the "bennies" arrived from the city.

Kristen checked for oncoming cars before crossing over to the boardwalk then made her way down to the beach. Most of the sunbathers were gone and the stretch of sand gleamed a warm topaz. She removed her flip-flops and continued to the shore. The wet sand cooled her feet as she slowed her gait to reminisce over the special times she and her mom had shared on their Sunday morning walks.

Lingering fear caused her to look in all directions for any sign of a suspicious looking person.

An older couple with a cooler set up beach chairs facing the sunset just a few yards from her. They provided a safety net.

The white crests of the waves took on a golden glint from the setting sun. The sky was a glorious shade of pink and orange. This is what Kristen wanted John to see. No description of it could compare with the real thing. Maybe he'd see it with her one day . . . everything was a *maybe* these days.

When would she feel sure of her role in this life?

She moved just a few more yards to the rocky jetty. The tide was low and there were plenty of rocks to sit on. She found one with a flat surface, set her flip-flops down, took another look around, then sat, and opened the envelope. A brochure was tucked into the center of the letter as she unfolded it. The letter was dated the day of the fatal accident. Nausea washed over her.

Dear Kristen,

Happy Summer Off!

I've decided to take the summer off, too. I want to spend some time at last, with you, my dear daughter.

We can visit Lancaster, Pennsylvania and see some of the Amish countryside and sample the wonderful food there. Then we'll go on to Upstate New York, and see more Amish settlements but without all the tourists and the shops that cater to them. Why the Amish? Because I'd like for you to see where I grew up in Stone Arabia, in Montgomery County.

I'm Amish, Kristen. And therefore, so are you. I've waited this long to tell you because you're finally at an age to understand things . . . my baby, only a few months until you're eighteen.

I'm sure you have many questions. Lancaster and Montgomery County are perfect places to fill you in about our Amish heritage . . . in the midst of rolling hills, pastures, barns, horses, and buggies, and a peaceful simple people. Our people, Kristen. I never want you to forget that. Deep inside, it's who we are, dear girl. Who the Lord created us to be.

This is my last week of work, so we finally won't be like two ships passing in the night. There'll be less notes and more talking face to face in the future. I promised Ross that I'd go with him on the boat to meet Mattie for lunch at The Seafood Harbor today to discuss our plans and theirs. Meantime, look over the brochure and itinerary and see what you think.

Love, Mom

"It's who we are. It's who I am." Kristen held the letter to her heart. "It's who You want me to be, Lord." She re-read the words again.

"Thanks, Mom. I think I know now what Jacob and my daed were trying to tell me that day we went for a walk."

Kristen folded the letter back into the envelope, picked up her flip-flops and ran barefoot all the way back to the house. She had much to do.

As the sun went down, John, Daniel, and Jacob washed up at the outside pump and headed inside, anticipating the delicious meal Katie and Aenti Miriam had cooked.

"Is that something blueberry I smell?" Jacob walked over to the stove.

Katie waved him off. "Jah, it's the blueberry cobbler Miriam made," Katie told him as she lifted the platter of chicken to bring to the table.

"Lots of blueberries this time of year, so we best use 'em up." Was Aenti Miriam blushing?

John enjoyed seeing his stoic aenti being young-at-heart and more than likely in lieb with Jacob Mast. He wondered what Kristen was doing. He missed her even more than he'd expected.

As if reading his mind, Aenti Miriam said, "I s'pose Kristen will be back before dinner on Tuesday. It'd be nice, Jacob, if you and Katie could join the familye for the evening meal."

"Jah, that would be gut, ain't so, Katie?"

"Jah, denki, Miriam."

They bowed their heads for meal prayer.

Afterwards, Katie passed the platter of chicken, followed by creamed peas, small roasted potatoes, pickles, and biscuits.

If he and Kristen became a couple, John would be at this table many more times. He was comfortable with Jacob and Katie. It would be a nice surprise for Kristen to learn that Jacob would live and work in Stone Arabia from now on. But did this mean that she would come to live here with her daed and her aenti? Seemed only right for a dochter to live in her vadder's haus. But it was also Katie's haus. John began to worry. *No more struggles for Kristen, Lord, please.*

The morgen was cool as John brought the buggy around for Daed, Mamm, Mary, Daniel and Anna to head out for Preaching at the Stoltzfus's place. As he hitched both horses to the larger buggy as he did every other Sunday for Preaching, he thought how Kristen would have to squeeze in . . . maybe next to him.

"A lovely morgen for the ride, jah?" Mary asked, settling in between Mamm and Anna.

"Jah. We'll probably eat the common meal outdoors." John turned to look at Anna as he said it. She loved eating outside. For

415

Anna, the common meal today would be a big picnic. In actuality, it was just that. Kristen liked picnics, too. Waiting two more days for her to come home would feel more like two weeks.

When they arrived at the Stoltzfus's place, fifteen minutes later, Tim Stoltzfus, the youngest son, was tending to the horses and buggies. It was still early so only a few families walked toward the large barn. The women and girls parted ways with the men and boys as they entered to sit on their separate sides.

John and Daniel walked with Daed toward their seats. John spotted Katie seated on the women's side quietly chatting with one of the other women. He was glad for that.

She'd sat alone for church services long enough. Although sometimes Aenti Miriam sat with her. Both unmarried, they'd become close friends through the years, especially after Jacob had left. Only difference was, Aenti Miriam had Mamm, nieces, and nephews. Katie only had Jacob, and he'd been gone.

The woman that Katie was talking to kept touching the back of her kapp, as if checking to see if her bun was still there.

He smiled to himself. Just like Kristen used to do. He walked on then stopped.

Daed and Daniel turned to look at him, puzzled.

John whispered for them to go ahead.

Daniel shrugged and walked on, but Daed hesitated. He looked in the direction John's gaze was focused on.

Katie caught their gaze first, smiled, and then fiddled with the Ausbund hymnal on her lap.

The young woman noted Katie's distraction and turned.

"Kristen!" John's voice was just a few decibels below being heard by all present in the barn.

A couple of heads turned.

"Shhhh, John. You'll speak with Kristen afterward. It's gut to see her at the service, jah?" With a pleased smile, Daed patted John on the back and steered him to their seats.

The cooler weather did nothing to stop the fire John felt run through his entire body. Perspiration trickled down the back of his neck.

A few minutes later, Mamm, Mary, Anna, and then Aenti Miriam, were seated with Kristen and Katie. John couldn't keep turning to look at them without attracting unwanted attention, so, he stared straight ahead, wondering how he could sit through the service for three or so hours with a calm composure.

She's really here, isn't she, Lord? It seemed too gut to be true. Kristen returned two days early. Is here at Preaching. And is dressed in the proper Plain church dress. Was this a dream? Had Kristen really given him such a radiant smile when she first turned and met his gaze?

The songs and the sermons seemed to take longer than any other time John had attended haus church. The chant-like tone of the singing soothed his erratic heartbeat. Kristen had looked genuinely happy to see him. He couldn't wait to hear of her plans and why she'd returned two days early. How did she get here? Where did she get the Sunday church dress?

The nearly three hours had felt like thirty when the last hymn had ended and the congregants began to get up and walk outside. He joined the men to set up the church benches to serve as long tables not far from the haus. He scanned around and saw Kristen walking with Katie just past the barn.

Kristen held a large ball, probably for the children to amuse themselves after their meal.

"Throw it to me, Kristen." Katie held out

her arms, laughing. Kristen threw the ball to Katie, but instead of catching it, Katie looked to her left, then ran over to Kristen at deft speed, knocked her to the ground and fell atop of her just as a gun shot went off. Katie didn't move.

Kristen screamed from beneath her.

John nearly turned the table over in his rush to get to them. The other men soon followed. Jacob, Daed and Daniel were at his side in what seemed like an instant. Women rushed the children inside.

"What happened?" Jacob's question sounded like the wail of a wounded animal as he knelt beside a limp Katie and a shrieking Kristen.

"Someone must have been aiming a gun Kristen's way, and Katie saw the shooter and jumped on Kristen to block the bullet." John's voice came out in rushed breaths. "We need to call the sheriff to stop whoever did this, or he might try it again."

Several men rushed away to get help.

Others began to search the area behind the barn and the corn field beyond it.

Kristen cried out hysterically. "Aunt Katie! Aunt Katie! Talk to me. Please don't be dead. Aunt Katie!"

Jacob and Daed lifted Katie off of Kristen. A splotch of blood darkened the left area of Katie's dress and the back of Kristen's.

Mamm and Aenti Miriam helped Kristen up from the ground and led her away toward the haus. Kristen kept turning back to Katie, sobbing and barely able to walk but for the support of Mamm and Aenti Miriam.

An hour later, John walked into the kitchen to find Kristen lying on the small sofa with a wet rag on her head. "I got news."

"What is it John? Is Katie . . ." Aentie Miriam turned her face into her handkerchief.

"She was taken to the hospital and is in surgery. The doctors think she will be OK. The bullet lodged in between the ribs and just missed her lung. Jacob and Daed will stay there until she is out of surgery."

"Who in the world tried to shoot our Kristen?" Mamm asked in nearly a whisper, as if Kristen might not hear.

"Seems that Alex Cook fellow got his bail after all. His daed put up the money. The police apprehended Alex in the cornfield. He was high as a kite and got disoriented."

"But John, how did he spot Kristen, dressed Plain like the rest of us?" Aentie Miriam stared at him with confused eyes.

"I heard Katie call out her name to catch

the ball. That must have been his cue while he watched from his hiding place in the bushes."

"And how did he know she was here to begin with?"

"Mattie Cook slipped up and told him. Said she would never pay his bail so that he could follow Kristen to Stone Arabia. Alex was doing a lot of talking, flying high as he was. Vell, no matter. He'll not be causing further trouble for anyone."

"Thank the sweet Lord." Mamm breathed a sigh of relief. "Did you hear that, Kristen? They caught the awful man who tried to shoot you."

"But he shot Aunt Katie. I might be dead now if she hadn't seen Alex. Then he'd have his wish. Poor Aunt Katie. I should have stayed in Bradley Beach and none of this would have happened here."

Mamm's lips pressed into a thin line. "Now you hush up about all of that. We're familye and any one of us would lay down our life for the other. Just like it says in scripture."

Kristen raised herself to a sitting position. "But my mom was shunned. And she was familye, too. What if she turned up here with me out of the blue? You wouldn't speak to her or have anything to do with her. And

421

Jacob was worried that some people around here would hold her past actions against me. That was why he wrote those notes."

"Kristen, your mamm did things in a hasty fearful way. Not knowing the truth, she panicked. If she would have returned after all these years with you and the truth she'd learned in tow, our bishop would velkum her back into the church and community for sure and for certain. And not a tongue would wag for it." Mamm sat down beside her now. Her face held a reassurance of her words.

"Can I go to the hospital to see Katie?" Kristen's eyes held a silent plea as she looked to John.

"Not today, Kristen. The doctor told us that only Jacob could go in to visit her after she comes out of surgery. Maybe tomorrow will be a better time. I'll see if Angela could drive us. Meantime, we'll all pray for Katie."

Kristen was worried about Katie. Truth be told, so was he. Of all the people to save Kristen — the one who'd kept her mom and Jacob apart. The Lord worked in strange ways.

At the crack of dawn John stepped into the kitchen to find the table set and pancakes sizzling on the stove.

"Kristen! Are you feeling up to this?" She

had on another Plain dress and a kapp. "Sure. I finally beat your mother down to the kitchen. Besides, I couldn't sleep worrying about Aunt Katie."

"We'll call Angela right after breakfast to drive us to the hospital. Where'd you get the black boots?" He'd never seen her wear those before.

"I found them in my mom's closet, along with the Plain dress and kapp I had on yesterday. It was like a small sign from God when they all fit."

"A sign?"

"Yes. That I'm to be Amish. Just like Mom intended."

John's sense of elation required a breath of fresh air. "If the pancakes are done, maybe you can come to the barn with me while I milk the cows. Can't have you forgetting how to do it if you'll be living Amish."

Just then Anna came down and began making the kaffee.

"While you do that, Anna, I'm going to help John milk the cows. Can you tell your mamma if she comes down before we get back?"

"I'll tell her, Kristen. But hurry back so the pancakes are still warm."

"Jah, little mamma," John teased.

Kristen wasn't sure that her ribcage would hold in her heart much longer, the way it pounded so hard. She stood and followed John to the barn.

When they entered, he motioned for her to sit on a bale of hay next to him.

"It's gut to see you looking calm and settled this morgen." His blue eyes searched her face, as if waiting for a confirmation of his words.

"Yes, I am calmer and feel more settled now. I just want Aunt Katie to be all right, and then I'll be OK, too. Right here."

He cocked his head.

"John, you know how hard I've been trying to find out who I really am? Right?"

He nodded.

"Well, this is where I'm supposed to be. Mom's journal and her letter helped me sort it all out. It was as if a light got turned on inside of me."

"Gott has answered your prayers — and mine. Jah?"

"Jah. I know now that God is guiding me." Kristen locked her gaze into John's happy eyes — eyes that turned their focus to her lips.

She drew closer to him and as his mouth touched hers, she sank into his warm loving embrace. Heartbeat against heartbeat, his kiss so intense yet gentle.

When their lips parted, John smiled and his words came soft and tender.

"I'm in lieb with you, Kristen Esh. I'm glad you're where Gott has willed you to be, here, in Stone Arabia. With me."

"I'm in lieb with you too, John Wagler. It's good to be . . . home. With you." She smiled back at him then settled into his strong arms. Complete at last.

EPILOGUE

October

Aunt Katie taught me how to make all things blueberry during her convalescence. She'd give the instructions with a watchful eye and I'd mix and bake.

We celebrated two birthdays in the same week this month. That meant two of Aunt Elizabeth's delicious birthday cakes to feast on . . . one for John's twenty-first birthday last Tuesday, and another for my eighteenth birthday that Friday. We both received homemade cards from each member of the family — so personal and special. There's no comparing those to elaborate gifts or delivered flowers.

I gave John my treasured little heart-shaped bottle filled with sand from Bradley Beach and the largest package of yellow cheese I could find. John gave me a small wooden box that contained a sparkling mica rock of the area and a lone white beach

426

shell. The words, *we complement one another,* were written on a small slip of bark paper he'd rested atop them.

I'm all finished with my baptism and German classes. John has polished the open two-seat buggy, and we're now officially a courting couple. By early fall next year Aunt Elizabeth will waste no time in planting the celery, which I'm told is a big part of an Amish wedding in our district. It grows well in the cooler climate here. I learn new things about the Plain life every day.

I showed Daed Mom's wedding quilt, and he confirmed that it had been theirs. All the women in the family had made it for them at a quilting bee to be given as a gift on their wedding day. It had never been used. But soon enough it will grace the bed John and I will share.

My cooking needs some work, especially my pie crust, despite Aunt Katie's lessons. No one has yet to utter a critical word while they labor through one of my disastrous rock hard concoctions with polite quietness. Although John's smirk always gives him away.

Daed and Aunt Katie offered us their home to live in after we're married. It seems that they'll live in Aunt Miriam's house. She and Daed are now a couple, too! It's so exciting to see them happy together. John and I enjoy watching Aunt Miriam giggle and blush. Although, in between her giddiness, she still pounds out a firm hand about things.

The Wagler store is doing very well, and most of our Amish and some Englisch neighbors shop there. I'm now officially the bookkeeper and word has it that come tax season, some of the locals will want my help with their income tax returns. Ross taught me well. My inheritance will be a nice nest egg for our kinner one day. And if the familye needs something repaired at the store, we won't have to worry about the expense, thanks to my mom's hard work all those years.

Anna calls herself the candy girl. She tries new flavors of fudge every month. The maple walnut holds first place to this day. She already has test recipes going for peppermint flavored fudge to be perfected by Christmas.

Life in Stone Arabia is busy and slow at the same time. I've unwound on the inside and am more energetic on the outside. Seems that's how it should be.

I had a lot of forgiving to do. After the shooting, Alex Cook was found guilty of rigging the boat that killed my mom and Ross.

Now, instead of resenting him, I pray for him. Thanks to John.

John not only gives me his love but leads me closer to God with each passing day. I bring everything to prayer. It makes all the difference.

I'm no longer a stranger to myself or to those around me. I'm Amish. And I can say that just fine these days — with a heap of gratitude and happiness.

Thanks, Mom. We've come full circle.

GLOSSARY OF AMISH TERMS

Abeer — Strawberry

Ach — Oh

Aenti — Aunt

Ain't so? Isn't that so?

Ausbund — Amish hymn book

Bitte — You're Welcome

Boppli — Baby

Briwwi — Restroom

Brudder — Brother

Budder — Butter

Daed — Dad

Dawdi — short for grandfather.

Denki — Thank You

Dochter — Daughter

Dummkopf — Dummy. Stupid.

Eheman — Husband

Englisch — English. Refers to non-Amish people

Familye — Family

Ferhoodled — Confused, mixed up

Frau — Wife

Goede Mariye — Good Morning
Gott — God
Grank — Sick
Grossdawdi — Grandfather
Grossmammi — Grandmother
Gut — Good
Haus — House
Hullo — Hello
It wonders me — I wonder
Jah — Yes
Kaffee — Coffee
Kind — Child
Kinner — Children
Lieb — Love
Lobbich — Silly
Maidles — Young ladies
Making down/Making wet — Raining hard
Mamm — Mom
Meidung — Under the bann
Melasshich — Molasses
Morgen — Morning
Mudder — Mother
Nacht — Night
Naerfich — Nervous
Narrish — Crazy
Nee — No
Onkle — Uncle
Plain — Amish and Mennonites, etc
Redd up — Clean up, straighten up
Schmart — Smart

Shunned — Banned
Sohn — Son
Unvelkum — Unwelcome
Vadder — Father
Velkume/Velkomed — Welcome/Welcomed
Vell — Well
Verboten — Forbidden
Verhaddelt — Mixed up
Voss iss diess — What is this?
Wutz — Pig. When someone eats a lot.

ACKNOWLEDGMENTS

Linda S. Glaz, my agent, who never gave up on me even when I did.

Scribes 202 Critique Group, for helping me to learn to write better in the proper style for fiction and keeping my project in prayer.

Fay Lamb, my editor, for her fine eye and insight that put my manuscript into its best shape.

Lue Shelter, former Amish, who patiently answered many of my questions about the Amish and even had a chat with me by phone.

Peter Maran, my husband, for resolving computer technical issues and financially supporting a freelance writer.

Lauren Futch, a close friend to an Amish family whom she sees regularly, who clarified many aspects of the particular sects of Old Order Amish in upstate NY and many other things I'd asked her about.

Brenda Nixon, author of Buggies and Beyond, for revealing many unknown facts about some of the stricter Amish sects, mainly the Swartzentruber.

To Peter, Amy Khan, and Sylvia Hasenkopf, for accompanying me to the Amish community of Stone Arabia in Palatine, NY, part of Montgomery County, for necessary research. Those were interesting jaunts.

To the memory of one of the best weekends I had at the Jersey Shore in Bradley Beach, at the home of Maryann Marchwinski Farrell and the late Charles (Charlie) D. Farrell in celebration of Charlie's last birthday. And all the other visits and weekends at the shore back-in-the-day in Shark River Hills with Charlie showing my husband and me his love for a place dear to his heart.

ABOUT THE AUTHOR

Linda Maran has authored a self-help book and numerous non-fiction articles prior to her endeavor toward fiction.

Fascinated by the diversity in culture and religion, she never forgot her first encounter with the Amish many years ago during a visit to Lancaster, PA. More recently she discovered that many Amish communities reside in her home state of New York, where she visits whenever possible, gathering information on the Plain life of that area.

The author is also an accomplished artist in oils and watercolor and enjoys playing the drums, contemplative prayer, cooking and is an avid reader.

She lives with her husband in both Brooklyn, NY and Maplecrest, NY.